Sixty-Six Chances

Nick Buxton

First published in 2013, this edition published in 2017.

Also available in all eBook formats

Typeset in 12/14pt Garamond by Blind Rabbit Books, UK

Cover design by BespokeBookCovers.com

eBook ISBN: 978-0-9956992-1-2
Print ISBN: 978-0-9956992-0-5

For Clara
'Whenever' you may be…

ACKNOWLEDGMENTS

Firstly, thank you to everyone who listens to my crazy ideas, whether you choose to or not - that includes Bertie the rabbit. And thanks to those of you who took an interest in one idea in particular... this one.

I want to thank Josephine for having the patience to read this story in its infancy. Thank you to Glenn for his continued encouragement, and all the ideas we came up with together - and then forgot - while consuming Boddingtons. Thank you to Lee for the same, plus his unique insight into all things! I'd also like to thank Phil for not finishing it; and John for not starting it! Thanks to all the others who showed support, and thank you to the people who didn't – it made me work harder. Thank you to John Jarrold and Andrew Wille for pointing a lost puppy towards home. Thank you to Sarah Herman for her expertise.

I want to thank my family, both near and far – especially mum and dad for teaching me hard work and dedication. Thank you to my sister Joanne for showing me what it means to never give up.

Thank you to the places, and the people, of north east England – who helped inspire this story.

ONE

I often wondered what makes us uneasy when we're alone sometimes. Without seeing or hearing a thing out of the ordinary, I'd still be spooked. I always assumed it was the sheer silence that did it. We human beings need something going on, someone to talk to, a pet to make a fuss of. Without it we seem unnerved. The thunderous rattle of a train blasting past our house is often more settling than silence, it reminds us things are normal.

I've felt a presence before, never seeing - just feeling, something lingering like a cold patch of air that has no place on a warm street. But I didn't think much of it; after all, I'm only human. People often turn, sensing someone behind them, only to find no one there. We're just wired that way, or so I'm told. Until recently, I never realised that there's more to it than that. Until recently, I never realised that those little chills - the ones that make the hairs on your arms stand on end – can be the signature of something life changing. Looking back, I didn't realise how little I knew about those unnerving moments. I'm still creeped out by them, even though I now spend most of my time chasing them – searching for the next one, then seeing how it unfolds.

The weak January light is fading from my home town of Durham. I'm back in the attic room, in the empty townhouse. I look out of the window at the cold scene, the ice on the inside of the window glass showing it hasn't been a kind winter so far. I've spent so long living in the past, I'm really not sure of the future. I think how at the age of twenty-nine, I have so much time left. Although time doesn't mean that much to me anymore.

I've spent endless hours analysing the last few months - what I've done and where I went wrong - the damage I've caused. My mind is racing and my heart is aching for many reasons. I've seen and done such amazing things lately that having an ordinary life now seems far too simple. I take a final look around the room that gave a beginning to my adventures. I kneel on the dusty floor and roll up my sleeves. I take a pen knife from my pocket. Heart racing, I extend the blade...

**

Four months earlier – 7 September 2012

I feel an extraneous chill as I scan the darkening university grounds for signs of life. Standing in the side doorway to the old science building, I see the square through the trees. It's quiet; I'm glad. Only the magpies cackling loudly on the nearby bell tower of Durham Cathedral spoil this summer evening's tranquillity. I also see John lurking by the gates; he looks like he's up to no good - even more than usual - dressed in dark clothing. His short frame casts a silhouette against the late summer sunset.

My attention turns to the mechanical keypad lock on the door. This is the first time I've ever broken into anywhere. Well, the first time I've done it and it wasn't my job to. Luckily the lock is a standard one – identical to many others I've defeated, at the care home, the local hospital, anywhere with someone willing to pay me the fifty pounds call out fee.

Suddenly, I'm startled. 'Right, coast's clear,' John whispers, appearing from nowhere. He stuffs a bin bag down the front of his jeans. 'So, can you get it open?'

'Jesus, John, do you have to creep up on me like that? I think so. I can't believe you roped me into this.'

'We're not robbing a bank, Si.'

'It feels like it.' I make a start on the lock with a few fine tools.

'Don't worry, we won't get caught,' John says, grinning.

I wish I felt as optimistic as my life-long friend. 'And what if we do?'

'Then we'll say we're just working late; I often stay late working on Fridays anyway.' He hovers behind me, shuffling around.

'Go and keep an eye on the path,' I say, surveying the grounds again.

John obliges and disappears around a mossy sandstone buttress.

After some effort, I eventually defeat the lock without breaking anything.

John returns just as I push open the door. 'Brilliant.' My accomplice hops over me and disappears inside.

I reluctantly follow. Our shadows dance on the red tiled floor as we jog the length of a gloomy corridor. Moonlight from narrow windows, set high in the walls, guides the way as we arrive at a timber-panelled lobby.

'There aren't any security cameras, are there?' I ask, flashing my eyes over the ceiling.

'Nar, don't think so.'

'You sure?'

'Yes I'm sure. I've been coming here every week for years and never seen one yet. Stop worrying, Si.' Across the lobby, there's a grand oak staircase, decorated with colourful patterns of light.

'So what is it we're looking for anyway?' I ask.

'Just some chemicals.'

'Chemicals? This is for your project and not bomb-making stuff for terrorists?' I joke.

'Of course. They just won't let me have them because of stupid health and safety. Come on.' John attacks the stairs, two at a time.

'Health and safety was invented for a reason,' I say, as loud as I dare. My sarcastic comment goes unnoticed and my friend is gone. I clamber after him. There's a large stained glass window responsible for the beautiful pools of light on the steps. Any other time I might stop to admire it. I find John at the first landing; his advance arrested by an impregnable-looking security door.

I'm relieved to see him produce a security pass and swipe it through the card reader. There's a bleep and the door swings open. He passes through without hesitation.

I pause.

John's face appears around the doorframe. 'I know you're not happy about this, Si, but I promise this stuff is so worthless it's not worth nicking anyway. I just can't ask for it, that's all.'

I can see the excitement in him. I follow. This

floor is even darker than the last – there's less windows for the moon to appease. The sound of the security doors closing behind me echoes around the old building. As I survey the way ahead, the oak panelling seems to close in on me. I feel like a hundred ghosts are watching me – unimpressed by my being here. We shuffle quickly along the upper corridor and arrive at what looks like the chemistry labs.

John stops me beside a door. 'This is it,' he says, taking a key from his pocket and unlocking it. Inside, I find a dark storeroom with wooden shelving and a small window at the far end. There's curious artefacts, dusty bottles and tins, and jars of liquid playing home to some particularly gruesome-looking specimens. Luckily I can't see well enough to identify anything. Halfway down one wall is a large glass cabinet; this becomes the focus of John's attention.

'The chemicals I need are in here. Can you get me in?' he says, skipping around the cabinet.

I approach, straining my eyes in the gloomy light. The front is frosted so I can't see its contents; I only see the brightly coloured warning labels. *Danger: heavy metals. Poison. Explosive substance. Ionising radiation.* 'What on earth's in here, John?'

My friend glides over to the window. 'Don't worry, mate, there's nothing in there that can kill you... not quickly anyway.'

'Oh, that's nice to know.'

'Jesus, Simon, stop worrying and get the cabinet open... please.'

'I know what you're like; I'll get it open if you promise not to blow anything up.'

'I promise. Honestly you can't do anything scary with the stuff in there.'

I take out my tools again.

'You'd better make it quick,' John adds, still peering out of the window. '"There's a few people in the square; if we don't get a shimmy on we'll be spotted on the way out.'

I work the small cabinet lock, trying my best to ignore the warning labels. I feel perspiration building on my forehead. I daren't remove my jacket for the need of a quick escape. Within moments, I have the cabinet open. I retreat.

John is straight in; rummaging inside. He bobs his head around checking each shelf. I watch as his eyes fall upon a pair of large metal flasks. He freezes. 'Bingo, a nice bit of mercury cad.'

'A bit of what?'

John takes one of the flasks from the cabinet and holds it out to me. 'Mercury cadmium telluride crystals to be exact. Or more commonly known as HgCdTe.'

'What on earth's that?'

John grins. 'It's what we make bombs out of.' He holds the flask nearer.

I take another step back.

He laughs. 'That was a joke, Si. It won't bite you.'

I take the flask. It's heavy for its size; I assume it has something to do with the mercury element as I inspect the label the best I can in poor light.

John picks two more items from the cabinet, stuffs them in the bin bag he brought, and closes the doors; they lock shut.

'Are we done?' I ask.

'Yep, we're done. 'Let's go.'

I'm relieved to be making my way out of the horrible room, even if I am carrying stolen goods. Back at the exit doors to the stairs, I wait in the darkness.

John swipes his pass. Bleep... nothing. He swipes it through the reader again. Bleep... nothing. 'Bloody security pass,' he says, frantically swiping again and again. Bleep, bleep, bleep... still nothing.

I look at my watch. It reads 9.10 p.m. 'It'll be on a time lock,' I say.

'A what?'

'You know, the swipe card system will go off at a certain time. Probably nine o'clock.'

'Damn. Now what do we do?'

'I don't know; this was your idea.' I stumble around the creepy corridor trying a number of doors. Not one of the ornate brass handles will budge. 'There has to be another way out,' I say.

'I don't think so.'

'There must be. What happens if there's a fire?' My words give birth to an idea. I scan the ceiling for a little red light.

'What are you doing?' John asks.

'I'm looking for a smoke detector.'

'Why?'

'So I can set the alarms off.'

'What? You can't do that.'

'It's the only way out.'

'You've gotta be kidding me.'

'Nope. If we set the alarms off the doors will unlock automatically.'

'Every man and his dog will descend on us.'

'We'll have a few minutes to get away.'

'For God's sake, Si.' He drops his swag on the floor and paces the corridor for a while - hands on head.

'I don't think we have a choice,' I say.

John lets out a strangled sigh. 'Alright, I'm not staying here all night.'

'Have a look around for a lighter or something.' I put my heavy flask on the floor and travel the corridor struggling to see. *There must be something lying about.* Eventually, our search brings us back to the macabre storeroom. We fumble around in the dark looking for something we can use to set the alarms off.

'I can't find anything,' John says, knocking tins and bottles onto the floor.

I discover a can of air freshener. 'This'll do.'

'How?' John asks, picking up various objects and dumping them back on a shelf.

'Ionisation; spraying this does the same job as a flame, right?'

'Good call.'

Back in the corridor, I'm staring at the smoke detector. My arm raised – can in hand – poised for action.

John has his eyes tightly closed and his fingers in his ears. I'm not sure what he's expecting to happen. This feels like a flash from a comedy sketch. The feeling soon evaporates as I think of the pending result. I grab my flask – ready to run.

'You sure this will work?' John asks, opening his eyes.

'Yeah, it should do.'

He takes a deep breath. "Do it.'

I spray the air freshener into the smoke detector and loud bells fill the halls. I head for the way out with John on my heels. I push at the security doors - they open.

'Sweet,' John shouts, scurrying past me, swag bag swinging.

I descend the stairs as fast as I can without falling, and run the blackened corridor to the exit. I burst out of the building, bells ringing behind me.

Out in the university grounds the air is fresh and comforting. I follow John through a little squeaky gate onto a footpath that leads down to the river - constant glances over my shoulder. None of the youths in the square seem to see us, or give a monkeys about the fire alarm spoiling their Friday night loitering. I toss the can of air freshener into a bin by the footpath. The more woodland I put between me and the university, the more I relax.

At the bottom of the hill, I almost swagger – pleased with myself. I must be flooded with adrenaline, and I like it. There's a small pub overlooking the river. John's red car is parked in the alley behind. We move towards it as fast as we can without drawing attention to ourselves, shuffling awkwardly along the wooded path. The heavy container isn't helping me remain inconspicuous. Finally at the car, I carefully hand over the metal flask I've been cradling.

John places it in the boot with his other items and locks his car.

I'm relieved; my part in this is done. I hear distant sirens on the late evening breeze. 'We should get out of sight, John.'

'Yeah. I think I owe you a pint,' he says, gesturing towards the public house.

Catching my breath, I have to agree. 'I think you do.'

**

My skull still vibrates - the effect from the fire alarm bells - as we leave the tired-looking bar and find a table. 'I can see the headline now,' I say, taking a seat by the window. 'Simon Benson, air-conditioning engineer arrested on suspicion of supplying explosives after helping college bum John Hartley pinch some nuclear stuff from his university.'

'It's not nuclear...' He leans in closer. 'Well maybe a little bit,' he whispers, with a grin.

I roll my eyes at him.

'Chill out, it's nothing to worry about,' he says, banging his pint glass against mine and spilling his beer. 'Cheers. And thanks for your help, there's no way I could have got that on my own.'

'I thought you'd finished your project anyway?'

John has a satisfying look that unnerves me. 'I finished the prototype. Now I can crank it up a gear.'

'So what are the chemicals for?'

'Well, you know the original idea, right?'

I do know. John's university project is all he talks about. Well, that and the girl who's been helping him build it. 'Yes, you've built a contraption that scans people for superbugs.'

John nods. 'That's right.' He pauses to flash his eyes over the pub. The place is rather dated and no longer a popular venue, so there aren't many ears to worry about. 'But it has a strange side effect,' he adds.

'What kind of side effect?'

'To be honest, we're not really sure yet. Emily suggested making some changes to the chemical mix so we could investigate it further, that's why I needed that stuff tonight.'

'Where's your female sidekick this evening anyway?' I've never met Emily, but I know from our past conversations that they've become great friends, and John's been hoping they'll become something more.

'She'll be here later.'

'So I finally get to meet her?'

'Yeah, so don't embarrass me.'

'Me? So has this college partnership finally turned into something a bit more exciting then?'

John sinks into his chair, eyes fixed on his beer glass.

'It has hasn't it? You shifty sod.' I'm about to quiz my friend further, when I'm interrupted by the squeal of the front door opening.

A pretty, young woman walks in. A blue summer dress hugs a short, but well balanced frame. Her light brown hair is straight and perfectly cut. John's face lights up as she enters. Her expression matches his as their eyes meet.

I realise this must be Emily. I stand as she approaches the table.

John remains seated. 'Hey, Em,' he says. 'This is my friend Simon.'

I offer my hand. 'Call me Si.' We shake.

'Would you like a drink?' John asks, pointing to the bar. Emily nods. 'Usual? Be back in a minute.' John heads for the bar leaving us alone.

'So, John's been updating me on your project.'

Emily sits bolt upright with her hands clasped tightly together in her lap. She smiles.

'He said you're making good progress.'

She nods.

She's so quiet. I find myself making patterns in the condensation on my glass. I'm glad when John returns and places a tall drink in front of Emily.

'I was just telling Emily that you've been updating me on the bug machine,' I say.

Suddenly, John's companion springs to life. 'It's a chemical reaction camera, well, technically a scanner really,' she says, softly. 'Not a bug machine.'

'Sorry. I err... I'm not really up on that sort of thing.'

John steps in. 'Si helped get the core chemicals.'

Emily quickly loses her nervous look. 'Oh wow, that's great,' she says, taking John's hand. 'Where did you get them from in the end?'

John gives me a sideways look. 'Si has his own business and knows lots of chemical suppliers, so he helped us out.'

I simply nod and smile. John's statement isn't far from the truth. I do work for myself, and I did help to get the chemicals, just not in the way Emily thinks.

'Well that's brilliant,' she says. 'Thank you. This'll really get us moving now.'

'John tells me your scanner has some side effects,' I say.

John and Emily glance at each other. 'It's nothing,' John adds. 'It should work fine now.'

The table falls silent. It seems John wanted to tell me something earlier, but now he's changed his mind. I'm intrigued, but I'm not going to press them.

'So, are you two... erm, you know...' I raise my eyebrows, theatrically.

'Yeah, we're seeing each other,' John says, slumping in his seat again. Emily blushes.

'Well that's great,' I say. 'And at least you can work on the... you know, camera scanner thing and still spend time together.'

'We call it the Human Aspect Scanner,' Emily adds. I sense she's taking the opportunity to change the subject.

I oblige. 'So what does it do then?' I ask.

'Well, unlike a camera, which just takes a still image, scanners can take an image and analyse it.

Depending on what parameters you set within the software, depends on what it tells you.' Emily seems far chattier when talking about work. She's clearly passionate about this, and being an engineer of sorts, I can relate to that.

She continues... 'It scans people. By looking at a person's face it can tell us their temperature, the pH of their skin, it can take measurements of their pupils, and so on. All this can then be analysed to give a picture of how healthy the person is. And if they have any underlying problems... all in a few seconds.'

'It could save a lot of time on blood tests and screening of patients when they go in hospital,' John says.

I nod, genuinely impressed.

'It's just not easy fitting it in around a full-time job,' John adds.

'Yeah, I know,' I say. 'I was only joking around with the college bum comment before.'

'I know you were,' he says, with a smile.

'Good luck with it all anyway, I know you've both been working hard on it.'

'Thanks, Si. Trust me, we'll get noticed with this one. And once the big boys get wind of what it can do, the cash will follow.

'I hope so, John, I really do.'

Emily stands. 'I'm just going to...' She gestures towards the toilets. John's eyes follow her as she travels the room.

I take my phone from my pocket and study the blank screen. My eyes return to the table to find John staring at me.

He's shaking his head in a pitiful fashion. 'Have you heard from her lately?' John's referring to my ex-girlfriend, Rachel.

‘No, it’s been a couple of months since her last text.’

‘Good. Stop looking then.’

I put the phone back in my pocket. ‘You’re right.’

‘If she text tonight what would you do?’ he asks. ‘Go running straight back to her?’

I shrug my shoulders. *Actually, I probably would.*

‘She’s not worth it, Si, she did nothing but treat you like crap for years. You’re better off without her.’

‘She did have some good points you know.’

‘I beg to differ, mate.’ He slams his empty glass on the table. His unimpressed manner breeds silence.

I’m embarrassed. ‘Will anyone know those chemicals are gone?’ I ask, eventually, wishing to change the subject myself this time.

‘No way, the stuff in that cabinet hasn’t been touched for years. Thanks for not letting on by the way.’

‘Just don’t blow anything up.’ It’s been a long night, I’m fading. ‘I think I’ll head off,’ I say, as Emily returns. ‘I’ll leave you two in peace.’

‘Do you want a lift?’ John asks.

‘No thanks, I’m happy walking. It’s a nice night. I’ll see you soon.’

‘Yeah. Come round for a beer one night,’ he adds.

‘I will. Thanks. Nice to meet you, Emily.’

She smiles, and with that I leave.

**

I stroll through town, jacket under my arm. There are plenty of people around. It must be the good weather bringing them out. I meet the river again. A young couple, standing by the footbridge, catch my eye. They stand close, and both are beaming at each other. The woman laughs and puts her arms around her man's neck. She moves in for a kiss.

Lucky boy. I pass and step onto the footbridge. Through the decking I see the dark water moving slowly – like treacle, far below me. There's a cooling breeze blowing downstream. I shiver as the cold penetrates my thin sweater. I put on my jacket. *A warm hug would be nicer.* I suddenly feel lonely as I leave the bridge and pass several couples obviously on a night out. The sound of laughter, and high heels on cobbles, fills the street - clip-clop. Rachel and I had been together for a few years, I always thought we were happy but it's comments like John's tonight that remind me our relationship wasn't all that good. It doesn't stop me missing her though.

I walk a couple of streets; it's quiet now I'm entering the suburbs. Street lamps illuminate large family cars with baby seats and little hand prints on windows. My head feels heavy. I cross the road and cut between buildings coming out into a small park area. It's well lit, but empty. I don't feel unsafe - as I often cut through here at night, but instinct has me looking over my shoulder. As I pass through the trees, the temperature seems to drop ten degrees in an instant. I feel uneasy.

Finally, I exit the park into my street, and I feel warm again. I still shudder as I take a final glance back towards the park. I'm just tired and edgy from our evening's exploits. The road is crescent shaped and lined with small elevated town houses. Each has a little garden to the front. I see my home in the distance. I feel sad seeing the place in darkness, just once it would be nice to return to a warm house and warm company.

Once inside, I switch on the lights and I'm reminded even more of my past relationship. I see the richly decorated interior. The house doesn't resemble a bachelor pad in any way. There's a woman's touch. It's a nice family home... minus the family. I leave my shoes untidily at the foot of the stairs and head to bed.

TWO

18 April 1912

The sinking of the White Star Line's Royal Mail Ship *'Titanic'* has sent shockwaves across the Atlantic Ocean. As the people of Durham talk furiously of the tragedy that took so many innocent lives, a far lesser occurrence passes nearly all of them by. The incident should have no effect on the future at all. However, unbeknown to most, it leaves just as much of an impression as the sinking of a great ship.

Four days after the shipping disaster, the Newcastle and Darlington Junction locomotive repair shed is busy as always. Located on the outskirts of Durham, it's a dangerous place to work. The grand Victorian building currently holds no less than three locomotives under repair: two inside, and one in the siding.

Although small, it's a relatively high-tech facility. The five skilled men that work here have an array of machinery at their disposal. Boilermaker, Robert Dodds is hard at work in the upstairs workshop. He's busy preparing a piece of cast iron to replace a boiler casing on a Pollitt Class D5 locomotive. Robert's a strong and capable man, but he's also experienced enough to know this is a two-man job. He's enlisted the help of Joseph Atkinson, the chief mechanical engineer.

'I think I'll stick to the railway tracks, Jo,' Robert says, looping a chain through a hole in the cast iron. 'None of this messing about on the sea business.'

Joseph sniggers and takes his pipe from his mouth with an oily hand. 'Stick to the railway tracks my eye, you've never left Durham.'

Robert shrugs and winches the heavy metal off the workbench, swinging it towards the drilling machine. Joseph steadies the load. A chain breaks.

Robert screams out. His hand is trapped under the weight of the iron. The room is blurry, his world suddenly clouded by pain.

Joseph does his best to free Robert from the weight of the metal. Two other colleagues rush to help. They lever the sheet metal from the bench with iron bars. Finally, Joseph pulls Robert free. Robert sits quietly on his workbench, his badly damaged hand wrapped in rags. Joseph runs to fetch help from the nearby infirmary.

**

12 September 2012

It's been five days since our antics at the university. I've been on edge ever since, worried we might be found out. John doesn't seem that bothered – so why should I be? My concerns are finally fading though, when I receive a phone call, on Wednesday evening…

'Hiya, mate, it's me.' John says.

'Hello. How's things?'

'Not bad.'

I can tell something's wrong. 'What's up? Have we been rumbled?'

'No, it's nothing serious.' John says. 'Are you free now?'

Luckily my plans for the night are only trivial. 'Yeah, I suppose so. Why?'

'Do you know where the university workshops are?'

I remember John once pointing out some old buildings on the other side of town. 'I think so. Do you need a lift or something?'

'No. Meet me there as soon as you can. I've got something to show you.'

I don't like the sound of this. 'Should I be worried?'

'I don't think so.'

'Great. That fills me with confidence.'

'It's not something I can explain... I need to show you.'

'Alright, I'm on my way.' I leave the house and jump in my van. The short drive to the other side of the city is peppered with glaring streetlights and thoughts of what trouble we might be in.

**

It's getting dark as I enter the industrial estate. I pull up alongside a collection of old, rundown buildings that don't fit with the others around them – the red engineering brick a stark contrast to the grey aluminium cladding of their modern counterparts. Fixed to a high chain link fence is a sign with the university crest on it';

the only indication this place is a teaching facility at all. I leave the van on the road and enter the deserted grounds.

I see John's car in the distance - parked by a small two-storey building which has a Victorian flavour. I head in that direction. As I cross the carpet of weed-infested gravel, a train thunders past. By John's car, I find an entrance door.

Inside, my lungs are tickled by musty air as I climb a timber staircase to an upper floor. 'Hello?' I shout.

'We're here; come up.'

At the top of the stairs I enter a grim looking workshop space. I walk the long room past a series of wooden workbenches, lathes, and pillar drills. *An engineer's paradise.* Rusty old gas heaters hang from the ceiling, and light fittings on chains swing in the draughts. The oak floor is black with oil. At the far side of the room I see John, Emily, and someone else - a clean-cut gent in his fifties I don't recognise. He's fashioning brown corduroy trousers and a woollen pullover.

'Alright, John, Emily? Is everything OK?' I ask.

'Yeah we're OK,' John replies. Emily's clinging to him, she looks rather uneasy. John introduces the stranger. 'This is Alan, our lecturer.'

That explains the clothes. I offer my hand. 'Nice to meet you,' I say. Outwardly I'm smiling, inwardly I'm not - I assume we're in trouble. We shake. I notice a large object on the floor covered by a white sheet. 'So is that the...'

'Yep, that's it,' John says.

I lift a corner of the sheet to reveal the Human Aspect Scanner, a contraption about the size of a washing machine. In fact it looks very much like one, without the outer casing.

'So why am I here?' I ask.

'I need a favour.'

'Go on.'

'We could do with a small chiller unit. Can you get hold of one for us?'

I nod. 'I might have something at home.' My worries of being in trouble over the stolen chemicals are fading, replaced with curiosity. Surely we could have discussed this on the phone. 'Why do you need a chiller?'

'Well, the scanner runs on a gas made from the chemicals you helped us with,' John explains, with his trademark sideways look. 'To get better results we need to cool the gas, I'll square you up with some money for your trouble.'

'You don't need to do that,' I say. 'When do you need it?'

'As soon as, mate.'

I notice Emily is looking more uneasy by the minute. 'Are you sure everything's OK?' I ask.

Alan finally joins the conversation. 'I think you should show him,' he says, handing an envelope to John.

'OK. See what you make of this,' John says, opening the envelope and handing me two photos.

Alan steps forward and explains. 'This is an image taken of Emily using the scanner earlier in the week.'

I look at the first glossy, black and white photo of Emily. She's sitting on one of the old workbenches, her legs dangling over the side, a smile on her face. I don't see anything unusual about it. The next image is the same, only Emily is covered with blotches of colour, like it was taken with a thermal imaging camera.

'Those were taken using the scanner primed with the old gas mixture,' Alan explains. This next image is taken using the new chemical gas mix.'

John hands me a third photo. It's similar to the

last, but with no blotches of colour. Emily is there, legs swinging, yet this time she's slightly out of focus. And she's not alone – for sitting on the bench next to her is what looks like a man in a boiler suit, clutching his hand wrapped in a bloodied rag.

I shudder as my blood turns to ice for a second. 'Who on earth's that?' I splutter. I expect John to suddenly laugh and admit he'd fooled me with some computer trickery. He doesn't. Instead, he shakes his head.

'We don't know,' Alan says. Suddenly, a loud noise beats up in the workshop and Emily jumps. A downpour is battering the roof. Water runs down the workshop's tatty windows. The vaulted ceiling seems to amplify the sound of the heavy rain. The growing darkness outside and the inadequate lighting around us, all adds to the tension.

'So that's supposed to be just a photo of you the same as the others?' I ask, addressing Emily.

'Yeah it is,' she replies, only just loud enough for me to hear her over the sound of the rain.

I can tell she's clearly unnerved by this and I can understand why. I inspect the eerie image more closely. I'm no expert, but it looks fairly genuine.

Alan moves to a workbench and hauls himself up with a groan. Emily stays clinging to John.

I continue dodging drips from the roof.

The lecturer explains the image. 'After Emily and John showed me those, I spent the majority of yesterday and today looking into it. In Victorian times this building was a railway repair shed. Looking at the photo, this chap's clearly injured so I looked at accident records from the period. I found one man by the name of Dodds who fits the description. He worked here many years, until he was forced to retire due to a badly crushed hand.'

I'm intrigued, and continue to watch Alan talk with his hands.

'Although this frightened Emily, she bravely carried on posing while John tried to capture something similar. They tried different angles but only this same image kept coming up, eventually this chap just disappeared.' John and Emily nod in agreement.

I'm sceptical. As an engineer of sorts, I believe in a logical explanation for everything, I would have expected John to be the same. I put on my scientific cap. 'I take it this guy only turns up on the scanned images then? Have you tried taking a photo with a normal camera?' I ask.

'We've tried a normal film camera, digital camera, and video camera,' John explains. 'He only pops up on the scanner.'

I study the images again. I grin. 'I'm sorry guys but I don't believe in ghosts. This is a wind up... right?'

Alan is quick to respond. 'It's not a ghost.' John's rubbing Emily's hand. She certainly looks genuinely frightened by this.

'So what is it then?' I ask.

Alan gives his analysis. 'I've not really spoken to anyone about this, that's up to John and Emily, so this is purely my personal opinion only. I think this is a rarely documented phenomenon known as relative haunting.'

'So you do mean ghosts then?'

Alan throws me an experienced glare. 'No, Simon, let me finish. Relative haunting isn't about ghosts. It's the term given to the theory that everyone leaves behind an energy residue, especially in highly emotional situations. In moments such as real joy, sadness, fear, moments of birth, death, and definitely at crime or murder scenes.'

'Would we not see many more people in a building this old then?' I ask.

'Because this chap is the only one to appear, it must be the only event in this part of the building's lifetime to be significant enough to leave a strong energy residue.'

However unbelievable, I'm processing this with an open mind.

Alan continues. 'The components and chemicals used in the reaction are all from the exploration of visual radiation and image capture. The Human Aspect Scanner could simply be a piece of equipment that can pick up this energy, and show it.'

'Is that really possible?' John asks.

'I think so, yes.'

'If that's the case, would hundreds of other scientists not have discovered this before when experimenting with this kind of thing?' I ask.

'Perhaps, but maybe these two are the first to test such equipment in a space with strong enough energy left by someone in the past.' Alan continues to gesticulate as he addresses John and Emily. 'Don't forget that most imaging equipment is developed in laboratories, under strict conditions, and in modern buildings purpose-built for the job. Buildings with no history at all.'

The room falls quieter as the rain outside subsides. 'Well, if that thing really can do what you say, then you might have finally hit the jackpot, John-Boy,' I say, slapping him on the back.

'Let's not get carried away people,' Alan says, getting down from his bench. 'You should chill the gas first. Then, take it from there.'

'What will that do?' I ask.

'It should make the image clearer,' John replies.

'I'll sort that out for you, no problem.'

'Thanks, Si.'

'Then what?' Emily asks.

'Then you need to take your scanner somewhere else,' Alan says, already turning out lights as he circles the workshop. 'Somewhere where there's lots of history. And most of all... highly emotional past occurrences.'

'I'm not sure I like the sound of that,' Emily adds.

'Don't worry babe, it'll be fine,' John says. 'Assuming we can find somewhere, and this happens again, what do we do next, Alan?'

'You keep testing, analysing, and recording until you can write a paper on it that will blow the scientific world wide open.' Alan says. 'And then you'll get a huge research grant and salary for years that will tick me right off.'

'Sounds good to me,' John says, grinning.

'Don't you think we could be... well, messing with things that we really shouldn't be?' Emily says, stuffing her hands in her jacket pockets and burying her chin in her collar.

'What do you mean?' Alan asks.

'Well, I could point it at the road where my little dog got killed and see the poor thing lying there suffering all over again. I'm sorry, but I wouldn't really want to see that, thank you.'

She has a point. That wouldn't be nice, and we're only considering the death of a pet. *What else could this thing see?*

Emily continues. 'I don't want to do that again, John. I'm afraid of what will appear alongside me next time.' She looks at her partner with glazed eyes.

I expect him to support her.

'I think this is too good to miss. I want to test it

more,' he says. 'I'm sorry babe; I just think this could be huge for us.'

'Do you even need anyone in the shot?' Alan asks.

'No. I suppose we don't,' John replies. 'There you go, Em, you can stick with me. It'll be fine.'

'I guess you'll just have to know when to draw the line,' I say.

John nods. Alan mirrors him.

'OK. You win,' Emily says, with a sigh. She points to the images. 'If you want to continue, we can, but I'd rather be behind the scanner with you than in front of it with that creepy fella.'

Alan's poised to turn off the last of the lights. 'I think you'd best keep this under wraps for now until we know what we're dealing with,' he says. 'I'll give you all the support I can.'

'Thanks, Alan,' John says.

We all head for the exit. Alan plunges the workshop into darkness. Emily is the first down the staircase and out of the exit. I'm not far behind. Out in the car park I bid everyone goodnight. I leave the three of them by John's car, still discussing the images.

**

I'm glad I have my van to get me home. I still feel uneasy about what I've seen and mull over it as I drive. I think I stand with Emily on this. At the same time, I'm also intrigued and excited for John. I know how hard he works; I never thought that doing a degree in the manufacture of photographic equipment would turn him into an inventor. And I could never picture him at university; his attention span is way too short. But he's always been determined to succeed, and I admire that.

From what I've seen tonight, it seems he may finally have his big break.

This could be a welcome distraction for me too. For the first time, I've spent an evening without thinking of Rachel. My record is soon spoilt as I return home. The little light on the answer machine is blinking at me. I press play and listen. I'm surprised to find Rachel's voice on the recording…

'Si, it's me. Ring me when you get this.' End of message.

Suddenly, I'm not sure how to feel. My heart thumps against my ribs. *Do I call back?* I check my watch. It's still before ten. I dial.

'Hello.'

'Hi, Rach,' I say.

'Oh it's you. Thanks for being so quick to ring me back.' I'm reunited with her sarcastic charm.

'I've been out,' I say.

'Did you do the CD?'

I'd promised to copy some old photos from my PC onto a disc for her. 'Yes, it's here waiting for you.'

Rachel's approach is direct as always. 'Good. I'm leaving Durham on Monday.'

'How come you're leaving?'

'Well there's nothing for me here so I've got a flat in Newcastle.'

'Oh right, that sounds nice,' I say, feeling awkward.

Rachel always had an unstoppable desire to climb to the top. I assume that's why she's leaving town. I never held anything against her for that. In fact, I was always proud of her. It's a pity she had little time for me, yet expected my undivided attention whenever it suited her. I realise she still has that hold on me.

'I won't be back for a while,' she says. 'And I'm not leaving my address.'

I'm upset knowing that my friend and partner of many years doesn't even want me to know where she's moving to. 'When do you want to collect it?'

'I'll be round at six tomorrow night.' The line goes dead.

The last of the evening feels tarnished by the call. Although I've secretly hoped for contact from Rachel, now it's happened I feel down again – like the day she left. I've just about got used to life without her, life without caring for someone each day. Now I'm reminded of what I'm missing. Her voice has muddied the waters of my emotions. I retire early and suffer a sleepless night.

**

Thursday passes quickly. My return home from work is overshadowed by the thought of seeing Rachel. I make a meal for myself, but don't eat much. At six on the dot, the doorbell rings. I answer to find my ex-girlfriend standing before me. Her high cheek bones and long blonde hair still top her six-foot frame. I remember how friends used to comment on her model-like features. Unfortunately, I also remember how her clinical personality always tarnished the look.

'You gonna let me in then?' she says, bluntly, dulling any shine that remains.

I move aside and let Rachel into the house.

She struts past me.

'I've done the CD's,' I say, handing over an envelope full of memories. 'Do you want a drink or anything?'

'No, just the CD's,' she replies, snatching the

envelope. She pops her head around the lounge door frame. I suspect she's expecting to find the place in a mess. *It was always her that made all the mess.*

'You look really nice,' I say. The second the words leave my lips I realise I shouldn't have said them.

Rachel smiles. 'I know. Think of what you're missing.' She flicks her hair like a show pony flicks its tail, and heads for the door. I've just fuelled her ego and given her a perfect opportunity to mock me. *This will be the last.*

'So when do you leave?' I ask.

'Soon. I'm off to Milan with Kelly for the weekend then I'll be gone.'

'Well, shopping always did come first,' I say.

With a frosty glance, Rachel leaves.

I watch her walk my garden path without so much as a thank you from her. I can see why we fell apart. I think I'm only sad that I'm alone – not sad that I lost Rachel. This will probably be the last time I'll ever see her. I slam the door.

**

It's Friday evening and I'm heading home for the weekend. Although my business is mostly refrigeration, I try to be flexible in my work. I've been self-employed for over five years now and I've learnt to be as versatile as possible to keep the work rolling in. This week has been busy; I've done everything from repairing fridges at a large supermarket, to fitting new door locks at a care home. I love what I do, but I'm ready for a break. My phone rings as I get out of the van…

'Hello,' I say.

'Si?' John's voice reaches me.

'Yeah who else would it be?' I say.

'Did you get that chiller sorted?'

'Yeah, it's in the van ready to go.'

'Spot on. We'll need it. Are you free tonight?'

'I've got no plans,' I say. 'Why? Do you want to try it out?'

'Not yet. I need to show you something first.'

'Not more scary scanner images?'

'No, something else. You wouldn't believe it, mate. I'll be round at yours in an hour.'

The line goes dead.

**

I barely have time for my shower and dried up microwave meal before John arrives. We sit at the table in my kitchen. As always I do my best to ignore the glossy white kitchen cabinets that Rachel once picked – I hate them. They really don't suit a Georgian town house.

'So what is it this time?' I ask.

John produces another envelope. 'Take a look at these.' He hands me a collection of newspaper cuttings and some old photos.

'Alright. What are they?'

'Just look through them,' he says, remaining vague. His mannerisms tell me to expect a surprise.

I spread out the items on the table. A newspaper cutting from the *Durham Chronicle* dated April 1912 with headlines of the Titanic disaster; an old train ticket; and another article documenting the Dodds incident. It's strange looking at the newspaper image of this person from so long ago, especially as I've seen him next to Emily.

'Alan did more digging today; everything in front of you is from the same year, 1912,' John explains.

I continue browsing the items. A faded flyer for a circus visit to Durham, in the summer of 1912; a black and white photograph of Durham police station; and an invitation to a garden party. Finally, my eyes land on what I guess John really wanted me to see – a tatty black and white photo of me.

'What the hell?' All the hairs on my body stand on end as I examine the photo. It looks very old. I'm dressed in old-fashioned clothes, and I'm standing in a street. Next to me is a woman, and she's kissing me on the cheek. 'What's this?' I ask.

'Dunno. Who is she?'

'I've no idea,' I squeak.

I scan the photo closely.

John looks over my shoulder.

The woman looks in her mid-twenties with long dark and curly hair. She's very pretty. She wears a heavy-looking long dress and dark boots. We stand beside a table with a gingham cloth draped over it and glasses and bottles on top. There's a handwritten sign on the wall behind us that reads, 'Lemonade – 1d.' We're holding hands as she kisses me.

'Turn it over,' John says.

I do. On the reverse of the photo in faded ink are the words: *Simon and Clara – Conley Hope Summer Fete, 1912.*

I throw the photo on the table. 'Right, you're taking the mickey now, John-Boy. This is definitely a wind up.'

John stares, straight-faced.

I stare back for a moment. Over twenty-five years of friendship ensures I can read his mind, let alone his facial expressions. He would have cracked by now.

'Is this for real?' I ask.

'I promise, Si. This isn't a wind up. Alan brought that photo to me two hours ago.'

'I've no idea who that is.'

'Me either.'

I can't believe what I'm seeing.

'Have you got any beer in?' John asks, already making the journey to the fridge.

'Yeah, help yourself. Get me one too.' While my friend harvests refreshment, I examine the photo further. It looks old – as the paper is really thick, and the image is yellow and grainy. It's dirty around the edges and smells fusty. Everything about the photo looks old... except me. Even the bottles and glasses on the table are quite obviously not of our time.

'Look at my clothes,' I say, as John hands me a drink. I point out the high, lace-up leather boots, corduroy trousers, light-coloured shirt with granddad collar and double cuffs.

'Was it fancy dress? That lass seems to like you,' John says, with a grin.

'I've never seen her before in my life. That can't be me.'

'It's definitely you.'

'It can't be, John.'

'Look at your ear.' John points out my left ear in the photo. It's my ear alright, clearly scarred from when I was a child. I cut it climbing over a barbed wire fence, trying to pinch apples from a garden. In fact, I'm sure it was John's idea.

I rub my ear. 'Bloody hell! How's that possible?'

'No idea, mate. Alan said he found the photo in the archives at the library. I don't even think he recognised you. He only gave it me because it was in with the stuff about Dodds's accident.'

'I want to know where this came from, John.'

'I don't blame you. It's proper weird.'

'You're telling me.'

I stare at the photo until my eyes dry out. It makes no sense at all. It's a frightening feeling not being able to remember a moment of your life.

'Why don't we hit the library tomorrow?' John asks.

'Definitely. I need to find out who she is.'

John's pocket vibrates. He looks at his phone. 'Damn, I need to go. I promised Emily I'd take her out.'

'You're joking. What are you doing here then?'

'Well, I wanted to show you that, 'didn't I?' he says.

'Don't mess things up with her, John, decent girls don't come along that often.'

'I know.'

'Can I hang onto this?' I ask, waving the photo at him.

'Yeah, keep it.' John takes the other items and makes his way out.

At the door, I watch John hop down my garden steps and out into the street to meet Emily's car as it pulls up. He has a noticeable spring in his step. I'm happy for my friend.

'I'll pick you up about nine in the morning,' he shouts, getting into the car.

'OK, see you tomorrow.' I wave as they drive away.

The rest of my evening is occupied by the photo John left me. I comb the tatty old thing for signs of mischief. I don't believe it's real, but I can't find any evidence to show otherwise. The person in the shot seems to be me. I'm not helped by the young woman; I still have no memory of her. I wonder if she's even real. *She's very attractive, in fact she's gorgeous.* She could just be a random person John found on the Internet and superimposed her image next to mine.

I'm confused... and tired.

Eventually, I head to bed and fall asleep, my head filled with questions about the mysterious Clara.

THREE

I wake on Saturday feeling strangely excited. Glancing at the bizarre photo, I'm still sceptical, yet far too curious. If it's real, I want to find out how it came to be. And I plan to do it today. I grab a shower and rush my breakfast. By mid-morning I'm sitting at a large oak table in the middle of Durham library's general archives.

John arrives with a cardboard box. 'The woman said this is everything from 1912,' he says, dropping it on the table in front of me.

'Is that it?' I ask.

'Afraid so. I'll hit the computers; I think we'll have more luck with that.' He wanders off.

After only minutes of rifling through the dusty box, it's apparent there won't be much to see. There are only old newspapers with hardly any photos, and parish council meeting minutes. I find nothing of the woman in my photo. I get up and take a walk through the quiet library.

John's sitting in a distant corner, at the end of a line of empty PC's. He has his hands behind his head, leaning back on his chair.

'Any luck?' I ask, as I approach.

'Nope. You?'

'Not a sausage,' I say, taking a seat next to him and turning on a PC. Once loaded, I begin my own online search.

'I'm just waiting for the census to load up,' John says, rocking back and forth. Why don't you look for that place name?'

'Already on it,' I say, typing in the words 'Conley Hope.'

After several dead ends I find a local tourism website. 'Hey, John, listen to this. "Nestled in the countryside, approximately twelve miles north of Durham, is the quaint village of Highfield. This small village was once the gateway to the Conley Valley, and the small mining town of Conley Hope."

John's leaning so far back on his chair, straining to see my PC screen, that the inevitable happens. He topples off the chair and lands in a heap, dragging several DVD's off a nearby shelf. His chair clatters to the floor.

The majority of the library's occupants look over.

'It's OK,' he says, 'I'm fine.'

I shake my head.

John remains on his knees in a pile of DVD's, and reads the screen over my shoulder. "A popular place for walkers, there's a beautiful picnic area at the start of a trail into the valley. A tunnel through the hillside takes you to a lake which was once the site of the Conley coal mine. Once only accessible by steam train, the secluded valley is a great place for a quiet walk. The old town of Conley Hope is now mostly in ruin, and largely underwater following severe flooding in 1912. Today the valley is a haven for wildlife."

'Interesting,' I say.

'Not really. Sounds like a crap place to me.' John sets about picking up the DVD's.

'Well one thing's certain, John; I couldn't have been there in the street with that lass if it's underwater. That photo can't be real. So, who's the joker?'

John is back at his PC. 'I don't know, Si, I really don't, mate. It's certainly not me. Great, the census has loaded; I'll search for that town in 1912.'

I study my friend's facial expressions as he takes in the information on his screen. He still doesn't crack. I shuffle my chair closer.

'Here we go, there's a list of residents so people must have still lived there.' John says, scrolling the data.

'Is there a Clara?'

'Can't see one... Nope, no one by that name lived there in 1912.'

I'm disappointed. 'That's that then,' I say, getting up. 'I'll take that box back and see if they have any old maps.'

John slumps in his seat. 'OK, mate.'

I return everything to the archives clerk. She directs me to a large cabinet, holding local maps, dating back to the 1200s. I'd be silly not to have a sift through them - Conley Hope must be shown somewhere. I shuffle the giant pack until my fingers feel strange from the dust. I do find a really good one of the Conley Valley dated 1905; the Clerk makes a copy for me. It must be nearly lunch time; I'm hungry. *I haven't seen John in a while.*

I'm just about to go in search of my friend when he comes jogging through the room holding aloft a sheet of paper. 'You won't believe how brilliant I am,' he shouts, attracting the attention of the other library's occupants yet again.

'I did an Internet search for one or two of the other people on the census and found this newspaper article from 1912,' he says, forcing the printed copy into my hand.

I read aloud... but quietly. "The garden party was a complete success with a delightful time had by all. At his home, Mr Raymond Cole, Mayor of Conley Hope, entertained a large crowd. There was many a noble face including Captain Pearson of the Durham Constabulary. He proudly exhibited his wife and youngest daughter. His eldest daughter, Clara, arrived some time later fashioning the latest in spring wear."

'That could be her,' John says.

'It could, but it's a long shot. How many Clara's would there have been back then?'

'Not many, by the looks of it, the name was rare.'

'Really? Is there anything else?'

'Yeah, I checked the census for Durham, for the same year, and found her. I've got her address and everything.'

So, I have the name and address of a girl who lived a hundred years ago… a girl who kissed me on the cheek. *This is crazy.* 'Where did she live then?' I ask.

John takes the paper from me and turns it over. He's written the address on the back. 'Number twenty-six, North Bailey, Durham.'

'That's just by the cathedral isn't it?'

'Yep, I think so,' John says. 'Why don't we have a peek on the way home? We won't find much more here.'

'OK. Let's go.' I collect my map and we leave.

**

It's trying to snow again. John takes a detour on

his way to dropping me at home. We travel along North Bailey, a narrow cobbled street near the castle and cathedral in the centre of the old city. There's a mixture of old shops and three-storey Georgian town houses. I make myself dizzy staring at the house numbers as they flash past in the cold afternoon light.

John stops the car outside number twenty-six – a large brown brick town house. It must be at least three hundred years old and has tall sash windows and a grand entrance doorway. It would certainly have been a fine and expensive residence in 1912.

'So that's where she lived, mate,' John says, staring out of the car window at the house. 'I wonder if it's our girl.' The place looks empty. There's a 'for sale' sign attached to the outside wall.

'This is nuts… do you think we could get a viewing,' I say. 'Have a snoop around.'

'Yeah, that'd be cool. Can you imagine what we'd see if we fired the Human Aspect Scanner up in there?' John's words breed an idea.

We look at each other. 'Are you thinking what I'm thinking?' John asks, with a huge grin.

'I am. But how?'

'Let me speak to Alan, the old git knows everyone in Durham. He might be able to get us in there.' John scribbles the name of the estate agent on his hand.

A car horn startles me. We hadn't noticed the traffic was building up in the street behind us.

'Crap.' John mumbles, driving away.

**

After being dropped at home I pack some things and set off to visit my parents near the Scottish border. I always look forward to visiting them; I miss them since they moved away from Durham. My dad is a keen walker and had grown tired of life in the city. My mum was happy following him to greener pastures. This is my first visit since my break up with Rachel. My mum will be happier to see me this time. Although Rachel played the perfect partner in my family's presence, my mum saw right through it.

As much as I enjoy seeing my mum and dad, this last week has left me with far too many unanswered questions - questions with answers I could be leaving in Durham. I'm still fairly sure the photo is a fake; otherwise I'd have missed a moment in my own life. And if the woman kissing me is from 1912, then it definitely can't be real, unless I have a one hundred year old twin.

I enjoy a cold few days, in good company, although I'm glad of a phone call from John on Monday to update me...

'Hi Si, it's me. You still away?'

'Yeah, I'm heading home later though. What's up?'

'Alan got us the house. The one on North Bailey,' John explains.

'Did you tell him about the photo?'

'No. But I said we're onto something big. He pulled a few strings and one of his mates at the estate agent has given us the key for the rest of this week.'

'Brilliant. I'll give you a hand then.'

'Alright. We'll get the scanner there tonight and set it up so we can get started early. Join us if you want.'

'I will. See you there.'

I'm excited. Luckily I've left most of the week free in case I'd decided to stay with my parents for longer. Tomorrow can't come quickly enough.

**

I arrive in the square early on Tuesday morning and find John's car parked at the side of the green, opposite the university. I park my van and take the small chiller unit from the back – a white plastic box around the size and weight of a DVD player. I walk down to North Bailey with it under my arm. I can tell summer is over; the breeze is fresh and cool.

John and Emily are waiting for me outside number twenty-six. They're both dressed in scruffy attire. John has a carton of coffee in one hand and a bacon sandwich in the other - which he's eagerly munching on.

'Hi John, Emily,' I say.

'Hi Si,' Emily says. She seems less shy than the last time I met her.

John just waves his sandwich in my direction.

'Will I need any tools?' I ask.

'Nar, I've got everything we need,' John mumbles, his mouth full of food. He leads me inside.

The town house is in a bad state of repair. It must have been empty a while as the floors and walls are covered with dust and cobwebs. The traditional leaded glass windows are so dirty, hardly any light penetrates them. I follow John up a creaky staircase to the first floor. Emily brings up the rear. The grey walls of the landing have large sections of plaster missing. The place feels quite creepy.

'They'll have fun trying to sell this,' I say, crossing a narrow landing.

'I think it's going to auction,' John explains.

'I can see why.' We climb another staircase to the second floor. I'm shown into a good-sized attic room with two windows set in the roof. The floor is as dirty as the brown-green walls. There isn't much in the room except for something in the middle, covered by a dust sheet.

'Is that the scanner?' I ask, pointing at the covered object.

'That's it alright,' John replies. There are a couple of milk crates in the corner of the room. Emily takes one and sits on it. She's very quiet again.

I stand by her. 'Are you OK, Emily?' I ask.

'Yeah, I'm alright. It's just so cold in here.'

I actually feel rather warm. I have a thick coat on so I take it off and hand it to her.

'Oh, thanks.'

John removes the dust sheet revealing the Human Aspect Scanner. He dances a lap around the machine, checking its position in relation to the rest of the room.

'What are you doing?' I ask.

'I need to make sure it's set up right,' he says, producing a spirit level and placing it on top of the frame.

'What made you pick this room?' I ask, looking around me.

'Just thought we'd start at the top and work down,' he says.

Emily explains the machine. 'All the stuff in the bottom is mostly processors and graphics cards,' she says, pointing to what look like computer parts and cables of varying colours. 'The bit above it is the main scanner.'

I see a stainless steel box with grilles in the front. *It's a huge toaster.* 'What's that space above it?' I ask. 'Is that where you put the bread in?'

John scowls at me. 'That's where your chiller goes.'

I hand him the unit I've been carrying.

'Cheers, Si. Here, make yourself useful,' he says, handing me a power extension cable. 'Find a plug socket, will you.'

I roam the room in search of electrical outlets. I find one and plug the lead in. I notice the horrible brown-green walls are actually wallpapered. There's a beautiful Victorian pattern on it almost completely hidden by years of grime. I return to the project.

My chiller unit is now in the frame. I watch, arms folded, as John connects several clear plastic tubes to the back of it. I'm not sure what John and Emily have built but I do recognise most of its parts, the pumps and valves, switches and cables. I can't wait to see what it does.

John plugs a few power leads into the extension cable and stands back, seemingly admiring his work. 'Have you got the cartridge, babe?' Emily pushes a small cardboard box across the floor. It looks heavy. John opens the box and passes me a well-wrapped item. It's about a foot and a half square, three inches thick, and covered with bubble wrap packaging.

'This thing weighs a ton,' I say.

'Yeah I know, whatever you do, don't drop it – it's glass.'

I hold the object tightly. 'What is it?' I ask.

'It's a kind of lens. I call it the cartridge,' John explains. 'It's basically two pieces of glass sandwiched together and sealed, but instead of being filled with air it's filled with gas.'

'The gas made from the chemicals?'

'Bingo.' John takes the object, unwraps it, and places it on top of the scanner. He stands it on its end and fastens it to the frame with bolts. 'Light from the scanner is projected through the chilled gases in the glass panel; it hits the target and is reflected back. The processor captures the image which the software then interprets. A bit like sonar but with light instead of sound.'

This all sounds very technical, but I can't help thinking if a tumble dryer and a toaster had a baby; this is what it would look like. 'Well, that's very impressive, John, but will it work?' I ask.

'You'll see in a minute,' he says, adding the final component – a laptop. He opens it up and plugs it into his contraption. 'Can't have a scanner without something to look at the image on, can you?' John sits on the dusty floor, the laptop on his knee. He taps away on the keyboard.

I make sure my chiller unit is switched on and check the tubes. It makes a familiar quiet hissing noise as it does its job. I know it won't take long to get to the correct temperature. As I wait I can't help but take interest in what's happening on the laptop screen. There's a fast-moving list of commands; it just looks like jumbled nonsense.

'What does that do?' I ask.

John stops tapping for a moment. 'It's pre-written commands from the hard drive to the scanner, a kind of recipe for the reaction that's about to take place.'

'Recipe for disaster if you ask me,' I say, jokingly. My humour goes unnoticed. Suddenly a series of tones emanate from the scanner.

John jumps to his feet. 'That's it. It's uploaded.' He tosses the laptop to one side as if it were worthless. A green light on the scanner unit flashes. 'You do the honours, babe.' John says.

I slowly back away.

Emily leaves the safety of her milk crate for a

moment, and presses a button on the equipment. We stand in silence for a few minutes – waiting.

Eventually, I hear a low faint crackling sound coming from the equipment. It reminds me of an open fire or something freezing very quickly. My heart thumps.

John and Emily also back away from their invention.

My heart thumps harder.

The crackling sound fades. Suddenly a loud pop startles us all. Emily heads for the far corner of the room.

I see the glass panel on top of the equipment turn opaque as if frosted up from the inside. There's a beep from the laptop.

John takes a closer look at the screen. 'Right, we're up to temperature, or down to temperature... oh, whatever. Hang onto your hats boys and girls.' He presses the return button on his laptop keyboard... nothing happens. He presses again... still nothing. He exchanges glances with Emily. Loud banging noises suddenly come from the equipment.

'Damn there's something wrong with the gas,' John shouts.

I recognise the sound and the problem that's causing it. 'That's thermal shock,' I say. 'The pump on the chiller's' stuck.' I step forward and thump the chiller with my fist. The banging noise stops.

I retreat to the corner with Emily as the scanner comes to life. The crackling sound returns again, although much louder. The glass cartridge is glowing with light. Multi-coloured patterns appear on the attic walls. The sight is actually quite beautiful. The patterns resemble the Northern Lights crossing the room in gentle waves.

The phenomenon is short lived; within seconds the whole effect calms and the room returns to normal leaving the colourful patterns between the glass only.

That's the weirdest thing I've ever seen. 'Is it supposed to do that, John?' I ask.

John looks at Emily again. She shrugs her shoulders.

'Well, we weren't sure what it would do with chilled gas to be honest,' he replies. 'That was just a bit stranger than I'd expected though.' John approaches the equipment. He waves his hand behind the glass cartridge.

Through the smoky colourful glass, I see blotches of colour clinging to his hand. Like the image of Emily from the workshop.

'Err, John. Should you really be that close?' I say.

'Don't worry, Si, it's fine.'

There's a loud bang. John runs. We all cower in the corner. Emily looks petrified.

After a few tense moments, John begins laughing. He hops about and rubs his hands together. 'It's fine.' The glass cartridge has gone dark. The equipment seems to have shut down.

John doesn't look disappointed, in fact quite the opposite. 'I think it worked,' he exclaims. He scurries over to the laptop. 'Oh God, please work,' he mumbles, as he taps away.

I hang back.

John's eyes don't leave the screen. 'Somewhere in here will be an image of my hand but I can't find it,' he says, frantically punching keys, with his tongue out. Emily leaves me and goes to help. Ticking noises come from the scanner equipment; the sound is similar to noises made by a car engine and exhaust as it cools.

'There it is!' Emily shouts, suddenly.

'So it is,' John says.

I join them at the laptop to see what all the fuss is

about. Looking at the screen, all I can see is a blurred image of John's hand with the room in the background. *It's not that exciting.*

He and Emily continue analysing readings on the screen and making adjustments.

'Look, the gas temperature was too low this time,' Emily says, pointing to the corner of the laptop screen.

'I need to adjust that,' John adds.

I still don't believe in ghosts but I find myself looking for one. The image is in a kind of washed out colour, and not very clear. I don't see much at all.

John continues making adjustments.

Just as I'm about to walk away, the image becomes much clearer. I see something - behind John's hand, the walls are clean. The wallpaper is bright and there are curtains up at the window. The wooden floor looks clean and polished, and by the window is a chair. No one speaks. All eyes are frozen to the screen.

I see something else. All the hairs on the back of my neck stand on end. 'What the hell's that?' I ask, pointing to the shadow of someone on the floor.

'It's the shadow from one of you two,' John says, straining his eyes.

'No it isn't,' I say. 'That shadow is coming from the door, we were nowhere near it.'

There's a moment of silence.

'There's only one way to find out,' John says, eventually. 'Let's point the other way and do it again.'

I'm not actually sure if I want to find out what the shadow is, and I'm not the only one.

'Is that a good idea?' Emily asks.

John gets to his feet. 'This is the reason we came here,' he says, turning the scanner towards the door. 'Come on, we can't chicken out now.'

He's right. I want to see what secrets this house might hold, and if any lead me to the woman in my photo. 'Alright, let's go again,' I say. 'Come with me, Emily.' I take the nervous little thing to the window, she has my coat but she's still shivering. 'You OK?'

'I'm fine. I just don't like creepy stuff. Can I hide behind you?'

I chuckle. 'Yeah, course you can.'

Emily stands behind me. She nestles into my back and peers over my shoulder. This is the closest I've been to a woman in some time. I feel I have something to protect for a moment, even if it isn't mine. I like the feeling.

John sets off the scanner again. Emily and I watch from the window. The scanner goes through the same sequence and produces a brief light show, although less spectacular than the first. Eventually the equipment falls silent. We all gather around the laptop. The blank screen has a progress indicator bar at the top.

I wait. My heart thumps harder and faster the more the bar changes from black to green. *Seventy per cent... eighty-five per cent... ninety-five per cent.* I'm breathless as it reaches one hundred.

The room looks the same as in the first image but in full colour. It's from a different angle, and without John's hand in it. There are more items of furniture including a bed and a side stand holding an old-fashioned china bowl and water jug. But this is nothing compared to what I see in the doorway... It's not perfectly clear due to the bad focusing of the image, but there's a man dressed in a dark uniform. His open hand is raised high as if he's about to strike the young woman standing before him. She has red curly hair and is wearing a long dress and a very frightened look on her pretty face.

'That's the girl in my photo isn't it? I ask.

'Yeah, that's her.' John says.

'What a bastard.' Looking at the faces of my friends, I think they share my thoughts.

'Oh my God! That's awful,' Emily adds.

'Sorry,' John says, quietly. 'I didn't expect us to see something like that.'

'It's not your fault,' I say.

We spend a good while looking at the image. Maybe Emily was right. This equipment could unearth things that are better left unseen. I'm amazed at what this thing is capable of showing us. Eventually I retreat to the milk crate leaving my friends to quietly chirp to each other over their invention's apparent success.

I'm not sure what to think. I think I'm angry. I think I'm also very sad. I think I shouldn't really be caring. *Why am I even bothered by this?*

Emily approaches the scanner and taps a fire-extinguisher-shaped object strapped to the frame. There's a hollow metallic echo. 'We're empty,' she says. 'We won't be able to do anymore today.'

I need fresh air. 'I've seen enough for now anyway,' I say, getting up. 'I need to do some things at home.'

'OK, Si,' John says. 'We'll hang around a bit longer and go over all this data. I'll give you a ring when we're ready to go again.'

'No worries, I'll see you both later.' I pause as I move through the doorway and onto the landing, quite aware of what I might be passing through. It's a strange feeling.

Once outside, I feel better. But what I've witnessed brings on a sombre mood. I don't feel like doing much else today. I drive home unable to remove the haunting image from my mind.

FOUR

6 May 1911

Edward Petersen is a proud father. Watching his daughter Ellie getting married is one of the happiest moments in his life so far. After the service, the chief executive of the railway company has arranged for her, and new husband Charles, to have the grand reception on a train.

The beautiful steam locomotive *Emerald Princess* has the honour of being the engine used for the occasion. As railway employees themselves, it seems a fitting tribute to Ellie and Charles's union to be celebrating it on the newest addition to the Newcastle and Darlington Junction Railway Company's rolling stock.

The newlyweds had hoped to be photographed on the engine in the central station at Darlington. However, due to the influx of spring bank holiday travellers, Edward has been forced to deny his daughter her primary wish. Instead, he's arranged for photos to be taken at the quiet and safer railway sidings at Durham. Luckily for him, Ellie has warmed to the idea.

Standing in the spring sunshine, Edward and his wife, Mary, watch their daughter, and new son-in-law, pose for photographs in front of a large crowd of family and friends.

**

19 September 2012

The following day I wait anxiously for news from John. I'm tempted to call him as I'm keen to know when we can scan again. The events, and discoveries, of yesterday are still fresh in my mind. I resist the temptation to press him, mostly out of respect for his and Emily's space.

In the early evening, I receive a call from him; he asks me if I would lend him the use of my van to collect the equipment from number twenty-six, North Bailey. He doesn't have time to explain why… typical of John. I'm disappointed; I hope this isn't the end of our testing there. I rush over to his house and collect him. Luckily my van seats two passengers in the front so Emily can join us.

'How come we're collecting the scanner already?' I ask, as we head into town.

'It's at Alan's request,' John replies.

'He's not stopping us from testing that thing already is he?'

'I don't know mate, he didn't say. I hope not.'

'Why would he do that?' I ask.

'Because he doesn't understand it. People are always frightened of what they don't understand.'

Emily springs to life. 'In all fairness, babe, we don't understand it either.'

'I understand it fine,' John snaps. 'And I'm not letting anyone pull the plug on me that easy.'

'Where are we taking it?' I ask.

'Back to the workshops. But not before we see Alan and find out why he wants us out of the town house. He should still be at uni now.'

We collect the equipment and drive over to the university. The dark and windy night adds extra tension to what's already a gloomy trip. We park in the square and walk through the university gates towards the old and imposing building. John wastes no time leading Emily and I to Alan's oak-panelled office on the ground floor. He throws open the door without knocking.

The lecturer is still at his desk. 'I didn't expect you lot so soon. What can I do for you?'

'I didn't expect to have to send my best invention back to the toy cupboard, Alan. What's going on?'

I close the door behind us.

'You'd better all take a seat,' Alan says.

I pull up a leather chair along with the others, but choose the one furthest from Alan's desk. This is John and Emily's project, not mine. I listen as the lecturer talks.

'Right, there are a couple of reasons I've asked you to remove the equipment from North Bailey.'

I listen harder. I'm hoping Alan doesn't know about the stolen chemicals... and the strange photo.

'Go on,' John says, leaning forward on his chair.

'Well, there are a few health and safety concerns.'

John's straight on the defensive. 'Health and safety? For God's sake, Alan, not again. We can't do anything without...'

'Just hear me out, John,' Alan says, with a calm tongue. He takes an envelope from a drawer and slides it across his desk. 'I've been going over your project notes and a few things don't add up. I'm not stupid, John.'

My friend remains silent and looks cleverly unconcerned.

I'm worried.

'I don't want to tie your hands on this one guys, but whatever you're running that rig on needs to be on our COSHH register, or I'm for the high jump.'

'COSHH register? You're kidding me, right?' John says.

'If someone gets hurt I need to prove I kept you on a leash.'

'A leash?' John splutters. 'What the hell's that supposed to mean? You were fully behind us a few days ago...'

Emily joins in. 'Please, Alan. You know we wouldn't do anything silly. The chemical quantities we're mixing are so small, there's no risk, honest. John knows what he's doing.'

'I'm sure he does, Emily. But the fact of the matter is; until you can supply me with a full chemical breakdown of what's being used, I can't let you continue.'

I feel my chance to find out more about the mysterious Clara slipping away. *I don't believe this.*

'I'll have to clip your wings until I know more. Have you taken it back to the workshops?'

'We're on our way there now,' Emily says.

'This is stupid,' John adds.

'It's the rules. You know you have to declare everything. Otherwise there's nothing to stop you all blowing each other up.'

I work with chemicals, and gases, so I see Alan's point. But I'm also concerned by the sudden U-turn in support for John and Emily's project.

John gets to his feet. 'Fine, I'll get you what you

need.'

Alan points to the envelope on his desk. 'Before you rush off, take that with you. It's more information about the town house. You asked me to try and find out more about the owners.'

'Bit pointless if we can't scan the place,' John says, making for the door. Emily gets up and follows her boyfriend, head down.

I take the envelope for them. It's probably not my place, but I'm too curious about the contents.

John storms from the building at pace. Emily scurries behind.

I rush to catch up.

**

Back in the van, there's a strained atmosphere as we cross town. I drive slowly so not to damage the scanner. I have a lot of my own equipment in the back and don't want anything falling on it.

'Here,' I say, taking the envelope from my door pocket and handing it to Emily. 'See what's in there.'

She opens it and takes out a piece of paper. It's from the estate agent by the looks of it. John stares out of the passenger window.

'So, what does it say?' I ask.

'It's a list of facts relating to the town house, dates and things,' Emily says.

'Anything about our girl?'

'Well, let's see... The house was only ever owned by two families, one being the Pearson's. William Pearson bought it in 1885 and lived there with his family. Apparently he was known for his rather brutal reform of the local police during the early 1900s. His wife was a retired schoolteacher. He had at least two daughters. And the eldest, Clara, was also a teacher at a small school out of town.'

'That sounds like her,' I say. I feel butterflies in my stomach as my imagination plays with the image of this girl's life. I struggle to concentrate on my driving. 'Anything else?' I ask.

'It just says that the family left the house in December 1912 when Captain Pearson retired from the police. There's no record of them in Durham after that.' Emily also produces a photo from the envelope and holds it out for me to see.

The black and white image is faded and tatty. But it's clearly the same woman as in my photo, and our scanned image of the attic. She stands alone in the doorway to a grand-looking stone building. The door is open and there's a small dog at her side. She wears a summer dress, and her long curly hair cascades down the front of it. She looks very unhappy.

'Is it the same girl as in your photo, Simon?' Emily asks.

'Yep. That's her alright.'

John takes the items from his girlfriend and spends the rest of the journey studying them.

We arrive in the compound of what we now know to be the old Newcastle and Darlington Junction Railway locomotive repair shed. All is in darkness.

I turn off the van ignition and open my door – the interior light comes on, spreading shadows across the gravel.

'I wonder why her dad was so angry with her.' John says.

'I don't know,' I reply. 'But there's no need for slapping her, I'm sure.'

'Definitely not,' Emily adds. 'Poor thing; she's such a pretty girl.'

I nod.

'She's not skinny. Is she?' John adds.

'What do you mean?' I snap.

'Well, you know... you always think of lasses in the old days being super thin don't you?'

'There's nothing wrong with her,' I say, defending the woman in the image. I snatch the photo. Looking at Clara, compared with little Emily, I can see why John might say such a thing. She does have a curvy figure, but one that looks perfect to me. I'm annoyed – it must show…

'Do you fancy her or something?' John asks, with a grin.

I feel my cheeks flush. 'Don't be silly. Come on; get this piece of crap out of my van.' I climb out of the cab hoping to hide my embarrassment with the night's darkness.

**

The university workshops are as uninviting as ever. A blown fuse means we have to store the Human Aspect Scanner in the downstairs workshop. The space looks similar to upstairs except it has a series of large, heavy-looking oak doors along one side. I guess this would have been the access to the train engines in the siding outside.

'Where do you want this scanner thingy?' I ask, as John and I carry it inside.

John laughs.

'Well I never know what to call it,' I say.

'Alan always calls it "the rig," John explains. 'So,

why don't we stick with that? It sounds a little more scientific.'

'Alright, where do you want your rig thingy?' I ask again, with a grin.

Emily giggles.

John rolls his eyes. 'Over there, by the big doors.' We place the equipment by the large oak doors.

John unclips the gas tank from the side of the frame. He shakes it in my direction. 'I'm bloody annoyed, I've made a new gas mix and I wanted to test it tonight.' He puts the tank in a cupboard nearby.

I glance around the workshop at all the old machinery. 'Well, why don't you?'

'What do you mean?'

I look at my watch. 'It's only nine o' clock, why not test it here?'

'But Alan says we're not to use it,' Emily adds.

John looks at me. There's defiance in his eyes. 'You're right. What Alan doesn't know won't hurt him. There's no harm in a few little tests, babe.' Emily shakes her head.

'So, are you giving us a hand setting this thing up, or what?' John asks, looking at me.

I need no persuading. 'Right you are, boss.' I want to see Clara again and this contraption is the only thing that will let me. I help set up the rig and watch John and Emily go through an efficient start-up procedure.

John places the gas cartridge on top of the frame and hands me a spanner. 'Here, tighten those up will you.'

I tighten the small bolts that hold the cartridge in place as John sets up the laptop and re-fits the fuel tank. Within minutes, we're ready to go. Emily and I sit on a long wooden toolbox which resembles a coffin; we talk quietly as John starts the equipment.

'I wonder what we'll see.' Emily says, looking around the room.

I find myself reassuring her. 'Nothing too scary, I'm sure. Maybe we'll see Clara getting up to no good with a train mechanic and that's why her dad was so angry.' I'm trying to lighten the mood, but my words only fuel my curiosity. I wonder how a girl could end up in so much trouble. Whatever she'd done, I find it unacceptable for anyone to hit a woman, in any time.

'Maybe,' Emily replies.

As always, I'm struggling to squeeze many words from little Emily.

'Right, we're off,' John shouts.

The loud crackling sound, and the familiar light show, recaptures my wandering thoughts.

'I've made a few adjustments,' John explains. 'We're now on what I call "live feed" meaning we no longer have to wait for the still image. Once we're in full swing we should be able to see the images as they're received – almost like a silent movie.' Emily and I join John at the laptop.

There's something on the screen within minutes, but nothing unusual so far - only scrolling images of the workshop walls, in colour, and much clearer this time. The place does look different; it looks newer.

John pivots the cartridge, or lens, to seek out something interesting. He leaves it pointing at the great oak doors.

'Hey look at this,' Emily says, tapping the laptop screen. Although in reality the doors are closed, on the screen they appear to be open and the space is now flooded with daylight.

I glance away for a moment at the dark workshop. What I see in front of me compared with what's on the laptop couldn't be more different. We wait, speechless.

Eventually, a crowd of people appear on screen, in the doorway. All are dressed in early 1900s attire. Without sound, I can only guess from their faces that the people are cheering. I follow their line of sight and watch a shiny green and black steam locomotive slowly passing the open doors. The steam begins to linger in the doorway; the sunlight creating beautiful patterns as it passes through it.

Suddenly, the crackling sound coming from the rig changes in tone. It increases rapidly, along with my heart rate. Then a horrible grinding sound follows, like something under great stress. The events unfolding on the laptop screen become secondary to the events unfolding in the room.

There's a loud smash as the glass gas cartridge explodes. Particles of glass fly all over. I protect my face with my hands. I grab Emily and push her away from the rig. I stumble and fall to the floor and catch a flash of John diving behind the toolbox. I think my ears have popped. I lift my head from the dusty floor. Emily's still standing. She looks dazed but unhurt. She's backing away towards the door.

I get to my knees, the rig behind me. 'Are you two alright?' I barely hear my own words, let alone any reply.

John's head appears from behind the toolbox. 'What? I can't hear anything.' He's muffled. He seems deafened too. 'What happened?'

Before I can answer, I have my breath taken away by a horrible acrid smell – like a mixture of paint thinner and bleach. The stench, along with the dull ringing in my ears, makes me feel sick.

John must be the same as he coughs and chokes.

I put my hand over my nose and mouth. *My God*

that's nasty.

'The gases have escaped,' John croaks.

I scramble away on all fours towards the exit.

'Don't panic, it's not harmful. It just has a strong smell that's all,' John splutters.

I catch sight of Emily standing at the door. Her eyes are as wide as saucers and her mouth wide open. I turn to check John's following, and then I see why Emily looks so shocked…

Behind a stupefied looking John, is the rig – the top section completely missing. A huge cloud of thin mist hovers over the equipment. As on the laptop screen earlier, sunshine is pouring through the cloud. But this time it's different. It's in the room. What was once only on screen, is now happening right in front of us.

This becomes even more apparent as my hearing returns and I'm overwhelmed with noise – people cheering and the loud hissing of a steam locomotive just outside. My eyes burn as the workshop fills with steam and smoke. As if this wasn't enough, there's bright sunlight streaming from outside in the middle of the night. I get up and make a run for the door. I grab Emily as I go.

We exit into the dark gravel car park. My heart is thumping so hard I have to hold my chest. I cough and rub my eyes.

Emily looks stunned, and teary.

It isn't long before John bursts out of the door. 'What the hell was that?' he asks, looking as horrified as Emily.

'I thought you knew what you were doing?' I rant.

'What? I don't what?' His hearing is obviously still impaired; he was the closest to the rig and must have felt the worst of the small blast.

'You alright, Emily?' I ask.

She nods.

I glare at John. 'You idiot, you nearly took our bloody heads off with that thing.'

Emily has an uncharacteristic outburst. 'Don't shout at him, Si, it's not his fault.'

'You were the one that tightened the bolts up on that cartridge, Si. You probably murdered them up too far.'

'What? I'm quite capable of using a spanner, John.'

'Stop it, guys, I think we have a problem,' Emily says, pointing to the doorway. What looks like smoke is bellowing from inside. John and I make for the entrance door at pace.

Inside, I expect to be met by fire and heat, instead the room is cold and filled with steam. It smells sweet and strange, it's unmistakably from the boiler of a steam locomotive. The workshop is gloomy once again. The rig must have shut down; it sits idly in the corner. Everything in the room glistens with water. John and I cautiously approach the equipment.

'Is it off?' I ask, still coughing.

John checks the rig. 'Yeah, it's safe.'

I slide open one of the great oak doors. The fresh air is liberating. It isn't long before the workshop clears and I can see and breathe more clearly.

'Wow. What was that all about?' John asks. He circles the rig with wide eyes. He's smiling.

I'm baffled by his reaction. I'm even more surprised that he's left Emily outside. His project seems more important than she does. I go outside and retrieve her. 'It's OK; it's safe now,' I say, leading her back in.

Emily joins her boyfriend who's still inspecting

his equipment. 'What happened?' she asks.

John gives her a brief hug then glances around the room. 'I'm not sure, but I'm going to find out.'

Emily picks up a piece of broken glass from the rig. 'Have we broken it?'

'No, babe, I think we made it better.'

'What do you mean?' I ask. 'How can it possibly be better?'

'You saw what it did, Si. Come on, you can't tell me that wasn't impressive.'

'Do you think the reaction can always occur outside the cartridge?' Emily asks John. She doesn't seem frightened like I would expect.

'Let's hope so,' he replies, poking at the equipment.

'Are you serious?' I say.

'Damn right I am. Do you realise how much this thing could be worth?'

'Christ, John. Is that all you're bothered about?' I say.

John points at the rig. 'This thing can look back through time. And not just on a computer screen but in real life. Right there in front of your eyes.'

'He's right,' Emily says. 'Commercially, people would fight over this.'

'Exactly,' I say. 'Anything that sought after could bring big trouble.'

'You're forgetting why you're here, Si,' John says, waving Alan's envelope at me.

I remember. I do want to figure out how I came to be in that photograph.

'This thing can tell you what you want to know,' John adds. 'In fact, it could tell us everything we want to know. We could solve half the world's unsolved mysteries with this... just point and fire. Bang! There's your answer. That's what happened.'

John's right. The shock has me missing the point. 'Yeah, well maybe,' I say. 'But you could have created a porthole into God knows what; one that you have no control over.'

'I can control it. We've just had a minor setback that's all.'

I sigh. 'I hope you're right, John.'

'Every energy can be harnessed, Si. You should know that. Wow! Imagine the possibilities.'

I do. As I calm down, the reality of what just happened sinks in. I help clean up and watch as they tinker with the rig. I'm surprised at Emily's reaction; she's usually frightened by her own shadow. Their enthusiasm seems contagious. Although unnerved by the experience, the more I think about it, the more I see the potential.

'Do you think you can make that happen again?' I ask. 'Safely, I mean.'

John lifts his head from his laptop. 'I don't see why not. Are you in?'

I shrug. 'Maybe, as long as it doesn't involve glass flying at my head.' I wonder what new possibilities this could offer me. 'Could you get it to do that back at the house on North Bailey?'

'I guess so,' John says.

'What about Alan?' Emily asks.

'What about him? I'll soon get him off our backs,' John says, slamming the laptop shut. He looks at his watch. 'Come on, I think it's home time.'

We leave the rig and head for the exit. John removes a circuit board from it. I'm guessing it's to stop anyone using it in his absence.

Outside, I watch the twinkling lights of the city as

John and Emily lock up. The nearby trees sway in a strong autumn breeze.

We talk of the night's events as I drive my friend's home. I drop Emily off at her parent's house first. On the way to John's place I find a chance to discuss the chemical situation.

'How do you plan to get Alan off your back then?' I ask.

'Dunno, mate. He's pretty good with that sort of thing so I doubt I can pull the wool over his eyes.'

'Why not just tell him you got the chemicals from me?'

'I did think of that. Would you mind?'

'Well he won't let you carry on otherwise. Will he?'

'No. Tell you what, I'll make a deal. If I can say you supplied the stuff, I'll make sure we get back in the house and find Clara.'

'Sounds good to me.'

'Imagine if it was like what happened today – you could see her in the flesh.'

'Do you think it's possible?

'I'll make sure of it.'

'Thanks for the lift, Si,' he says, as we pull up outside his house. 'I'll speak to Alan. I won't be giving him the exact chemical breakdown though. We need some insurance.'

'What if he doesn't let us back in there?'

John takes the town house keys from his pocket and jangles them in my face. 'Then we go to plan B,' he says, grinning. 'See you later.' He jumps out and disappears into the house.

Shortly after, I pull up to my own house and realise John has left Alan's envelope in the van, I take it into the house. I now have two photos of Clara Pearson: one of her in the doorway, and one with me. I can't stop looking at the images. Although I wouldn't admit it to anyone, I'm really attracted to this woman. There's something about her eyes that makes me feel like I know her - like she knows me. She's that pretty, kind girl, the one my mum would love me to be with.

I eventually crash out – exhausted from the evening's events. Tonight I dream, something I rarely do, and I dream of a woman I've never met.

FIVE

9 August 1912

Peter Brown sits on a wooden bench outside The Sun Inn enjoying the evening air. The warm summer breeze on his face is a welcome contrast to the cold damp coal pit. The main street of Conley Hope is quiet.

George Taylor appears from the public house and joins his friend. He hands Peter a glass of dark ale.

Peter takes a gulp from his drink and lights his pipe. 'Aye aye,' he says, nodding towards the street.

Clara Pearson comes into view. She walks the pavement on the opposite side of the street, ducking every so often to avoid the blooming baskets of colour that hang from the shop canopies.

The two men watch as the young lady passes Henry Wiseman's general store and crosses the cobbled street.

'Maybe she'll come over for a drink,' Peter says, with a chuckle.

'Far too proper for us, Pete.'

'Don't be fooled.'

'Whatever do you mean?' George asks.

'Well, it's not proper for a lady to be out walking alone in the evening.' Peter says. 'Yet Miss Pearson often does.'

'That doesn't mean a thing.'

The men hush as Clara approaches.

'Good evening, gentlemen,' she says.

'Evening, Miss Pearson,' George says.

Peter takes his pipe from his mouth and tips his hat.

Clara smiles briefly and continues her walk towards the setting sun, head down.

Once Clara's out of range, Peter continues. 'Shall I tell you what I heard?'

'Go on,' George says, watching her walk the remainder of the street. His eyes transfixed on the pretty summer dress and fiery red curls.

'Well, some say that Clara Pearson came to live here to get away from her family in Durham. Apparently her father is furious with her for leaving.'

'She did look troubled.'

'She never used to. She's usually a happy sole, and a playful one at that, so I'm told.'

'I bet,' George adds, with a grin.

'Some folk say she plans to live as a spinster and has no interest in a companion, even though she might be considered the prettiest girl for many a mile. But I know differently.'

'Tell me, Pete.'

'She had a gentleman from out of town - they used to meet here often. I saw them.' Peter says. 'I saw them holding hands and carrying on.'

'Did he break her heart?'

'No. He disappeared.'

'What do you mean, he disappeared? What happened to him?' George asks, breaking into a cough.

By now, Clara is gone, leaving behind only gossip.

'Well, I heard that Miss Pearson was set to marry one of the policeman in her father's constabulary, but fell for this other chap,' Peter says.

George is listening intently. 'So, what happened?'

'The story goes that her father was so furious that he had her lover done away with,' Peter says - quietly, flashing his eyes over the street.

'I've heard none of this.'

'That's because the murder was covered up – by the police.'

'I don't believe it,' George says.

'It's true. Folk say that the only men who know what really happened are the Atkinson brothers. They were the last ones seen with her lover when they rode out to Durham with him in their stagecoach.'

'Has anyone ever asked them?'

'Would you? Anyway, it's not to be talked about.'

With that the conversation ends. Peter ushers his friend inside the inn. 'I think you owe me a drink for that information, George.'

The door to the public house swings shut.

**

29 September 2012

I've had over a week to think about what we saw the last time we tested the rig. And it's been a week of looking at the old photographs and thinking of the young woman in them. The accident in the university workshops could have easily brought about the end of our experiments with the so-called Human Aspect Scanner. But in fact, it's had quite the opposite effect. Maybe we should be more concerned about the consequences of its use, considering what happened. Instead, we've been motivated to use it again.

John has supplied a fake set of study notes stating the contents of his gas mixture. I'm not sure how accurate they are, but he seems to have convinced Alan to let us continue. I'm listed as the chemical supplier, which could get me into bother, should anything else go wrong. But today I don't care, for today is Saturday, and the day we return to the house on North Bailey.

I look out of the attic window at the gloomy street and see rain blowing sideways across it. John and Emily set up the rig. I'm hoping we get a similar reaction to that in the workshops. I can't wait to finally find out what happened to Clara Pearson in the early 1900s.

'Right, we're ready, Si,' Emily says.

I join my friends.

'I've modified the rig so that a constant flow of gas is pumped into the immediate atmosphere,' John explains, handing me a face mask.

We put our masks on and start the equipment. I wait with anticipation as the rig begins to crackle. It seems quieter now, and there's very little of the usual light show. I'm nervous. As safe as John tells me this is, I'm still not convinced.

At first nothing much happens. I can smell the gas through my mask, but it's nowhere near as bad as last week. I turn and push open a window, when I turn back I'm shocked to find the view very different to before.

The room is now decorated, furnished, and clean. But I'm struggling to focus on anything properly; it's like looking around a bathroom full of steam whilst drunk. The bed and nightstand have returned along with many ornaments and cushions in colours I can't quite make out. Clearer focus comes and goes in clouds which I assume are the concentrations of gases moving around the room in the air current from the open window.

My heart beats furiously as I wait patiently in the unpleasant conditions. After several minutes I'm ready to give up as the smell from the gases and the constant blurring of my surroundings leaves me dizzy. I'm making for the open window when Emily stops me.

'Wait, Si, someone's coming,' she whispers.

The small hairs on the back of my neck stand on end. I hear loud and erratic footsteps on the staircase. We all stare at the doorway.

A young woman rushes into the room and heads straight for me. John and Emily stumble away.

I'm frozen. Clara Pearson stands before me. She's within inches of me. *I'm finally face to face with her.* She's almost real, but not quite – like a hologram. I don't dare move or look at the other two.

Clara is nearly as tall as I and has beautiful long curly hair. She has plump lips and clear pale skin. She's crying. Seeing her like that so close to me is rather moving. I have an urge to reach out, but resist.

John speaks but I can barely hear him over the sound of the rig and the sobbing of the woman before me. She's just staring straight at me from a distance of inches; if we were of the same space and time I'm sure I would feel her breath on my face.

John speaks louder. 'Si, just back off a bit and I'll shut it down.'

'No, wait.' I'm speaking from the corner of my mouth. I don't know why. *What if Clara can see or hear me?*

No, that's just stupid. My fears are vanquished as she moves away with no reaction to me at all.

She collapses onto the bed and curls up sobbing.

Patchy waves of colour and greying image pass before me. I don't dare move to make any adjustments to improve the situation. One factor that is constant, like the incident with the train in the workshop, is the sound quality – it's perfect. It's as if everything I'm watching is real. This is demonstrated further as an angry male voice is carried up the stairs.

'Clara. Where are you? Do you hear me?' The voice is followed by more loud footsteps ascending the wooden staircase.

My heart thumps faster. I put my hands in my pockets to stop them from shaking.

A burly looking man in his fifties bursts into the room; he's wearing a pre-First World War policeman's uniform. *He must be Clara's father, William Pearson.* I don't move or make any sound as I wait to see what happens next.

'I cannot believe you have behaved like this Clara, telling everyone tonight. You show no respect for me or your mother. What will the commissioner think of me? How can he trust me to control his officers when I cannot even control my own daughter?'

Clara sits up on the bed. 'Control me? Oh, so it would be better to lock me away and stop me from thinking for myself would it, Daddy?'

Her father stomps the room continuing his lecture. 'Why could you not have warned me before I made it public that you and Walter may have a future together?'

Clara looks at the floor. 'I didn't mean for this to happen. I didn't expect to fall in love like this. Not in my wildest dreams. Not so suddenly.'

William isn't impressed. 'I'm sorry Clara but I don't accept that. I fear this has been going on for some time and that's what makes me look such a fool.'

'That's not true; we met only two months ago, in Conley Hope. Honestly, Daddy.'

'I will not allow it! You're my daughter, and I know what's best for you.'

'He is what's best for me. He's a kind and caring man who loves me as much as I love him – with all my heart.'

'I know nothing of him, Clara,' her father says. 'And neither must you.'

'I don't care what you think. Every moment I'm with him I'm happier than I've ever been. He gives me everything I need.'

'I don't wish to know about such things.'

'He has always been a perfect gentleman.'

William laughs as he walks to the door. 'In that case you'll have no problem informing him that you have no interest in continuing your friendship.'

Clara leaps from her bed. She rushes to her father who stands in the doorway. 'I won't, Daddy. I love him. I want to give him everything of me. You have no right to stop me.'

I know what's about to happen but I'm frozen in time and space, unable to stop the inevitable. I feel horribly helpless.

Clara's father erupts. 'What? You want to what?' He slaps her firmly across the face.

Clara's head jolts to the side. Her body goes limp for a moment.

'You will obey me or leave my house forever, Clara. My word is final.' He leaves the room.

More than ever I want to rush over to her.

She has her hands up to her face. She's sobbing frantically.

I head towards her passing through the mist emanating from the rig. I reach the doorway to find Clara has vanished. My movement across the room must have disturbed the flow of gases and the whole image has disappeared. I lean against the door frame.

Emily puts a hand on my shoulder. 'There's nothing we can do, Si, maybe we shouldn't have watched it.' As soon as John has the rig shut down, Emily grabs him and hugs him tightly.

I feel awkward standing alone by the door.

Eventually, we pack away the equipment in silence. Clara seems in so much trouble. I'm worried for her. I forget that all this happened so long ago. Even if I wanted to help her there's no way science would allow it, although six weeks ago there was no way science would have allowed me to witness it.

We leave earlier than planned and I'm invited to John's house for dinner and an evening of watching football. I'm not really in the mood, but I accept. At least it'll take my mind off all this for a while.

**

October brings with it a dramatic change in the weather and many changes in my life. I now spend the majority of my weekends with John and Emily. But I've made a point of giving them space and in return they don't make me feel like a spare part. I've always been invited to testing sessions and despite my efforts to limit my involvement, I usually give in.

We've made great progress since our encounter

with the *Emerald Princess* back in September. I've taken more of a role over the past weeks and I've been lucky to witness some amazing events from the past. John's fed Alan just enough information to encourage his continued approval of the project, but not enough to give him cause to make it public yet. Most of our testing has been limited to Clara's house, but we've also managed to scan other buildings including the university and even part of Durham castle, thanks to Emily, who called in a favour with a family member who works there.

We've seen happy moments from several different years, but unfortunately, the simple fact that the Human Aspect Scanner feeds on pure emotion means we've also encountered some sad and frightening events too. This includes an accident in which two people were killed. Luckily, John shut the rig down before we witnessed too much of the tragic event.

I now have a good understanding of the equipment. I know how to adjust various factors to improve the performance and receive a near perfect representation of the past. I've worked hard to learn from the other two. I'm happy with my contribution to the equipment's evolution. We've made good progress and together we've learnt a lot, not only about the equipment, but about ourselves and each other. I'm now good friends with Emily and she's definitely come out of her shell. Despite being saddled with me, probably far too often, the two are still hitting it off nicely.

We've discovered that it's impossible to photograph or video the effect the rig produces. And we've shown no one else what it can really do, not even Alan. Keeping it a secret has given us more freedom.

The biggest difficulty is the unpredictability of what we see. We have no way of picking a date, a time, or a particular event to re-visit. One day we witnessed a couple having sex in a university storeroom sometime in the 1960s. It left Emily a little red faced. We endured a couple of minutes of embarrassment before the rig was shut down, despite John's best efforts to do it sooner... or so he made out. We had a good laugh about it afterwards.

We've also found that if we visit the same event more than once, it eventually fades. It's as if we've used up all the energy that was left behind. One such event is the episode in the attic. On the third time of our viewing it, the images faded and they were eventually unrecoverable. We haven't seen Clara Pearson since, and although I wouldn't admit it to anyone, I feel like I miss her. The attic now feels very different to before; it feels as empty as it looks.

At some point we've all been moved by something we've seen. I don't think one of us has escaped a bad night's sleep thanks to the Human Aspect Scanner, although this hasn't stopped its continuous development. I've built an extra storage tank where compressed gases, mixed by John, can be stored. This cylinder can be fitted to the rig later to give us far more viewing time. This, along with other modifications made by my friends, has streamlined the whole process and improved its potential.

We had planned to test the rig in the university again during the mid-term break, but unfortunately John's had an accident that will keep him out of action for a while. Bouncing around on a trampoline with his young nephew must have seemed like a good idea at the time. However, catapulting himself off and landing on the patio certainly wasn't. I didn't realise ankles could break in so many places.

My friend is now up to his knee in plaster and very unhappy to say the least. He's even more annoyed that he can't attend the university's award ceremony with Emily; his ankle is still just too painful. It's a pity because she's up for an award – best student or something, I don't know. I've never been invited to anything like that, until I receive a call two days before the event.

'Hello,' I say, picking up my phone.

The quiet voice on the other end is that of Emily. 'Hi, Si, sorry to bother you but I need to ask a favour.'

'No problem, Em. What is it?'

'Are you free on Friday night?' she asks.

'I think so. Why?'

'Would you like to accompany me to the uni awards?'

'What about John?'

'He can't go because of his foot.'

'I don't think he'd be too impressed if I took you while he sits at home.'

'Actually it was his idea. Do you want to go or not?'

'You must have run out of names if you're asking me,' I say, making a joke.

'Don't be silly, Si, you were my second choice.'

'Thanks... I think.'

'Besides, all my other male friends are out of town and my dad's busy.'

'Great.'

Emily giggles. 'Do you have a suit?'

'Course I do.'

'Good. You'll need it.'

'What colour's your dress?' I ask.

'Why?'

'So I can wear a shirt to match.'

'Wow. I didn't know you had it in you, Mr Benson.'

'There's a lot you don't know about me, Miss Marks.'

'Well I've got a whole night to find out. Pick me up at seven?'

'I'll see you then.'

'Thanks, Si. I owe you one.'

'You don't owe me anything. It's nice to be asked.'

We say our goodbyes and I hang up.

**

By ten thirty on Friday night I'm clapping furiously as Emily leaves the stage of the Fonteyn Ballroom. She has an award in her hand and a huge smile on her face. I've rarely seen her out of a pair of jeans so it's a pleasure to watch her crossing the room in a figure-hugging silver dress.

I pass my friend a glass of champagne and kiss her on the cheek as she takes her seat. 'To the student of the year,' I say, tapping my glass against hers.

'How embarrassing,' she says, slumping in her chair.

'It's not embarrassing. You should be proud of yourself.'

'Thanks, Si.'

'You'll get another one of those for your project this year.'

'Well if we do, John can collect it; I'm not standing up there again.'

I laugh. 'I don't know about you but I miss using the rig.'

'I know what you mean. It's addictive isn't it?'

'Definitely. Where shall we scan next, the

university as planned?'

'Maybe. John will be out of action for a while though. I thought about scanning the classroom where he and I first met,' she says.

'Why?'

'To see if we left an impression,'

'What does that matter?'

'You know how the rig works, Si. I'd love to see if it left a strong enough impression. It would show how special the moment was.'

I'm concerned. 'Look, Emily. You don't need to see anything with the rig to rubber-stamp you two you know; I can tell you far more than that machine ever will.'

'Really?'

'Yes. John might not be the most expressive person when it comes to stuff like that but he thinks the world of you... trust me. I've known John far too long.'

'That means a lot. But I'm not sure.'

'What makes you think any different?'

Emily surveys the contents of her glass.

'Sorry, you don't have to answer that.' I say.

'That's OK. I just feel I'm too far down his priority list.'

'I'm sure that's not the case, Em.'

My thoughts turn to my own situation. After Rachel's last visit, I now know I'll never see her again. And I'll probably never see Clara Pearson again either. Now I'm the one staring into my drink.

'You're thinking about her aren't you?' Emily asks.

'Rachel? No, not really.'

'I didn't mean Rachel.'

I smile. I can't hide it.

'On the subject of first meetings and falling in

love, I wonder if we'll ever see why Clara got herself into so much trouble.' Emily asks.

'I doubt it.'

'I'd love to see her meeting her man. The one she fell in love with. Sorry, Si, but it did sound so romantic.'

'Do you think it would have left an energy impression?' I ask.

'I wonder if it made an impression the moment you first saw her.' Emily says, looking smug. 'I had noticed you know.'

I know how daft this whole thing is. I'm falling for a woman who I've only seen in a photo and in a strange animation from nearly a hundred years ago. I'm about to brush the subject off when I realise we've both had enough champagne to warrant a few stupid questions.

'What had you noticed?' I ask.

'I saw your face, Si. Don't worry, I won't say anything.'

'Thanks, Em. It's a bit embarrassing really. What kind of nutter falls for a lass in an old photo?'

Emily grips my arm. 'Oh, Si, I don't see it like that at all. You haven't just seen some lass in a photo; you've interacted with her in real life.'

'Not really.'

'You did, in a way, back in the attic.'

'I just wanted to go in and rescue her. It was horrible.'

'You've taken quite a liking to that girl, haven't you?' Emily asks.

'You know what... I have, but I don't think I'll be doing much about it do you?'

'Hmm, I guess not.'

'So, how weird am I then?' I ask.

Emily giggles. 'You're not weird... Well, maybe just a little bit.'

I smile. 'I'd love to know more about her though, just out of curiosity.'

Emily nods towards a group of young women on a table close to us. Two of them have red hair. 'There's plenty more attractive redheads out there, Mr Benson.'

I shake my head. 'Not like Clara. I don't know what it is about that woman that's got me so hooked.'

'OK. I'll ask you a boy question,' Emily says, with a mischievous look. 'How attractive would you say she is, on a scale of one to ten?'

I picture Clara in my head. I remember the feelings I had in the attic. I take the opportunity to justify my crush. 'Twenty.'

'Oh shit.' Emily drops her empty glass on the table. 'That's not good.'

'I know.'

'I've been thinking... Instead of scanning the university next time, we could take the rig and find Conley Hope,' she says, out of the blue.

I smile uncontrollably. I've been hoping for weeks that someone would suggest that.

'It's probably the last thing you want to see, but we might find where Clara met her true love. I think that would definitely show up on the scanner. At least you'd see her again.'

My smile dissolves as I think of Clara meeting her future lover.

'Sorry, bad idea,' Emily says.

'No. I want to see her again, Em. I'll take what I can get. Sorry that sounds a bit creepy doesn't it?'

'No it doesn't. I'll speak to John. Well I'm drunk; I think you'd better take me home.'

'Yes, I better had.'

'When I say take me home, I didn't mean...'

I laugh. 'I know what you mean, Em.'

As we get up from the table, Emily leaves her award behind. I pick it up and we exit the party, far from gracefully.

SIX

6 May 1912

Clara Pearson steps off the train at Conley Hope station. She's excited. It's not her first visit to the town; she has an old school friend who lives on a small estate within this pretty and relatively unknown little valley. Clara's friend, Josephine, married Mr Raymond Cole, the aptly named owner of the local mine. She's visited often ever since. Clara's not on a social visit today, she's here in the hope of filling a vacant position at the local school. Following an interview with the parish council last week, she's returned to discover the outcome.

Despite their friendship, Josephine hasn't pulled any strings for Clara as her husband is very strict in such matters. Mr Cole has a lot of say in what goes on in the town, but likes to do things by the book. That's how he's earned the respect of the town's people. Clara would also be displeased at the thought of someone doing her a favour. Although she's grown up in the shadow of her father back in Durham, she's determined to stand on her own two feet from now on - an independent streak that sets her apart from her female acquaintances.

Although nervous, Clara feels confident. She's received a good education, and studied hard to a high level, despite her gender and the obstacles against her. Since the age of fourteen, she's worked part-time in one school or another. As she leaves the train behind, she thinks about her interview and how it went well.

Clara makes the walk from Conley Hope train station to the little school on the edge of town. As she follows the grassy lane uphill she hears the whistle of the train pulling away. Clara can't help but smile as she passes a meadow filled with wild flowers, she loves it here. Her cream dress blows in the warm breeze as she walks.

On Schoolhouse Lane, Clara sees clouds of white smoke in the distance. It's the main transportation of the day continuing on to Durham, which lies behind the distant hills. The air smells sweet; birds sing in the young oak trees surrounding the school and little church next door. The only thing spoiling the tranquillity is the distant squeaking of pit machinery.

The school is a lovely building with polished stone walls and large mullioned windows. The church next door is similar, although taller due to the bell tower with its green slate spire.

As she enters the school hall, her nerves build.

Four stiff-looking members of the council are seated at a table.

Clara waits patiently in the doorway until a grey haired gentleman stands. 'Take a seat, my dear.'

Clara sits at the sole wooden chair laid before the council.

'How are you today, Miss Pearson?' the man asks.

'I'm well, thank you, Mr Daniels.'

'Good. Thank you for returning to us. We've considered all the applicants, and you outshone the rest by far, young lady.'

'Oh my, I'm so pleased.'

'It seems you have all the credentials, and certainly the right attitude,' he says. 'However, we don't believe you should be travelling from Durham each day to teach our children. We would prefer to have you living in our community.'

Even more good news for Clara; she's been looking for a reason to leave the city for some time. 'Well, I have every intention of taking up residence here in Conley Hope, sir.'

'Wonderful,' he says, sitting back on his chair. He looks relaxed. The three women on the council mutter and whisper to each other for a moment.

'When would you be intending to move here, Miss Pearson?' bellows a large lady seated on the end.

'I've been offered lodgings with my friends, the Coles, for the time being. I shall hunt for a house as soon as I'm settled.'

'No need. There's a small property that comes with the position, so finding a home won't be necessary,' the lady adds. 'It does need some repair work though, so it isn't available just yet.'

Clara can't believe her luck. Not only has she got the job she wanted, she also has a new home in her favourite place. 'Thank you. When would you like me to start?'

'As soon as you can,' the man says. 'It seems we have a new teacher and a new member of our family. Welcome to Conley Hope, Miss Pearson.'

Clara moves to the table. 'I can start next week. I promise I'll make a difference here.'

A tall thin lady with wiry white hair looks over her spectacles at the town's newest teacher. 'Don't get carried away, Miss Pearson. Just work hard and show our children the ways of our Lord and you'll fit right in.'

Clara beams as she curtseys and shakes the hand of each member of the council in turn. 'I can't wait.' Leaving the room, she strides out into the sunshine filled with excitement – almost to the point of bursting. She heads quickly across the schoolyard towards the little church. Out of sight of her new employers, she picks up her dress and runs as fast as she can down the lane to tell Josephine the happy news.

**

4 November 2012

I meet Emily at the university workshops. It's two days after the award ceremony and Durham University's Student of the Year has agreed to help me find Conley Hope. Armed with a few scraps of information, we're ready to begin our search for the mysterious Conley Valley.

We're also taking the Human Aspect Scanner with us in case we find something interesting. Although complicated and bulky, the scanning rig is surprisingly light and easy to move around. Two people can easily carry it a good distance. Emily and I load it into my van; luckily, it's a quiet Sunday so there are no curious onlookers.

'That should do it,' I say, as I tighten a strap to hold the equipment still. Are you sure John was OK with this, Em?'

'Of course. He's disappointed he can't be here but

he doesn't want that to stop us. He just said to ring him if we find anything.'

'I'm sure we can manage that.' I pause before closing the rear doors.

'What's wrong?' Emily asks.

'I just don't know if we should do this or not.'

'Don't be so serious, Si. We'll have fun.'

That's a surprising change in attitude. 'You're right. Let's go,' I say, getting into the van. 'So, do you know where we're going?'

Emily puts on her seat belt and takes a notepad and map from the dashboard. 'I looked up the places you said and I think we're in business.'

'OK then, off we go, Miss Marks. Point the way.'

**

We leave the city via the dual carriageway in the direction of Newcastle. Before long I'm negotiating the twisting green lanes of the countryside north of Durham.

Emily navigates. 'The little village should be here somewhere,' she says, scouring the horizon.

We round a bend in the road and pass a road sign – Highfield. 'That's it,' I say.

'There should be a picnic area on the other side of the village,' Emily explains.

'That's as far as we'll get in the van, I think.'

'Oh right, can't we drive straight there?'

'No, apparently the mining town of Conley Hope's completely gone now,' I explain, recalling the information I'd found at the library. 'I think it ended up under a lake or something.' I'm reminded of how impossible it could be to get another glimpse of Clara.

'Oh dear.'

'I know. We're not going to have much luck are we?'

'You never know, Si. Anyway, we might as well have a look around.'

Emily's probably right, finding the town gone may at least give me closure if nothing else. Coming out of the village I see a parking area with wooden seats. I pull in.

'What's that over there?' Emily asks.

I cut the engine. In the distance is a hill with a large red-brick tunnel disappearing into it. 'That must be the old railway tunnel. I think it's the only way into the valley,' I say.

'I guess we're walking from here.'

'Looks like it.'

I'm not sure who's more excited of the two of us as we walk the grassy disused railway track towards the tunnel's mouth. I survey the track as we walk.

'What's up?' Emily asks.

'Nothing, I was just thinking we could probably get the van down here if we need to. We can't exactly carry the rig all this way. Can we?'

'Good point.'

After a few minutes we come to the brick tunnel which passes through a section of rocky hillside. The van would easily fit through but I don't want to risk it in case someone comes the other way. It's a good job I don't as a couple walking their dog emerge from the opening as we enter.

'Hello,' they say, as we pass.

Emily and I return the gesture. I suddenly feel cold as we walk into the tunnel. Like Emily, I'm dressed warmly yet I feel a chill. My anticipation grows. I'm curious to know what's on the other side.

'Are you OK, Em?' I ask, as we reach the heart of

the dark tunnel.

'Yeah, I'm alright, just cold. This place is a bit weird isn't it?'

'Just a bit.' The old Victorian brick walls are damp and the roof is black, probably from the soot of old steam trains. We eventually reach the other side and come out into the welcome sunlight. My eyes adjust and then I see the beautiful valley filled with autumn colours; to my left is a small lake.

'Wow,' Emily says, running to a fence that marks the edge of the blue-green water. In the centre of the lake is an old rusty steel structure. It reminds me of a modern art sculpture.

'What do you think that is, Si?'

'It's probably part of the old mine or something,' I say, joining her. In the distance is a small wood and behind that an overgrown structure. 'Hey, let's have a look over there.' We walk towards the trees along what looks like the old railway line. Eventually it veers off along the side of the lake. We follow a smaller path towards the wood.

'Is it me or is it getting even colder?' Emily asks.

We're in a valley with hills on all sides so we're well sheltered from the wind, yet I too feel a definite change in the air temperature as we get closer to the trees. We make our way through a little parting in the wood. I now have a better view of the ruined building which looks like an old church.

'That doesn't look in a good state,' I say, as we walk through the woodland.

'No, it doesn't,' Emily replies, slowing her pace. 'Do you feel that, Si?'

'Feel what?'

'The air here is suddenly very thin and it's gone

really quiet,' she says. 'This place is full of hot spots, Si. Something happened here – I can feel it.' Emily takes my arm.

'Come on, let's get to that building and see what we can find.' We pass through the wood and come out the other side. The land slopes gradually downhill further into the valley. Beyond is a mixture of woodland and farmland, covered with sheep. I can't see any roads in the valley, so this must be the only way in or out.

Nestled on the edge of the woods is the ruined building. It's definitely a church of some sort, with a crumbling little bell tower and overgrown grave stones dotted around it. The building's heavily damaged and covered with ivy and brambles. Further into the valley I see lumps and bumps in the grass - rough square and rectangular shapes, also the remains of field boundaries and stone walls. If this is the site of the town of Conley Hope, it seems there's not much left.

We approach the church, most of the roof and windows are long gone. Timber boards are fixed at the main entrance and front windows. Broken green slates barricade the front door.

'Let's go around the back,' I say, hoping for a way in. 'If we can get in we'll go back and get the van, and the rig.' I leave Emily investigating a small set of steps leading down at the base of the bell tower. I continue fighting my way through undergrowth.

'Hey, over here,' Emily shouts.

I double back. 'What have you found?' I ask, descending the steps.

Emily points to a timber door at the base of the tower. 'It's open,' she says, peering through the gap. A piece of masonry falls. Emily screams and leaps back almost knocking me over.

'You alright?' I ask.

Emily looks embarrassed. 'Yeah I'm OK, sorry.'

'Don't be daft. Here, let me go first.'

I push open the door keeping an eye on the crumbling stonework. The timber door looks only a couple of years old but has a corroded lock. There are small footprints on the face. *Kids must have kicked it open.*

'Be careful, Em.' I enter the building. It's surprisingly light inside as much of the roof is missing. I cautiously climb a few steps into the main body of the structure.

Emily follows close behind.

I navigate bits of fallen masonry and timber that lie on the floor. I see the occasional cider bottle and plastic bag showing we're not the only recent visitors. There's a faint smell of urine. The layout is much like any other little church, containing a main hall with an altar at one end. There's a passage out to the boarded main entrance, and remains of a timber staircase leading up to a gallery. There are no pews or furniture left and everything looks water damaged and mossy.

I look up at the greying sky above us. 'What do you think, Em? Should we have a go at scanning this place?'

Emily looks uncomfortable.

'Maybe we won't see anything anyway,' I say, 'we could just go?'

'No, I think we should try it.'

'Are you sure? It's no big deal.'

'You'd like to see Clara again, and if she lived in this town there's a good chance she came here at some point.'

I don't need any encouragement. 'True. Come on then, let's get the stuff before it gets dark. We won't hang around too long.' We head back to my van at pace. The path through the trees is quite wide. I'm confident I can drive my van all the way to the church. We collect the vehicle and head back into the valley.

Emily looks vacantly out of the passenger window as I negotiate the grassy path. I can tell she's nervous. I've seen her like this before when we've used the rig; she loves experimenting with it but seems equally as worried about what we might see.

I'm nervous too, but excited about scanning here. Luckily we don't encounter anyone else on route to the little church. We manage to get the equipment inside. We set it up in front of the altar. I'm not religious, but scanning here feels a little weirder than usual.

'I hope we don't see anything horrible,' Emily says, putting on her face mask.

'Don't worry, Em. Churches are happy places. Aren't they?'

'I suppose.'

'Yeah, course they are. We might see a nice wedding.' I say, putting on my mask and beginning pre-start checks. I connect a large car battery taken from the workshops. 'I hope this'll supply enough power to start the reaction.'

'It should do. The gas tank is full but the consumption will be huge due to the open roof,' Emily says, looking up.

'Yeah, I thought that. Fingers crossed.'

Emily hits a couple of keys on the laptop. The familiar crackling sound begins. The latest addition to the equipment is an emergency stop button which can be held in the hand. If something should go wrong, like back in the railway workshop, it can be pressed to shut the reaction down. Emily takes the button and moves away.

Standing at the altar, I feel like I'm waiting for a service to start. I glance at my watch. As the gases from the rig begin to linger, an image appears almost immediately. Through the haze I see a church in a far better state than its present-day equivalent.

There are painted plaster walls, varnished pews and beautiful stained glass in the windows. A grand staircase leads to the gallery, and above my head is a stunning and completely intact timber roof. I look around the room for obvious evidence of extreme emotion, and my eyes settle on the front row of pews.

Seated there is a man. He wears dark clothing of the era we've come to recognise from Clara's time, and has his head in his hands. *He must be mourning someone.* As I make adjustments to get a clearer image, I feel water droplets on the back of my neck.

Emily doesn't seem to have noticed it's now raining; she's some metres away under a section of roof that's still in place.

I abandon the scan as rain is now pouring through the missing sections of roof and onto the equipment. I zip my jacket up and gesture to Emily to hit the stop button.

'Shut it down, Em!'

My friend doesn't seem to hear me.

I blame my face mask for muffling my cries. I throw it to the ground. 'Shut it off Emily,' I shout, louder. I'm still not sure if I'm heard. I think the gas is having an effect on me. I'm feeling dizzy. It's as if I'm in a dream, one in which I can't seem to speak or move properly. The air around me is getting thicker and thicker, like I'm suffocating. I feel like I'm underwater – I hit the floor.

**

I'm not sure where I am – my eyes are closed. I'm hot. I must have passed out. I feel around with my hands, open my eyes, and slowly get to my feet.

I'm confused. I look around the church and find it hard to accept what I'm seeing. I'm standing in the same spot I was a few moments ago, but I'm no longer getting wet. As I look up I see why – the roof is now completely intact. There's bright sunlight streaming through the stained glass windows. The floor is clean; everything in the room looks almost brand new. The walls are painted white, and the air smells fresh. And then I notice the most unsettling thing of all – the rig and Emily have disappeared.

The man at the front of the room still has his head in his hands. I find my legs and run to the spot where Emily was standing. My whole body is jelly-like as I hobble into the main entrance vestibule. This isn't like watching the past through a cloud of gas; I feel a real part of it. But this can't be real. *Am I still unconscious? - I must be dreaming.* I can't make much sense of it, something's gone very wrong. With no Emily to consult, my gut instinct is to head for fresh air and find somewhere where I can think for a minute – so I leave, quickly.

I'm blinded by an unexpected hot sun out in the churchyard. I cover my eyes as I scurry along a short path and onto a lane, both of which I don't remember seeing on our way into the church. Suddenly, I run into something and I hit the ground again. I land flat on my back looking up at a blue sky.

A face peers down at me. 'Oh my, sir. I'm so sorry I bumped into you. It's my fault entirely, please let me help you.'

I scan the woman's face.

'Are you alright, sir? I was rushing down the lane and I wasn't looking where I was going, it was terribly stupid of me.'

I remain stunned, doped, for another moment. As I sit up, she kneels down on the dirt track beside me. My brain eventually catches up with my eyes – it's the beautiful Clara Pearson. I simply stare at her. Not only can I see through time... I can travel through time. And it seems I can stop it dead, as this moment just hangs awkwardly for an immeasurable length of time.

'Can you not speak?' Clara says, eventually.

My brain doesn't seem to be working right. I just can't process what's before me. So far, I've only had old photos and a cloudy face to face encounter to show this woman's beauty, now I have clear proof. Long curly red hair partially covers a very pretty pale face. She has huge bright green eyes, and her plump lips seem to glisten in the sunlight as she speaks. 'Are you alright?'

I have to pull myself together, but can't seem to manage it.

Clara gets to her feet, her cream dress covered in red earthy dust. 'Well if you're not going to speak, mister, then I'll be on my way. I only wanted to make sure you weren't hurt.'

I get to my feet. I can imagine the dumb look on my face. 'Err, I'm sorry,' I stutter. 'I'm fine. What the hell happened?'

'Excuse me?'

I get up. 'What?'

Clara looks at me questionably. 'There's no need to be rude.'

'I wasn't being rude,' I say. 'Are you OK?' My reaction is slow but I feel I'm making sense at least.

'I don't understand.'

I guess I'm not. 'Are you alright?' I ask.

'Yes, I think so, but my dress is ruined,' Clara replies, brushing the dust from it.

'Here let me...' I help brush dust from her dress.

'Do you mind?' she says, sharply, backing away from me. 'I don't think that's appropriate.'

I look at the dress. 'Sorry I...' Without meaning to, I catch sight of the curvy figure within it.

Clara tugs my sleeve. 'I'm sure you wouldn't take too kindly to me looking and grabbing at you, sir.'

'Honestly, I wasn't...'

'I'm sure you weren't. Why are you wet?'

I can't get a word in.

I back away. She must be looking at my clothes – they're different to any she will have seen before. 'I didn't mean to grab at you,' I say. 'I only wanted to help.'

'What happened to you?'

I'm forgetting I was in the pouring rain a moment ago. 'It's a long story.' I say, still backing into the churchyard.

'You seem nervous,' she says, following me.

'No, not really.' I suddenly feel I'm being analysed. *I have to get it together.* 'I'm sorry; I'm just a bit shaken up, that's all.'

'You talk strangely; you must not be from around these parts?'

'No, I... err... I'm from the south.' I say. 'I was visiting a friend and fell off my horse. That's why I'm so wet.'

'I've been to the south; you don't sound like a southerner. Are you hurt?'

'I'm fine. Horses and I just don't mix, it was rather funny really.'

'I'm sure it wasn't, you could have been killed.

You should go to the doctor's house; he can examine you.'

'No. No, I'll be fine, really.' Luckily the man from the church appears and breaks up the interrogation. Clara and I stand aside as he passes. The man tips his hat at Clara and looks me up and down before walking out into the lane.

I rest against a nearby gravestone; I notice the name *Barnes* written on it.

'If you're in trouble with the law, I promise I won't tell,' Clara says.

'I'm not in trouble with the law,' I reply, quickly.

'You're a strange man, Mr...?'

Normally I would simply ask her to call me Simon or Si, as I hate being called Mr anything. But today, I think I'd better play along. 'Benson. And what do I call the stunning young lady who I bumped into?' I ask.

'That's rather forward, Mr Benson. My friends call me, Clara. You may call me Miss Pearson. I'm the new schoolteacher as of a few moments ago.'

'I'm sorry, Miss Pearson. I didn't mean to offend you.'

'I'm sure you didn't. But you have, so I'll be on my way.'

A long glancing look with those gorgeous green eyes nearly knocks me unconscious once again. 'But you are stunning,' I say, stupidly.

'I think I shall make a point of avoiding you in future, Mr Benson. Goodbye.'

Why did I say that? I'm stuck for a reply. I can't believe I finally get to talk to the woman I've been searching for and make such a mess of it.

With a flick of her hair, Clara leaves. She quickly glances back at me as she enters the lane.

I have that helpless feeling again. It might just be the reality of my situation sinking in, as the shock wears off. *Is this real or a dream? Have I died?* I stand in the little churchyard, hands on hips, butterflies and bees whizzing around me. I watch Clara disappear down the lane and into the lush green valley. *What a prat I've made of myself.* As I look at the picturesque landscape, flooded with hot sunshine, my thoughts turn grey. *How on earth do I get out of here?* I head back to the church.

Once inside, I remove my jacket and sweater. I'm roasting hot. I scan the sunny room for signs of a way home. I walk the aisle scouring the floor and pews. I feel panic setting in; I don't even know what I'm looking for.

After several minutes of scratting around, I sit on the front row clutching my head. *How the hell did I end up here?* I lean back and see a figure on the cross before me. Ironically it's only now I see the light. Not the light that shines on righteous believers, but the light from the Human Aspect Scanner. Above the altar is something that has no place inside a church. I stand and move towards the phenomenon. It looks like a pool of water suspended upside down about three feet above my head. Dim light emanates from it.

I look up into the swirling apparition and see similar characteristics to the clouds of gas formed by the rig. Not completely transparent but not obviously there – like heat that can be seen coming off a tarmac road surface on a very hot day.

The hovering pool is as wide as my arm span. Inside it are flashes of the grey October day I'd left behind. *The way home.* I grab a small wooden chair from the side of the altar and stand on it, but I can't quite reach the portal. *I need something else.* I find a long wooden pole with a hook on the end, it must be for opening the windows or something; I grab it and poke at the cloud. The end disappears through.

I spot the wooden staircase leading to the gallery and race up it. The swirling cloud is close to the staircase, it looks the same from above. I pick up a hymn book that's been left nearby and throw it into the cloud. It doesn't drop to the floor, instead it disappears into what I hope is home. As I look over the balustrade I realise if I'm wrong I could simply fall to the floor and break my legs, or even my back. *I might not even get home, I could end up anywhere.* I hear a faint crackling sound; it's familiar enough to make me take the chance. I grab my jumper and jacket and climb up onto the ledge. I leap.

**

I feel pain in my knees and hip as I hit the hard floor. I don't dare open my eyes in case I'm still trapped in the sunny blur I've been trying to escape. I suddenly feel cold, very cold. For the second time in an hour, I wonder if I've died.

When I open my eyes, I'm met by a welcome sight – a dull, damp, half destroyed, vandalised structure with rain pouring from the roof and rubbish all over the floor. I'm back. It's amazing how much I missed the world I live and belong in, despite how bad it might be. I feel even better as a familiar face appears.

'Si, are you OK?' Emily asks.

I get up feeling sore. I look into the air to find no gas cloud or church roof. I'm so relieved. 'Holy crap, Emily. I got sucked into that thing.'

Emily grabs me. 'Si, I said are you OK? Are you hurt?'

I'm shivering but don't feel like I've broken any

bones. I'm dazed. I look at my legs – I conclude that all the right bits are in all the right places. 'Yeah, I'm OK, I think. Give me a minute.' I stumble around putting my sweater and jacket back on. I notice the hymn book on the floor, the one I tossed through. Both Emily and I watch as it turns to dust before our eyes – like it aged a hundred years in a second. *Maybe it did.*

Emily grabs me again. 'What's going on? I thought you were electrocuted, oh my God, Si. I thought you could be dead.'

I have a sudden fear that someone could follow me through. 'Is the rig shut off?' I ask. I may have just opened a rather spectacular can of worms and damage limitation is my first priority.

'Yes. It's shut down,' Emily says. 'The button didn't work so I knocked the gas off manually. There was a flash. What happened? Please tell me.'

Would Emily believe me? After my ordeal, I'm left feeling strangely claustrophobic. 'I need to get outside; I'll tell you out there.'

Emily follows me closely, out into the grey winter day.

'How long was I gone?' I ask, once outside.

Emily looks confused. 'Gone? You didn't go anywhere. There was a flash and I thought you'd been fried. I shut the rig down and found you on the floor.'

I glance at my watch. "What time is it?'

Emily checks her watch. 'Ten past. Why?'

I show her mine. 'Look.' The watches are different. It seems only seconds have passed for Emily. But by my watch, nearly thirty minutes have gone by.

'What are you trying to say?' Emily asks.

I take a deep breath. 'I think I've just been back in time.'

Emily stares at me. 'Don't be silly.'

Maybe I was electrocuted. What I saw could have just been a vision. My watch could be faulty because of the current running through me. *No, it happened.* 'I'm pretty sure I did,' I say.

'What do you think you saw?'

'I didn't just see something. I was talking to Clara Pearson.'

Emily shakes her head. 'You must be in shock.'

'No, Em. I just met Clara, honestly. I stood and spoke to her, she even touched me and I could feel her. She was real; she was alive.'

'I'm getting you to hospital.'

I'm still shivering. I can see Emily isn't sure of my sanity, or my health. 'It all happened in a flash. Right?' I say.

'Yes.'

'So, how did I have time to remove my jacket and jumper? And why would I, if I was this cold?'

Emily hesitates. 'I don't know. But time travel is not, and never should be possible, Si.'

'Looking back through time isn't possible either. Is it?'

She hesitates again. 'You must have inhaled the gas. I know what that stuff can do; it's not nice.'

'I didn't inhale anything, Em. I was talking to Clara. I somehow got sucked into that thing and it spat me out the other side.'

Emily still looks unconvinced.

I point to the church. 'That place looked brand new, and it was summer...' I wander the overgrown patch of land around the church until I fall upon the flat area I think was the lane. I see a line of bumps in the grass. 'Hey, look over here. See that? That's what's left of the churchyard wall.' I follow the bumps to a patch of large shrubs. 'In this corner is a grave with the name Barnes on it, I saw it.'

I pull at thick shrubs revealing a gravestone; it has *A. J. Barnes* carved into the green mossy stone. 'That's it. This is where I stood talking to her. How would I know this was here?' Now I'm ranting. 'I ran straight into her. We were practically rolling about on the road, Em. I had to give her a stupid story about falling off my horse so I didn't look like a bloody weirdo.'

'Calm down, Si.'

'I thought I was stuck there. I thought I wouldn't get back. I know I was there and it was real, I wouldn't make something like that up.'

'I don't think you made it up, Si. I just think you maybe thought it happened, when it didn't.'

'It did happen. It was real. Look.' I point to the grave again. 'I've never been here before, Em. How could I know about this?'

'I… I don't know.'

'I'm sorry; I'm just really freaked out.'

Emily gives me a hug. 'You're shaken up. Look, I believe you, but it's a big claim. You'd think the same if you were me right now.'

It must be getting colder, I'm shivering even more.

'It's nearly dark, we should go home,' Emily says. 'We can talk on the way.'

'Good idea.' We hastily pack the equipment into my van under a darkening sky. Luckily, all the moving around warms me up.

'We'll figure out what happened to you, Si. I promise,' Emily says, as we climb into the van.

I'm happy to be leaving the Conley Valley and

heading home. It's getting late and I feel exhausted. I think of Clara as we drive through the valley. I can't believe what a mess I made of our meeting. *She probably thinks I'm an idiot.* Emily and I talk about what happened as we suffer the winding road home. We muddle over the swirling gas cloud and the rapidly deteriorating hymn book. *She can't argue with that – she saw it too.*

'So what do you think caused me to cross over to the other time?' I ask, still hoping she believes me. 'Sorry, I'm probably looking for answers too soon, aren't I?'

Emily looks deep in thought. 'Hydrogen,' she blurts out, unexpectedly.

'Hydrogen?'

'Yes, it must be.'

'What do you mean, Em?'

'Well, unless there was a major malfunction with the rig, which there wasn't, the only thing different today was the rain.

'So...'

'So, it must have been the hydrogen in the rain. It could have mixed with the other elements of the gas and changed the reaction,' Emily explains.

'But how on earth will we know?'

'Don't worry, Mr Time Traveller, the laptop records everything, I'll get the data we need. I'll just need some time to look at it.'

'You do believe me, don't you?'

'I'm trying my best, Si. Honestly, I am. Besides, I've seen some pretty weird things since we've known each other, I'll never dismiss anything. OK?'

'OK.'

'If you're right, Si, that's amazing what happened today, and you're pretty amazing for finding your way back. I would have just gone to pieces.'

'I'm just glad I got back.' We're nearing home. Rain starts to beat hard on the windscreen. My eyes feel heavy looking at the streetlights passing.

'Would you do it again?' Emily asks.

'Travel back? Maybe. In fact, I think I do.'

'What do you mean?'

'Well, that photo of me and Clara makes a bit more sense now, doesn't it?'

'Oh my God, I forgot all about that. It must be real.'

Emily's right. The events of today have shown that kissing Clara Pearson back in 1912 is actually possible for me. I wonder how that photo came to be, especially after the mess I made of our meeting today.

'Was she as pretty as you thought?' Emily asks.

No hesitation. 'Yeah, she was stunning. More beautiful than I imagined.'

I'm greeted with a grin. 'Well, you know what they say... If you want something, you should just go right after it.'

'A one-hundred-year-old girl is a bit different to a new kettle, Em.'

Emily laughs. 'Yeah, I guess so.'

I drop Emily off at her parent's house and head home. I make a cup of tea and phone John, filling him in on all the day's events. He's excited about my claim, yet sounds sceptical. I'm hoping his laptop and the data Emily mentioned will back me up. After an hour-long conversation, I take a shower and get something to eat. I'd planned to have a lazy evening watching a film. I don't make it past the halfway point. By nine, I'm in bed. I fall asleep thinking about that sunny churchyard, and those huge bright green eyes.

SEVEN

It's been a few days since I last saw Emily or John. I've not been feeling well since Sunday. It may be the effects of my adventures with the scanning rig, or simply a cold. I've been to work, and bed, and done little else.

I've stored the rig in my garage as I haven't had a chance to meet Emily at the university workshops and drop it off. I've thought about Clara non-stop. I keep replaying our conversation over and over in my head. There are so many things I could have said differently, so many ways not to have made a fool of myself. John still doesn't want to make our findings public, not until he's seen proof for himself. I feel sorry for him; he missed the best moment in the life of his invention. But his absence ensures another visit to find Clara at least. That's if I can pluck up the courage to do it again.

The plan is to meet up at the weekend, to go over the data from the church scan, and discuss our next move, but things are brought forward on Thursday night. John calls me and asks me to meet him at the university straight away. He doesn't say why, but Emily's sobbing in the background makes me expect bad news.

**

I rush through the gloomy university grounds with my mind and stomach churning like washing machines. I'm worried about the fake chemical purchase orders I signed. I'm worried about my friends. I burst into Alan's office in similar fashion to John the last time we were here. I'm greeted by a very worried-looking Emily.

'Are you OK?' I ask.

She puts her arms around me. 'Yeah, I'm OK.' John looks out of the window at a dark night, his ankle still in cast. He's tapping nervously on the timber sill.

'So what's happened, John?' I ask.

His eyes don't leave the window. 'They found out I nicked the core chemicals.'

I can tell he's upset. 'How did they find out? I can't believe they're bothered after the results we were producing,' I say.

John shakes his head. 'That's the problem though, Si, we shot ourselves in the foot.'

'How?'

John turns. 'If I hadn't kept the results from them, I might have got more support.'

'So who's pulling the plug?'

'Alan.'

'Why? I thought he would back you up.'

'We lied to him, Si. He's not going to risk his neck for someone who lies to him.'

'Tell him it was my idea; tell him it was my fault.'

'He's not stupid, Si.'

'The police are involved,' Emily adds.

'Shit. What have they said?'

'They want to charge John with breaking and entering, and maybe even manufacturing explosives.' Emily says.

'What? You're kidding?'

'It won't be that bad, babe,' John says. 'I told them I did it during the day, and the cabinet was unlocked. They can't prove it wasn't.'

'That still leaves bomb making, John,' Emily says, beginning to cry.

'This is crazy. So, who called the police?' I ask.

'Alan, I think,' Emily says, sobbing. 'It's university policy.'

I shuffle about impatiently, wanting desperately to confront someone. 'All this over a couple of chemicals?'

'They're pretty scary chemicals,' John says.

'How scary? And how did they find out it was you?'

'You were right at the start, Si. Those chemicals can be used for making home-made explosives. So when they found them missing, they had to investigate it. Alan recognised the compounds from my notes.'

'Jesus, John. You plonker.'

'This is serious, Si. They're talking about kicking me out. I've been working four sodding years towards this degree. I could lose my job too.'

'Sorry, I know. What about Emily?'

'I told them she had nothing to do with it.'

'Good. Did they believe you?'

'Yes.'

'They can't put us in prison for walking into an unlocked storeroom and borrowing some stuff for your college project, John.'

'No they can't, but what if they think we were

making a bomb? They've been waving the terrorism act at me.'

'The what? This is nuts.' I wander the room, trying to take this all in. 'So, who do I speak to? I'll tell them what happened. I'll bloody show them if they want. I'll take Alan back to 1912 and scare the crap out of him if I have to.'

'You can't do that, Si,' Emily says.

'Damn right I can.'

'They won't believe you anyway,' John says. 'I told them. They think we're lying to get out of trouble. And we don't even know if we could make it happen again, anyway.'

'They think the rig's dangerous,' Emily adds. 'They want it dismantled and all parts returned to the workshops by tomorrow night.'

I don't believe this. 'I'll see you tomorrow then, for the dismantling party.' I storm out.

As I approach the university gates, a young woman crosses the square. She has long curly red hair and a cream coat. She walks upright and swiftly. I watch her for a moment through the gaps in the wet iron. The gates squeal as I push them open and pass through. Thin mist surrounds the cathedral towers on the other side of the square. The building looks less impressive than usual, somehow. Everything is beginning to look rather ordinary compared with the events of the last few weeks.

I walk through town, burying my chin in my collar to avoid the cold wind. The cobbles beneath my feet are glowing with warm yellows and oranges from the lights of little shop windows. At the bottom of the hill is the bridge over the river. I head that way.

There's a man standing by a street lamp. He claps his hands to keep warm, his breath clearly visible in the evening air. A woman approaches him. She laughs at something he says as they meet. As I pass them, they embrace, exchanging excited whispers and giggling like children.

Will I ever be that happy with someone?

**

I wake suddenly and sit up in bed. The bed sheets are damp; I've been sweating. It must be the cold still coming out of me. I head to the shower. When I return to the bedroom I notice three missed calls from the previous night, and a voicemail. I listen to the message.

'Hey, Si, it's John. The police want to meet us at the workshops at ten tomorrow morning to see us dismantle the rig. Can you make it? Let me know.'

Not a chance. I dress warmly and rush downstairs. The digital clock on the oven reads five forty in the morning. I brave the cold and skip quickly to my garage. Once inside, I turn on the lights and an electric heater to soften the cold air.

I begin piling junk by the garage door – metal framework, lengths of hose, brackets, nuts and bolts, old air-conditioning unit parts, and cables. I remove any labels and distinguishing features from the rig and place them on the parts I've collected. I find an old PC under the workbench. I pull it to pieces and add the internal parts to my collection. Finally, I remove the distinctive gas tank from the rig; I check it's empty and put it with the rest of the junk.

By seven o'clock I have the real rig loaded into my van. My garage now only holds useless parts that wouldn't even build a good sci-fi film prop, let alone a Human Aspect Scanner. I have three hours to get to Conley

Hope, hide the rig in the church, and get back. I set off at pace.

**

At 10.10 a.m., I back my van up to the great oak doors at the rear of the university workshops. There's a police car parked with other vehicles close by. I wish we'd shared everything with Alan now, maybe this wouldn't have happened if we did. I have a plan though; I just hope it works.

I turn the engine off and take a moment to compose myself. For my plan to work I need to do some acting. I take a deep breath and get into character. As I climb out of the vehicle, one of the great oak doors slides back to reveal John on his crutches.

He hobbles over.

'Just go along with whatever I say or do,' I whisper, as we meet. I open the rear doors to the van and reveal the great pile of junk. 'Here's your scanner, mate. Where shall I dump it?' I ask, at the top of my lungs.

John looks around the van interior. He looks mortified.

I'm not sure if he's acting too, or I've actually fooled him. I don't care which.

'You've already stripped it,' he says.

'Well, I told you I would.'

'But...'

'The job's done, John.' I jump into the van and clamber over the junk in the back.

Emily arrives. 'What are you doing, Si?' she asks. 'What's that?'

I start kicking all the random electrical and mechanical components out onto the old gravel railway sidings. 'That, my friends, is your Human Aspect Scanner.'

John inspects a couple of the parts. He gives me a sideways look - I think he's caught on. 'I can't believe you dismantled it without me,' he says, also raising his voice. Emily looks confused. Two police officers and Alan arrive on the scene.

'No point in hanging around, John,' I say. 'If these idiots want the best thing this university ever produced to be destroyed then I'm happy to oblige.'

'What's going on?' Alan asks.

'You wanted this destroyed didn't you?' I say.

'Well yes, but...'

'But nothing. I know John couldn't face pulling it apart himself, and I know he's worried you'll just keep it and sell it, so I did him a favour.'

'We wouldn't sell it.'

John joins in. 'You might do,' he says.

'Why would we do that?' Alan asks.

'Because it's the most amazing scientific machine I've ever seen,' I say. 'Or did you still think it was a bomb?' I glare at the police officers.

'I don't think it's a bomb.' Alan says.

'No, but they do.' John says, pointing a crutch at the officers. 'And you have my notes, you didn't tell them any different.'

'That's because I thought you lied.'

'Those chemicals are no more valuable than kitchen oven cleaner,' John says, his words clearly aimed at the police. 'And I wouldn't have a clue how to make a bomb with them.'

'You don't have any idea what this machine can do, do you?' I say. I take the black and white photo of Clara and me from my jacket pocket and hand it to Alan.

'What's this?' he asks.

'That's me being kissed by a girl a hundred years ago.'

'What?'

'That's right. You've just demanded your best students destroy the world's first time machine. We all had a lovely day out in 1912. John and Emily went for a walk in the countryside and I popped in on a village fete. That's where I met her. She was lovely, we drank lemonade and talked, she even kissed me.'

Alan inspects the photo, open-mouthed.

Both police officers step forward to look.

'Anyone can produce this on Photoshop,' one officer says.

'No they can't. Take it to your forensics lab and let them test it,' I say. 'You'll find it's genuine. Here's another one... same girl.' I give Alan the other photo of Clara.

'We don't waste our budget on student pranks,' an officer says.

Alan looks shell-shocked. So does Emily. The two police officers whisper to each other.

'These two worked their butts off day and night on this project,' I say. 'Not once did they take any stupid risks, not once did they intend to do anything wrong.' I'm boiling over. I point at Alan. 'All they wanted to do is impress you.'

John looks at the parts lying on the gravel. 'I wanted to make sure it was working perfect before I showed you. That's all.'

'If you find any evidence of bomb making you can lock us up,' I say, addressing the police officers. 'But you won't.' I slam my van doors. 'I'm sorry I dismantled it. But you'll be even sorrier you wanted it that way. All because you want to make an example of John for pinching some useless bottle of liquid that's been locked in the cupboard for ten years.' I approach the police officers. 'Do you need my details regarding the chemical supplier forms?'

'I don't think that's the issue here.' One officer says. 'We're only concerned about the potential threat from this invention.'

'Well, as you can see, it isn't much of a threat anymore,' I say, pointing to the junk scattered all around me.

'You realise we have to file a report with MI5,' the other officer says.

'Fine with me,' John replies.

The officer turns to Alan. 'I think this is an internal matter. I'm satisfied with everything here. MI5 may be in touch, they'll probably want to inspect this.'

The second officer glares at John as they walk to their car. 'Don't stray too far, Mr Hartley.'

John gestures towards his foot in cast. 'I won't be running away, will I?'

'Let's leave this crazy lot to it,' one officer says to the other. They get in their car.

'What time is it, John?' I ask.

He checks his watch. 'Not far off lunch time. Why?'

'I'll take you both for a pub lunch,' I say. 'I'm not planning on working this afternoon. And I don't know about you two, but I could do with a drink after that.'

'Yeah, why not,' John says. 'I'm off for the rest of the day. Unless you want me for anything else, Alan?'

'It would be nice to find out more about this?' Alan says, waving the photos.

John takes them from him. 'You weren't

interested yesterday, Alan.'

John tucks the photos in his jacket. 'If you want to kick me out, go ahead. No point in me being here now is there?' He hobbles away leaving the lecturer in a car park littered with useless rubbish.

**

As I drive the short distance to our local pub, black clouds gather over us. Although I may have come across as in control back at the workshops, it certainly didn't feel like it.

'I think we'll be alright,' John says.

'I hope so,' Emily says.

'So, where's the real rig?' John asks.

'I'll explain over that beer,' I say, with a grin.

The weather is deteriorating fast. The wind is blowing the van around on the road. We arrive at a pub close to all our homes. It's a new building made to look like an old country pub. On leaving the van, I pause to respect the phenomenon unfolding in the sky. I've always been touched by two things; a golden dusk, and the beginning of a storm. I love the change in atmosphere; I've always seen it as the coming of the next chapter in life. Today I hope it is.

**

We sit at a table in a large bay window overlooking the car park. It's wild outside. Rain pours down the glass. I can't help thinking about my visit to the sunny Conley Valley. It seems so far away now, not only in time, but in contrast to this. I notice my friends are holding hands under the table, it makes me smile.

'So I guess it's in your garage then?' John asks.

I assume he's talking about the rig. 'It was. I moved it to the little church in case the coppers came looking.'

'Good thinking,' Emily says.

'So what's our next move, John?'

'I've no idea, Si.'

'You're not going to let all this set you back are you?' I ask.

'I just hope they don't kick me out of uni.'

'They'd be pretty stupid if they did.'

'What makes you say that?' he asks.

'Did you see Alan's face when I showed him the photos? Think about it. If you build another rig and go public with it, they'll want some credit. They'll want to say you studied with them. They won't kick you out.'

'I hadn't thought of it that way,' John says.

'There's no way they would pass up that kind of publicity.'

'You're right. All I can do is wait and see.'

'I'm sure it'll work out, babe,' Emily adds.

'Do we carry on?' John asks.

'Well, we can't stop now, John. You haven't seen what I've seen,' I say.

'I'd love to see 1912,' Emily says.

There's a flash of lightening that lights up the car park.

'I'll take you to meet Clara,' I say. The thought alone has me smiling from ear to ear.

'I think you need to get a grip,' John says, bluntly.

'What do you mean?' I ask.

A loud roll of thunder covers the pub.

'You know, Si. Your thing with that lass is silly.'

I'm embarrassed. 'This isn't about Clara, John. It's

about you getting recognition for the rig instead of grief.'

'I know. Thank you for what you did today, Si. I just don't think you should be putting too much emotional effort into this, if you know what I mean.'

'I just want to know where that photo came from, nothing else.'

'Good,' John says. 'As long as that's all it is.'

'We've found a way to travel back through time, John. I want to see more.'

'So do I. But we need to be careful.'

'We do,' Emily adds.

'In what way?' I ask.

'You've seen the films, Si. If we go changing anything in the past it could have consequences in the future.'

'Do you really think history can be changed?'

'Well as far as I know, what you did has never been done. So, who knows?'

'If it's happened, it's happened, John. I doubt the past can be changed.'

'Well until we know that for sure, we should assume it can be.'

'I don't believe that. I made a right mess of meeting Clara, if what you say is true, that photo should have disappeared. There's no way she would want to kiss me now. She probably hates me.'

'So, that's why you want to go back?' John asks.

I see the point. *Are my feelings for Clara clouding my judgment?* 'No, not at all.'

'Another accident at this level could leave us with more than a mouth full of gas, or a broken cartridge, mate. Is it worth the risk?' John asks. 'Would you be so bothered if it wasn't for Clara?'

'Maybe not. Look, I know I can't be with her, and

I know I should be careful what I do if I meet her again. Let's just not think too deeply into this and remember that you two have invented the best thing ever. And you should get to enjoy it.'

John nods. 'OK. I'll drink to that,' he says, lifting his glass.

'So, what's the next move then?' I ask.

'Back to that church, I guess,' John says.

'By keeping the rig, are we not still stealing?' Emily asks.

'Most of the stuff we used to build it was from home anyway,' John says. 'If you want we can replace anything we got from uni, then the whole thing is ours.'

'What do we do about the core chemicals; they've taken everything we had,' Emily says.

'Can we not buy the chemicals on the Internet?' I ask.

'You can't just buy them, Si. Most of it is used in military equipment like guidance systems and night vision. We could already have MI5 after us, if we try buying that stuff online they'll be all over us.'

'I'll have a think.' I say. 'There must be someone I know who can get hold of what we need.'

'Trust me, you'll be very lucky,' John says.

'No harm in trying.' I accept this won't be easy. But I'm not giving up.

'OK. To trying then.' John lifts his glass again. Emily and I do the same this time.

We spend the afternoon relaxing and chatting about the project that's no longer a project... but a quest. For John and Emily, I imagine it's a quest for recognition. For me it's a quest for Clara Pearson. Maybe ambition is ruling all our morals.

EIGHT

15 May 1912

The sun feels warm on Clara's back as she walks from the Cole Estate to town. The dry dusty lane shows the lack of rain this summer. The hawthorn bushes are alive with small birds fluttering in and out. Even the loud humming of bees and horse flies doesn't spoil the tranquillity for Clara. After growing up in the city, living here is simply heaven.

She leaves the lane and enters town, walking briskly, even though her dress feels hot and restricting.

'Afternoon, Miss Pearson,' a gentleman says.

'Good afternoon, Henry.' Clara pauses to cross the road as a tram passes.

Ornate cast iron posts line the Victorian street. Thick electric cables hang between them high overhead. They buzz as the tram moves by. It squeaks and clanks on its rails. Clara heads across the road to a row of red-brick shops with cast iron canopies and brightly painted signs. She enters the general store – a large shop filled with dark oak shelving from floor to ceiling. Once inside, she approaches the counter.

The shop keeper is smartly dressed with a shirt and tie and a white cloth apron around his waist. 'Afternoon, Miss Pearson,' he says.

'Afternoon, Mr Wiseman.'

'Have you come to collect the food hamper?'

'I have.'

'Everything's in the back; I just need to wrap it up for you.'

Two men enter the store and move to the counter.

'I won't be a moment, gentlemen, I'll just finish serving the lady,' the shopkeeper explains. He looks flustered.

Clara assumes he doesn't want to leave his shop unattended. 'No need, Mr Wiseman. I'll just put everything in my basket, you carry on.' Clara walks around the back of the counter.

The shopkeeper shows her to a storeroom. On a bench is a small stack of fruit and vegetables, ready to pack.

'Just those items there, Miss, are you sure you don't want me to wrap them?'

'Don't worry, I'll manage. I take it they'll be added to the Coles' account?'

'Yes, Miss Pearson. No payment needed today.' The shopkeeper returns to his other customers.

Clara takes a cotton cloth from her basket and puts it on the bench. She fills her basket with the items. She leaves the storeroom and travels the length of the shop. 'Goodbye, Mr Wiseman.'

'Goodbye, Miss Pearson.'

As Clara reaches the door, she realises she's left

her cloth behind. She places her basket on the floor and heads back to the storeroom. She'd explain her mistake to the shopkeeper, but he's busy talking with the two men at the counter. Clara doesn't want to disturb them; she goes back into the storeroom. She collects her cloth and is about to leave when she hears one of the men speak her name. She waits, out of sight, and listens.

'Miss Pearson's a very pretty girl,' the first customer says.

Clara's face flushes, she smiles.

'She's a bit odd though. Don't you think?' the second adds.

Clara's smile soon dissolves.

The voices fall silent. Clara hears slow distant footsteps on the wooden floor of the shop. A third customer must have entered.

'It's alright gentlemen,' she hears the shopkeeper say, quietly. 'Carry on.'

'I was just saying, I think Miss Pearson's a little strange,' the first customer says, again.

'In what way?' the shopkeeper asks.

'Well, don't you think she's a little forward to be teaching our children?'

Still hiding behind the storeroom door, Clara can hear the footsteps of the silent customer still moving around the shop.

'How do you mean "forward," Jack?' the second customer asks.

'You know. She's not as proper as we might like.'

'How do you know that?' the shopkeeper asks.

'I've just heard things, that's all.'

Clara is annoyed. She's ready to burst into the shop. But she waits to hear more.

'I did hear that her father isn't happy she moved

here,' the second customer adds.

'I see what you mean. She's far too ambitious for a woman,' the shopkeeper says. 'That only leads to trouble.'

'What's wrong with an ambitious woman?' Another man's voice joins the conversation. 'I'm sure she can live whatever life she chooses. And I don't think you should be discussing being proper while talking about a women behind her back, gents,' the stranger says.

It must be the third customer. Clara recognises his voice, but can't recall where from.

'I don't think our discussion is any business of yours, sir,' the shopkeeper says.

'It is when you insult someone I know,' the stranger says.

'I'm sorry, I didn't realise you knew Miss Pearson,' the first customer says.

'It wouldn't matter if I didn't,' the stranger adds.

'Can I help you with anything?' the shopkeeper asks.

'No, thank you. Just browsing.'

'Well if you're not here to buy, I suggest you be on your way.'

Clara chooses this as the moment to reveal herself and steps out from the storeroom.

**

17 November 2012

It's been over a week since our encounter with the police and Alan at the university workshops. From what John's told me, the dust seems to have settled. The university won't be pressing charges, but John's future has been put on hold until after a meeting with an MI5 agent at the end of the month. Alan says it's just to explain a few things. *I'm not convinced.*

Alan himself has been apologetic. I think my little speech at the workshops has him thinking about what might have been. John remains uncooperative.

We think we've solved the puzzle of my visit to 1912. What we now refer to as a 'crossover,' seems to have definitely happened. The data from the rig confirms it. Emily was right; the introduction of extra hydrogen found in the rain water changed the reaction enough to cause it. John is confident he can recreate it. Over the past week John and Emily have been working hard to get the equipment ready for another run. Some parts of the rig have been replaced, some modified and new bits added, including my gas tank, which is far bigger than the old one. This means the rig will operate for much longer, even outside.

Meanwhile, I've taken on the lifestyle of a desperate actor. I'm working twenty hours a day – repairing air-conditioning units by day and studying the early 1900s by night. I spend all my free time watching old films and scouring the Internet for information on how people looked, walked, talked, and generally behaved in the time that Clara was alive. I'm determined to return to Conley Hope. I've spent many moments mulling over the risks to my health and considered the damage I could cause by visiting Clara again. But I keep arriving at the same conclusion – I must see her again. Emily thinks it's a crush, John thinks I'm obsessed. I don't know what it is, but I know I can't walk away without making some attempt to reverse that disastrous first meeting. I've visited a tailor in town and they've made a few items of period costume for me. I made out I'm into amateur dramatics.

We've made every attempt to find out if anyone owns the little church, but have drawn a blank. We've decided to risk it and replace the lock on the rear door with our own so we can leave the equipment there permanently. I still think the police could come knocking one day, so it seems the best thing to do. I realise John was right when he said the core chemicals would be hard to get hold of. We can't find any of the compounds needed to make the gas required for the rig's reaction. Even careful searches online have brought nothing. We're at John's house discussing the situation when I remember Faza...

John almost spits his tea back into his mug when I mention our old school friend's name. 'You're kidding me. Right?'

'He might know someone who can get what we need.'

'He probably would. But, do you really want to get involved with him? Jesus, Si.'

I understand John's reaction. The last time we saw Faza he was in the middle of a busy shopping centre trying to get his arm through the steel mesh fixed over a wishing well. I presume he was stealing the money. 'You've got to admit, he'll know some shady character that can get hold of that kind of stuff.'

'Yeah... very shady. I don't fancy dragging him into this, Si.'

'Me either. But what other choice do we have? We don't have to tell him why we need it,' I say. 'We could make it clear it's a one-time thing. Offer him some cash for the favour and have no contact after that.'

John stares into his mug for a moment. 'Alright. But I hope you know what you're doing, mate. Where will we find him?'

'I'm guessing he still hangs around his old haunt.'

'Oh great. It's alright for you, you can run. I've got a cast on remember.' He points to his ankle.

I laugh. 'It won't come to that.'

'Don't be so sure.'

**

By half three, I'm parking my van behind the grottiest pub in the greater Durham area. I help John out. Looking upon the peeled, lime green paintwork of the bar door, I prepare myself for an unpleasant experience. I enter, with John hobbling behind. The stench of warm ale hits me. The room is small and dark.

Two men sit at a table in the corner; their eyes follow us to the bar. The rest of the place is empty.

'What can I get ya?' a scruffy, overweight barman says.

I scan the bar pumps and choose the cleanest looking. 'Two pints of that, please.'

'No bother.'

'We'll sit over there,' I say, to John.

John shuffles over to a table by the bandit machine.

After paying for the drinks, I sit opposite my friend. We're still being watched by the two guys in the corner. The barman looks uneasy.

'Guess he's not here then?' John says.

'Doesn't look like it. Do we ask around?'

'Don't know if that's a good idea, Si.'

I sip my drink. It's warm, flat and bitter tasting. 'You'll have to bring Emily here for a night out,' I say, with a grin.

'Yeah, right. Don't think so, mate. What do we do now then?'

'Hang around for a bit I suppose.'

'Well I'm only having one of these. It tastes like fish tank water filtered through someone's underpants.'

'It's worse than that.'

We don't need to hang around long. After fifteen minutes or so of chatting, but not much drinking, the bar door opens and a familiar lanky character enters. Faza strolls to the bar. He flicks his greasy black ponytail and scans the room. His eyes widen as they fall upon the guys in the corner.

'Can I put that on my slate,' he says, as the barman slides him a pint of something dark and flat.

'You can. But you'd better clear it by the end of month.'

'Chill, Tony. You know I'm good for it.'

John and I remain silent, watching. I feel kind of sad looking upon Stuart Phasacklea – someone I remember well. A bright young lad, adopted as a child, with parents so strict they tipped him over the edge. I remember him when his clothes weren't hanging off him – when he didn't talk in a slow, low drone, when he was intelligent and interesting.

He catches sight of us and rushes over to our table. 'What the hell are you two doing 'ere?' he asks, sitting next to me.

I smell alcohol on his breath, and sweat on his clothes.

'Looking for you,' I say.

'Christ. You must be desperate for something.'

John laughs. 'Not really.'

'I don't believe you,' Faza says. 'One of you hooked on smack or something?'

'Maybe we just missed you,' I say.

'Don't pull my chain boys. Whatever you want you'd better ask for it quick cause those two meatheads over there are after me.'

'What do you mean?' I ask, looking over at the corner.

'Don't look,' Faza says. 'You'll piss them off even more.'

'What do they want?' I ask.

Faza gulps down half his drink in one go. 'Never mind what they want. What do you want?'

'Just some chemical compounds,' John says.

'You building a bomb or something?'

'No, nothing like that,' I say.

'Growing pot then? Poisoning someone?'

'No. But if you can get what we need, we'll pay you well not to ask.'

'I see. Not like you to be up to this kind of business, Si.'

'It's a boring story,' I say.

'I get the picture. What do you need?'

John takes a list from his pocket and hands it over. 'Everything's on there.'

Faza pulls faces as he reads. 'Looks like expensive stuff,' he says.

'Can you get it or not?' John spits.

Faza laughs. 'I don't remember you being the assertive type, Hartley.'

I see the two guys in the corner are finishing their drinks. 'Can you help us or not?' I ask.

'Yep. But do me a favour...'

'Go on,' I say.

'Distract those two for a minute.'

'How?'

'Don't care,' Faza says. 'You got a mobile number?'

'It's on the bottom of the list,' John says.

'Good. I don't have a phone so I'll be calling from a pay phone.' Faza gets up. 'Just nipping to the little girl's room,' he says, loudly. He disappears into the toilets.

'What on earth are we doing?' I say.

'Don't look at me. This was your idea.'

One of the guys from the corner follows Faza. He's twice the size of both of us.

'Shit. What do we do?' John asks.

I notice the remaining guy hovers by the door. He's huge too. 'I don't know. I'd better see what's going on. He could be knocking the hell out of him in there.'

John shrugs. 'Leave him to it.'

'I can't do that.' I head into the toilets. My heart's pounding as I open the men's toilet door. The big guy's trying to look out of a high-level window. The window's wide open and the rest of the toilets are empty. *Faza must have bolted.*

The guy lunges at me. 'Where's he gone?' he screams.

I put my hands up. I back into a wall. 'I don't know,' I say.

'I think you do. And you're gonna tell me or I'll beat the crap out of ya.' He raises an arm – fist clenched.

'I said I don't know.'

He punches me in the face. I lose vision in one eye. I'm dizzy. I stumble. A hand dryer stops me sliding any further down the wall.

He grabs me by the throat and presses me hard against the dryer.

I try to struggle free but I'm helpless with the sharp corner of the hand dryer jammed between my shoulder blades. *Great, I'm going to die in a pub bog at the hands of a Neanderthal.*

'Tell me where he lives,' he says; his rank breath in my face.

'I haven't seen the guy in ten years,' I say. 'How the hell would I know where he lives?'

My sight's returning to normal. There's two teardrops tattooed on the face before me. John once told me that's a gang symbol to show how many people you've killed. *I don't fancy being his third tear.*

I dig deep and find some anger. 'Get the hell off me,' I say, shoving the guy off with every bit of strength I can rally.

He lets go of my throat.

I can breathe again now the pain in my back has subsided. 'You think you're a tough guy picking on someone half your size do you?'

By the look on his face I think he's about to hit me again.

'I don't know that idiot anymore,' I say, pointing to the window. 'I only came here to cash in a favour. And he ran off because of you. So thanks a lot.'

'What kind of favour?' he asks.

'None of your business. So go on then, hit me again. Knock the hell out of me in a pub toilet just because I said hello to someone. Lovely boy you are, aren't you? Your mum must be so proud.' I'm speaking loudly on purpose.

The guy looks that shocked I think I've knocked him off his stride. It's as if he can't decide whether to hit me or not.

Suddenly, the toilet door flies open and the barman bursts in. 'Right, out of my bar both of you.' The thug gives me a steely glance then pushes past the barman.

I follow. I cross the room straightening my clothes.

John's already waiting by the exit with his crutches. The two big guys have now left.

'You alright?' John asks.

'Yeah, I think so,' I say, rubbing a sore temple. We wait a few moments then exit.

Back in the van, I move the rear view mirror and check my face. I have a big lump on my temple but nothing else.

'What happened in there?' John asks.

'Faza jumped out the window,' I reply. 'That big dumb bastard thought I'd tell him his whereabouts if he ruffed me up a bit.'

'You sure you're OK?

'Yeah, I'll be alright.'

'So, what do we do now then?' John asks.

'Go home and put frozen peas on my face,' I say.

'And after that?'

'We wait.'

**

The next few days drag. We can't make any progress without the core chemicals. Luckily, I don't have much of a black eye – it would only be noticeable if I mentioned it. I haven't heard anything from Faza, John put my mobile phone number on the list he gave him so not to worry Emily.

After five days, my phone eventually rings…

'Alright, Si. It's Faza. Got your bomb-making shit.'

'It's not for a bomb.'

'Whatever.'

'Did you manage to get it all?'

'I did. When do you want to meet?'

'As soon as you can.'

'Tonight. Eight sharp. Phone box by the old railway bridge.'

I think I know where he means. 'How much money do you want?'

'Bring three hundred.'

I hear a bleeping noise as if the money's running out. 'OK. See you then,' I say.

'You will.' The line goes dead.

**

At eight sharp, I'm waiting in my van opposite the meeting point. It's a cold, dark night and the rain pours down the windscreen making it difficult to see the phone box from across the street.

John sits next to me, nervously tapping a crutch on the dashboard. It's annoying. 'I still think three hundred quid is too much,' he says.

'We don't really have much choice. Here he is,' I say, spying a lanky figure through the wet blur.

Faza is rounding the corner carrying a large sports bag.

'Wait here.' I get out and jog across the road.

We meet under the bridge, out of the rain.

'Alight, Si?' Faza says.

'Better after getting away from your buddies in the bar,' I say, with sarcastic flavour.

'Did they give you shit?'

'Just a bit. What did they want?'

'Does it matter?'

'I guess not, but thanks all the same. Have you got the stuff on the list?'

'Yep.' He hands over the bag.

It feels heavy. It reminds me of when John first handed me the flask back at the university in the summer. 'Is it exactly what we asked for?'

'Yes, Si. I don't rip people off.'

'Judging by the sophisticated way you left the pub last week, I seriously doubt that,' I say.

'I don't rip off mates.'

That's reassuring. I open the bag. The chemical containers look the part but I'm no expert. 'Can I show these to John just to check?' I ask.

'Be my guest, but I want my money first.' He holds out his hand.

'You can have half now, half after John's checked this is the real thing.'

'That's fair.'

I take an envelope from my pocket and roughly split the notes in two, giving Faza half. I then take the bag to the van.

Faza steps into the shadows as the van interior light illuminates the wet road.

John looks over the contents. He opens a container and sniffs what's inside. 'Yeah, that's the stuff,' he says.

I return to Faza, and hand over the rest of the cash.

He tucks it in his jacket.

'Thank you,' I say.

'You're welcome,' he says, shaking my hand.

'How can we find you if we need more?' I ask.

'Just leave a red apple on top of the phone in that box over there. I'm here most days. I've got your number, if I see it, I'll ring you.'

'A red apple? Seriously?'

'Yeah.'

'OK. I guess I'll see you later.'

'Don't blow yourself up, Si.'

I return to the van wiping my hand on my jeans. By the time I get in, the lanky figure has slipped away.

John's still looking over the contents of the sports bag.

'Are we in business then?' I ask, as I start the engine.

'Looks like it,' John replies. 'Give me a day or two to turn some of this into a gas, and we're ready to go.'

I'm grinning from ear to ear as I drive away. I might actually make it back to Conley Hope after all.

**

Two days later, it's the weekend again. We've made the trip to Highfield or Conley Hope as we know it. I've parked my van to the rear of the broken church. There's a gap in the dense woodland which hides the vehicle perfectly from anyone passing by. John and Emily get the rig set up and start testing while I change into the clothes I'd purchased.

I fumble around in the back of my van in poor light. The dark corduroy trousers seem a little short; I guess that was the fashion. The white and cream striped granddad shirt fits perfectly, as do the black ankle boots. I sit on a toolbox for a while mulling over the things I've learnt about how to behave in 1912. I feel I'm ready to go. I eventually join my friends in the church.

'Wow. You look the part,' Emily says.

'Thank you.'

'The rig's fuelled up with more than double what she's used to carrying,' John explains. 'And there's the additional tank of hydrogen.' He taps a small cylinder at the base of the rig. 'That should hopefully send you on your way.'

'Great. Hope it works.'

'Well, we've done a kind of virtual test run with the software and the results look like yours from your trip to the other side. So it should work,' John says. He looks at his cast. 'I just wish I was going with you, Si.'

'That thing will be off soon,' I say. 'Then we'll go together.'

'You're not there yet,' he replies.

'I know. So what do you need me to do?' I ask.

'Nothing,' Emily says. 'You just remember not to mess it up this time.' She winks at me.

'Right, Si,' John says. We won't shut the rig down unless you're back; I'm assuming we need to keep it running so the gate stays open, so to speak. If this works, don't hang around long.'

I nod. 'OK.' I have terrible butterflies in my stomach.

'Emily has modified the stop button,' John says. 'When she presses it, the hydrogen solenoid valve will open and hopefully that will give the same effect as the rain last time you were here.'

'Alright. Let's get on with it,' I say. If I'm made to wait any longer I think I'll back out.

John hits a few keys on the laptop.

I hear the usual crackling sound.

We all keep our distance as the mossy walls turn to fresh white plaster before our eyes. John and Emily have face masks on. I don't wear one in case that was a factor in my crossover last time.

'Hey look at that,' Emily says, pointing to a noticeboard on the rear wall. At the top is a simple handmade calendar. It looks like it was made by a child. *The vicar's son or daughter, maybe.* The days are scored through up until 15 May. *I wonder if that's today's date on the other side?*

'Will it be 1912?' John asks.

'Well, this place looked brand new when I met Clara, and that was 1912. If the church was flooded later that year then that's the only year this place existed.'

'Good point,' Emily says.

'What do you think then, Si?' John asks.

I fill my lungs to bursting with damp air. 'Good enough for me. Hit it, Em.' I step into the gas cloud. I watch Emily press the hydrogen input button. Nothing seems to happen. I just have a horrible taste in my mouth from the gases. I check a few readings on the laptop which sits on top of the rig. Everything seems normal. *Maybe that's the problem.* I'm annoyed that nothing's happening.

'Do you want me to check the data?' John shouts.

'No. No, stay there,' I say.

Suddenly there's a familiar loud pop. I feel weak at the knees. I also feel a kind of force drag me sideways.

John, Emily, and everything else from 2012 disappears.

**

I open my eyes. The church looks almost new again. The miserable future of this place is replaced by its radiant past. I've appeared by the doorway out to the churchyard. I see a family huddled together at the altar, a vicar is blessing a small child wrapped up in blankets before him. The child looks very sick. Its mother is clinging to the child and the last moments of its life.

My heart's thumping. *That's awful.* I feel so sorry for them. I flash my eyes over the rest of the room. Above my head is a pool of swirling gas only just visible. I relax knowing I have the same chance of getting home as before. Again, it feels weird being a part of the past – rather than just watching it. Luckily, no one has seen me. I quietly slip away.

The sun is bright and it takes a few moments for my eyes to adjust. I move along the path to the dusty lane. I stop at the gate and look around. I see a cluster of buildings across the lane that look like timber houses or shelters for animals. There's a road of sorts leading down the gradual slope further into the valley. I see many houses dotted about the greenery. All is quiet.

I hadn't even noticed the school next door the last time I was here. I was too busy talking with Clara. The thought of seeing her makes my heart skip three beats. I hope I don't make a mess of it this time. The school looks deserted. I hope I have the right month; I hope I have the right year. I head down the lane towards town in search of clues. I pass several cottages on my way, not recognising anything. In my time none of this exists anymore.

The whole valley seems peaceful. The air smells of flowers and freshly cut grass. The warm breeze soon blows away my sombre mood and the walk settles my stomach. I guess it's midday as the sun is high and hot on my back. Most of the pretty houses lining the lane are built from stone, but as the dusty dirt lane becomes a cobbled road, I find Victorian style red-brick buildings rising up around me. A flagged pavement begins. I pass a bridge on my left which spans the railway line. A small sandstone station sits nestled in a wooded hollow. The road flattens out and tram tracks appear.

I see people milling around ahead.

I reach what looks like the centre of town and pass the entrance to a park. There's a cast iron bandstand with wooden seating around it. Children play nearby. I hear dogs barking. *Time to get into character.* Everywhere is clean and bursting with colour. Flowers hang from baskets on the lampposts and outside the red-brick houses. I pass a grand looking bank with stone pillars straddling a pair of huge oak doors. *I have no money; I hope I don't need any.*

Leaving the shadow of the bank, I head across the street to a row of shops. I stop at the first and peer through the window. My curiosity gets the better of me and I can't resist the chance to look inside. The blue and cream sign above the window reads 'Wiseman's General Store.'

I'm uneasy as I enter the building. There's a basket full of food by the door, I step over it. Inside I find floor to ceiling shelving packed with all kinds of products. At the far end is a large mahogany counter complete with traditional balance scales and cash register.

A smartly dressed shopkeeper is serving two customers.

I wander the shop, my boots sounding loudly on the polished oak floor. I read many labels as I pass. *Salt, custard powder, cocoa, toffees, tea.* I'm amazed by the attention to detail on every tin. The place even smells interesting. As I get closer to the counter, I hear the two male customers talking with the shopkeeper.

'I was just saying,' one man says. 'I think Miss Pearson's a little strange.'

'In what way?' the shopkeeper asks.

'Well, don't you think she's a little forward to be teaching our children?'

I move closer.

'How do you mean... "forward," Jack?' the second customer asks.

'You know. She's not as proper as we might like.'

'How do you know that?' the shopkeeper asks.

'I've just heard things, that's all.'

They're talking about Clara. This isn't on.

'I did hear that her father isn't happy she moved here,' the second customer adds.

'I see what you mean. She's far too ambitious for a woman,' the shopkeeper says. 'That only leads to trouble.'

I can't hold my tongue. 'What's wrong with an ambitious woman? I'm sure she can live whatever life she chooses. And I don't think you should be discussing being proper while talking about a women behind her back, gents,' I say.

'I don't think our discussion is any business of yours, sir,' the shopkeeper says.

'It is when you insult someone I know,' I reply.

'I'm sorry, I didn't realise you knew Miss Pearson,' one customer says.

'It wouldn't matter if I didn't,' I add.

'Can I help you with anything?' the shopkeeper asks.

'No, thank you. Just browsing.'

'Well if you're not here to buy, I suggest you be on your way.'

A woman steps out from a side room. I find myself looking upon Clara for a second time. Her facial expression matches her fiery curls. I'm glad I'm not to blame for it – she looks furious.

'Are you enjoying your gossip, gentlemen,' she says.

The shopkeeper is a rabbit in Clara's headlights. The two other men back away from the counter.

Clara wades in – hands on hips. 'I didn't expect that kind of talk from you, Mr Wiseman.'

'I apologise, Miss Pearson,' the shopkeeper says. 'It was wrong to speak about you while not in the room.'

'I'd hope you wouldn't speak about me like that while I am in the room.'

The two customers linger with their heads hanging.

'I apologise to you both,' the shopkeeper says, nodding in my direction. 'You're welcome to browse.'

'No. I was just leaving,' I say.

'I think I'll join you,' Clara says.

'We apologise too, miss,' one of the other guys says, quietly.

'I should think so too.'

Clara and I leave together. At the door, I wait while Clara collects her basket. She throws a cotton cloth over the top and struggles to carry it out of the door. It looks heavy.

'Can I help you with that?' I ask.

'No. I'm fine, really.'

I walk along the pavement at Clara's side. We're heading in the opposite direction to the way I should be going. But I don't care.

'I'm sorry about all that back in the shop,' I say.

'No need, Mr Benson, you defended me. Thank you. You didn't have to after the way I spoke to you the last time we met.'

She remembers. 'Yes, well maybe I deserved it,' I say.

'No you didn't. I'm afraid I can be a little hotheaded at times.' She's starting to sound out of breath.

'Please let me take that,' I say. 'I won't tell anyone.'

Clara laughs. 'Thank you.' She hands me the basket. Her angry expression has subsided. She touches my sleeve. 'You're not wet today,' she says, with a grin.

'No, I'm a little more respectable,' I say.

'I didn't say you weren't respectable. Besides, I might not like respectable.' Clara gives me a playful look.

I'm not sure how to react.

'Don't worry, Mr Benson. I'm teasing.'

I smile. 'Call me, Si.'

'Si? That's an unusual name.'

'It's short for Simon.'

'It's still unusual,' Clara says. 'I think I prefer Simon, Si sounds rather oriental. You don't look oriental.'

'No, I don't. And what do you prefer to be called?' I ask.

'Miss Pearson,' she says, with a flick of her hair.

I get the message.

As we reach the end of the street Clara skips a few paces ahead of me. 'Come on; hurry along... before your arm drops off.'

She's nuts. I pick up the pace.

We turn into a lane edged with plump hawthorn bushes. It winds its way downhill through lush green fields.

'I hope I'm not taking up too much of your day?' Clara asks.

'No, not at all.'

'Isn't this place simply beautiful?' Clara says, closing her eyes and taking in a huge breath.

I scan her pretty face, her lovely big smile. 'Very beautiful,' I say.

'Where do you live... if you don't mind me asking?'

'A long way from here, I'm afraid.'

'You are a mystery, Simon... I like that.'

I've never been keen on the longer version of my name, back in the future only my mother calls me Simon, and only when I'm naughty. Today though, I'll happily put up with it. We arrive at the gate to a small estate.

'Well this is my home,' Clara says. 'At least for now.'

I hand over the basket.

'Thank you. That was very sweet of you,' she says.

'You're welcome.'

'Will I see you in town again?'

'I hope so.'

Clara throws me another smile. Her plump lips part revealing perfect teeth.

My heart skips another three beats. 'Goodbye, Miss Pearson.' I look back more than once as I walk briskly up the lane. Each time, Clara's still standing at the gate watching me. I leave the lane and enter town. Eventually, I break into a light jog. *I hope the rig's still working.* I must look strange running along the street. No one else seems in a hurry to get anywhere.

Once I've passed through town, I speed up. I'm panting as I run uphill to the little church. I'm hot. *I need a drink.* Luckily, the church is still empty. I'm relieved to see the swirling gas cloud by the back wall. I compose myself before moving a pew so I can climb onto a ledge sticking out of one of the stone pillars. I clamber up so I'm almost above the cloud.

I hear crackling. I leap through.

**

I roll along the cold floor landing at John's feet.

'You alright, Si?' he asks.

I stand. I'm still out of breath.

'Jesus, I guess not.'

'It's OK,' I say. 'I'm fine.' *I feel fantastic actually.*

Emily arrives. 'I've shut the rig down, Si.'

'Thanks, Em.'

'Did you get there?' John asks.

'I sure did. I annoyed a couple of locals, but also managed to see Clara, and I think I might have made a decent job of patching things up with her.'

'Brilliant,' Emily says, her face alight.

'Did you get a kiss in front of a lemonade stand?' John asks.

'Nope.'

'Shit.'

'Why, what's wrong?' I ask.

'Nothing, I just know what you're like. You won't give up until that happens, will you?'

'Well it must happen at some point.'

'Thought you'd say that.'

'How long were you gone, Si?' Emily asks. 'It was just the same as before here. A loud pop, then a flash, and you hit the floor.'

I check my watch. 'Nearly an hour,' I say. I'm shivering again.

Emily hands me a jacket. 'Wow. Did you explore?'

'I did. How much gas was used?'

John checks a level gauge on the tank. 'Only about half.'

'So we'd easily get a two-hour run from one tank?'

'I guess so,' John says.

'I think I'll build a bigger tank,' I say.

'I don't like the sound of that,' Emily says.

I laugh. 'Don't worry, Em. I'm getting the hang of this now. I'm having fun.'

'Glad someone is,' John says. 'We've only been here a minute.'

John's words hatch interesting questions. *Does this mean I'm now an hour older than I should be?* I'm fascinated by the possibilities.

'Well, why don't we have a brew in the van to warm up? Then we'll do it again,' I suggest.

'You haven't even told us what happened yet,' John says.

'Yeah, Si. What did you see?' Emily adds.

'I'll tell you over that brew. Come on, I'm freezing.' I bounce down the rear church steps and battle though the brambles to my van. Once inside, I dish out hot tea from a flask and begin my story...

NINE

25 May 1912

The Conley Hope annual village fete is a great occasion and one that's planned carefully for many months. The main venue is the town park. Each year there are stalls tempting the town's people to buy a multitude of goods. It's also a chance for exhibitors to show off anything they fancy, from Mrs Attley's award-winning cakes to young Arthur Trumper's prize pig. Other activities include free train rides for the children and sporting competitions for the men. The school play is another attraction for young and old. It's performed several times in the school hall during the afternoon and early evening. It's a glorious warm day.

Clara has the unenviable task of keeping the child actors in check. She's enjoying playing a game in the schoolyard while the town's bank manager and his son change the scenery for the second performance of the day.

Suddenly she hears a commotion out in the lane –

horse's hooves pounding the dusty road, wagon parts rattling, men shouting.

'Please look after the children a moment, Sarah,' Clara says to another teacher, and goes to investigate. She doesn't rush as she's already out of breath from running with the children. She walks through the crowded school and out into an even busier front yard.

Two Black Maria police carriages are at the school gates. The four horses, two apiece, strain at the hands of their drivers. Children run around them with excitement. Clara soon realises this spectacle is all for her benefit.

A smartly dressed policeman climbs from the first carriage and opens a door to the second. A gentleman in a police captain's uniform steps down. Clara goes to greet her father.

Captain William Pearson is highly respected in Durham, and well known here. Unfortunately he also possesses an angry streak and he doesn't look happy today. He greets his daughter with an officer at his side.

Clara hangs her head. She feels like she's in trouble.

'Hello, my dear. I must say this village fete looks to be as good as I'd heard it was.' He manages a wry smile for the benefit of onlookers. He continues to address Clara from the corner of his mouth. 'It would have been far better to receive an invitation rather than have to come here unannounced.'

Clara rolls her eyes.

'Don't pull that face with me young lady.'

'What am I to do father? Every time I find happiness you arrive with a hundred men to spoil it for me.'

'Let's not talk out here like this, for goodness sake.' William ushers his daughter inside. 'Wait here,

Charles,' he barks at the officer accompanying him. His eyes fall upon a photographer setting up his camera by the gates. He points. 'Make sure he takes no photographs of me.'

Clara leads her father to her classroom. The captain's boots ring loud on the polished wood floor. Clara offers him a chair and they sit together in the sunlight from the tall sash windows.

Clara's father looks around him. 'Look at this place, as my daughter you don't need to work. So, why are you here?'

Clara doesn't want to cover a subject already exhausted. 'You know why, Daddy. I love it here and I'm happy. Why can you not be happy for me?'

'I cannot stand aside and watch my daughter waste her life, it's time you came home.'

'But I don't want to come home. Why do you not pick on young Annie? She's to travel the world with no particular direction in life and you approve. You always pick on me, Daddy. Why?'

'Your sister is travelling with her fiancé; there's a difference.'

'Annie's only ambition in life is to be looked after by a wealthy husband,' Clara says. 'What a bore.'

'There's no wrong in that.'

'I wish to plan my own future, not have a man do it for me.'

'And what of Walter?'

Clara pauses. 'Walter is a nice man, Daddy, and I know you trust him, but...'

'I do trust him, and his intentions towards you are clear. He's one of my best officers and it would be stupid of you not to accept his hand.'

'His intentions are only clear to you, Daddy. If

Walter wants to marry me then he should ask me. He should stop trying to impress you and do something to impress me.'

Sarah appears in the classroom doorway. 'I'm sorry to disturb you, Miss Pearson, but everyone is waiting for the play to start. I fear we may be keeping folk waiting too long, Miss.'

'I'll be right with you, Sarah.'

The woman disappears.

'You're making your mother ill with this behaviour,' William says.

'That's not true and you know it, Daddy. And I'm not something to be offered to your best officer.'

Captain William Pearson stands, his face turning plum.

'Please don't spoil my day, Daddy. Why did you have to come and discuss this today, of all days?'

'You're right. I have other business to attend to. I shouldn't keep you from your fete, especially as it will be your last.' He makes for the door. 'We'll discuss this next week when you come home. Walter will be there to greet you and I promise he will ask you for your hand. And I'm sure you will accept.' And with that, he leaves.

There's further commotion out in the lane. Clara watches quietly from the window as the police carriages are pulled away by their horses. Today had been the happiest of her life before her father arrived. Now she has a hollow feeling inside. She wipes a tear from her cheek and returns to the children.

**

24 November 2012

John and Emily are hanging on my every word as I finish the tale of my last crossover to Conley Hope. The van windows have steamed up, and we're all out of tea.

'That must have been amazing,' Emily says. 'I'm so glad you and Clara made up.'

'So, shall I go back again? I ask.

'It's up to you,' John says.

'Do you feel up to another trip today?' Emily asks.

'Yeah, definitely.'

Back in the church, there's no work to do as the rig is still set up from my visit to Wiseman's General Store. John types a few commands into the laptop.

I hear the gases filling the tubes from the fuel tank to the scanner unit.

'Ready when you are,' John says. He taps the fuel tank. 'And don't forget you only have half a tank of gas. Don't be longer than an hour.'

'Yes, boss.' I take off my jacket to the sound of crackling.

John and Emily put on their masks and retreat. The damp mossy rear wall turns white and clean as the gases drift across it. The noticeboard and calendar we used to determine the date last time, appears again. I see the days are struck through up until 25 May. That's ten days after my last visit to Clara.

'It's the wrong date,' Emily says.

'That's OK. I don't want to access the same day anyway,' I say. I want to see Clara again, but I see no point in reliving the same moments as before, if that's even possible. I'm hoping to access another point in Clara Pearson's history. *Later is fine*. 'Go for it, Em.'

Emily presses the hydrogen input switch.

I step into the gas cloud. I feel the temperature rise. The crackling sound fades. All goes quiet.

**

I stumble into a pew. I manage not to fall over it. The church is warm and bright again. I hear children laughing. I duck behind a pillar so not to be seen.

In the sunny entranceway, stand a boy and girl no older than thirteen. They're dressed in summer clothing. The water-damaged window boards of the present have disappeared revealing the grassy churchyard beyond. The children whisper to each other and kiss quickly.

This must be the cause of the energy I've accessed. Maybe it's a first kiss I'm watching.

The young boy and girl run out into the sunshine.

After a moment, I follow them into the church yard. My stomach's churning again. It feels like late afternoon; the sun is hot. I hear crickets in the meadow grass and birds chirping in the trees. There's a chorus of flying insects buzzing around the flowers that grow at the edge of the churchyard. There's a group of people congregating outside the school.

I follow the lane in front of the grey stone schoolhouse and stop at the gates. I see a table with a gingham cloth draped over it; on top are bottles of cloudy liquid.

'Would you like to buy a bottle of lemonade, young man?' an elderly lady says.

'No, thank you,' I say. 'Maybe later.' I see a handwritten sign on the schoolyard wall behind. *This must be where the photo of me and Clara was taken.* It's a strange feeling knowing I'm here, in a moment I've already seen. But I don't see a camera, and I don't see Clara. I enter the schoolyard.

'Are you here for the play, sir?' a man in a brown suit asks. 'Admission is free. I'm told it's a marvellous show.'

'Erm, yes I am.'

'Find yourself a seat in the hall then, sir. Not long to wait now.'

'Thank you.' I feel like everyone's looking at me as I walk a beautifully tiled corridor and enter the school hall. There aren't many free seats – the room is busy. I find a space among the many wooden chairs laid out in rows in front of the stage and sit down. Suddenly, people get up from their seats and head to the windows. Something's happening outside.

I hear shouting.

'Don't worry, dear,' the middle-aged lady next to me says. 'Someone always gets too excited at the fete.'

I smile and stay seated. After a while things appear to calm down, and there's activity on stage as final preparations are made. I hope I'm blending in. My butterflies subside.

'Are you new in town?' the lady next to me asks.

I take the opportunity to find out more about this place. 'No, just visiting,' I say. 'But I'm thinking of moving here. Would you recommend it?'

'Oh yes, definitely. Conley Hope is a lovely town. Everyone is so friendly.'

'How long have you lived here?'

'I've lived in the valley all my life. But I moved into town when my husband died.'

'Sorry to hear that,' I say.

'That's kind,' she says. 'I'm happy though. I now have a lovely new house in town.'

'How long has the town been here?'

'It's been springing up over the last few years, as the mine has expanded. My family used to own the land we're now sitting on.'

'Really? So are the school and church both new?

'The school has been here two years I think, but the church was only opened at the beginning of the year. We're still missing a full-time vicar. You don't happen to be one, do you?'

'No, I'm afraid not.' At least I know the church has only been around several months. All the energy left in there must be from the time Clara was here, or later. I still haven't seen her. *I wonder where she is.* 'I think I'll take a walk,' I say. 'Stretch my legs.'

'It was nice meeting you,' the woman says.

'And you.' I leave the hall and wander along the corridor in the hope of finding the reason I came here. Suddenly, a door is thrust open and a woman emerges, bumping into me. I end up with a face full of curly red locks.

'I'm so sorry,' she says. It's Clara. 'Simon. Oh dear, that's the second time I've done that.'

I notice Clara looks upset. I think she's been crying. 'Are you alright?' I ask.

'Oh... yes. Sorry.' She takes a hanky from her sleeve and dabs her cheeks with it. 'It's nothing to worry about, silly really.'

'Are you sure?'

'Yes, really.' Clara glances along the corridor. 'Do I look dreadful?'

'Of course not. You look lovely.'

She smiles. 'You're sweeter than I thought. I'm sorry but I have to dash, please stay and watch the play. I'll come and find you.'

My heart races and the butterflies return. 'I will.'

I find my way back to the hall, but all the seats have been taken - so I stand at the rear. I simply take in the atmosphere, smiling at everyone who smiles at me.

Clara appears by the stage with a small group of children dressed in colourful costumes. She ushers them on stage. One little boy looks nervous and upset. Clara kneels before him. After a few words from his teacher, the boy ends up laughing.

I watch with admiration.

The play begins and after a few minutes of keeping a watchful eye on her tiny actors, Clara looks over - our eyes meet across the room. She heads in my direction. Clara joins me and stands close. She whispers scraps of information about the children in my ear. She tells me a little bit about each child as they say their lines. I can tell she's proud of them all.

I look interested but really I barely hear a word. I just feel her gentle breath on my face and smell the soapy scent of her skin – I can concentrate on nothing else.

The play is only short. And when it's over I applaud along with the rest of the room. The children look rather unorganised as they leave the stage.

I nod towards the children. 'It looks like you're needed, Miss Pearson.'

'I feel so rude,' she says.

'Don't be silly.'

'But I'm always rushing off...' Clara says, edging away.

I'm encouraged by her indecisiveness. 'Off you go,' I say, waving her away.

Clara takes charge of the children as the room begins to empty.

The commotion gives me a chance to check my watch. I see that over half an hour has passed since I crossed over. I can't hang around much longer. I wander over to the window and watch the people outside. I'm intrigued by their clothes and mannerisms. I hated school. *This is the best history lesson I've ever had.* After a while, I feel a pinch in my side.

It's Clara. 'Come with me,' she whispers. 'I have something I want to show you.'

I follow her out into the corridor and through a door into another passageway.

Clara skips ahead. I rush to keep up.

She leads me through a door into a large classroom. It's fascinating, just how I imagined a 1912 schoolroom to be - polished wood floors, rows of little wooden desks, and a great blackboard at the head of the class.

'This is my classroom,' she says. 'Do you like it?'

'I do,' I say. 'Aren't you a little old to be still at school though?'

Clara giggles. 'Do you like my children's drawings?' She shows me to a section of wall covered with colourful sketches and paintings. 'Aren't they wonderful? Such imagination.'

'Yes, they are.' I see a painting of a woman's face; I think it must be a portrait of Clara. 'Someone's painted the teacher,' I say.

'Clara nods. 'Yes, I think little Jessica likes me.'

'I'm sure they all like you.'

'I hope so.'

'I know so. I see how you are with them; you're a very good teacher… and a special lady.'

'My father doesn't think so. He wants me to return home.'

'Your father's an idiot.' I've forgotten my etiquette – it just came out.

'Pardon.'

'I don't mean to be disrespectful,' I say, digging my way out. 'But if this makes you happy, then carry on and don't let anyone ruin it. That includes your father. He doesn't own you. No one does.'

Clara cocks her head to one side.

'Sorry. I've offended you again, haven't I?' I say.

She smiles. 'No, I'm just surprised that's all.'

'Why?'

'Because you're the only person I've ever met who agrees with me.'

'Really?'

'Yes. Everyone thinks my father knows best.'

I stand nose to nose with Clara. 'The only person who knows best is you.'

A perfectly timed train whistle blows in through the open window. 'That sounds like my train,' I say, seizing the opportunity to slip away.

'Oh dear, do you have to go so soon?'

I sense disappointment in her voice. 'Yes, I'm afraid I do.'

Clara sticks out her bottom lip in a childlike manner. 'I must not make you late then. I'll walk you to the lane.'

Out at the school gates, I see a man with a big camera on a tripod. He's taking a photo of the elderly ladies selling lemonade.

'I don't think you should be pointing that contraption at us, young man,' one of the women says. 'You should take a photograph of this lovely couple instead. Look at them, they're so sweet.'

'Oh, we're not...'

The lady puts her arm around Clara and hustles her in front of the camera. Clara grabs my hand and pulls me with her. We huddle together.

'This will be a perfect photo to accompany my story,' the photographer says, before putting his head under the camera hood. He holds up a tray of flash powder.

I glance at Clara. I see mischief in those bright green eyes.

'Let's make it an interesting story then,' she whispers. Clara then promptly kisses me on the cheek. There's a flash from the camera.

I can feel my face flushing.

'Can I take your names please? For the article,' the photographer says.

'Simon, I say, Simon and Miss...'

Clara interrupts. 'Simon and Clara,' she says, smiling at me. The photographer scribbles some notes.

We walk along the lane until we reach the edge of the school boundary. Clara leans on the school wall.

'I'm sorry I have to go,' I say. 'I'd like to stay longer.'

She plays with her hair. 'Will you be returning any time soon?'

'I will, very soon.' My statement is a bold one as it's pure luck that I managed to get back here today.

Suddenly I'm startled by more shouting. People scatter in all directions. I hear a tremendous rumbling sound as a cloud of dust rolls along the lane towards us. A dark blue carriage, pulled by four huge horses, hurtles past. Turning my back on the lane, I grab Clara and use my body to protect her. I feel several flying stones hit me in the back. I watch the coach disappear down the lane to town. There's a man seated at the rear wearing a dark mackintosh and a scarf pulled up over his nose and mouth. He carries a shotgun.

I cough with the dust as the lane falls silent again. 'Are you alright?' I ask. I realise I've taken hold of Clara – I quickly let go.

She bites her lip. It makes her look frighteningly attractive. 'Yes, thank you,' she says, brushing dust from my shirt and shaking it from her hair.

We laugh together.

'What on earth was that?' I ask.

'The stagecoach.'

'I've never seen anything like that before in my life.' I say, honestly. 'Why does everyone seem so afraid?'

'They're afraid because that was the Atkinson brothers' stagecoach,' she replies.

'Oh right. Is that a bad thing then?'

'The Atkinson brothers run a small stagecoach company from town.' Clara explains. 'Quite famously they are the safest and most reliable stagecoach in the north of England. However, they're feared by many for their underhand ways of keeping the competitors at bay.'

'So definitely ones to avoid then?'

'I actually quite like them,' Clara says, to my surprise.

'Well, I really do have to go. I'm sorry it's only been a flying visit,' I say, genuinely not wanting to leave.

'Flying visit?' Clara asks.

'Yes... err... I mean a short visit.'

'Please promise me you'll come back to visit our lovely town again soon.'

'I won't come back to visit your town, Clara, but I'll come back to visit you.' That amazing big smile develops before me. I love it. I take Clara's hand and kiss it. Her skin is soft on my lips.

'Goodbye, Simon.'

I leave quickly making it look like I'm rushing for

my train. I run down the lane and duck behind a timber shed. I wait a few moments. I think about my last moments with Clara. *I can't believe I came out with that line.* I take a peek around the corner of the shed; I can see the schoolhouse and church from here.

Clara's gone.

I make a run for the church.

**

I lie still for a moment until I feel the biting cold return. Looking up at a grey sky, I know I'm home.

On the way back to Durham I tell my friends all about my third trip to Clara, but I leave out the part about the photo in front of the lemonade stand. I hesitate when they ask me if she's kissed me yet. *If I tell the truth, will John and Emily think I've reached my goal and pull the plug?*

'No not yet,' I say.

'Well if you're going back again, you need to be careful,' John says. 'The gas tank is completely empty. The rig could have shut down any minute, you're lucky you got home.'

The discussion continues at John's house until I'm ready for home. I have an early night. I'm excited about the events back in Conley Hope, but thinking and talking about it has left me drained. I've reached my goal. *So what now?* I know how the mysterious photo came to be, but there are still so many unanswered questions. *Could I have altered Clara's history?* I know nothing about time travel, but then I probably know more than most. I like to think I'm a considerate person but I know I haven't thought this through enough. If John's right I could be doing immeasurable damage by meddling in the past. I fear my attraction to Clara may be leading me off the moral path.

Never the less, I fall asleep remembering only the soft touch of Clara's hand and the feel of her breath on my face.

TEN

8 June 1912

Today is Josephine Cole's twenty-fifth birthday. One of the first to deliver good wishes is her close friend Clara. The two ladies walk the kitchen garden of the Coles' residence.

'Isn't it peaceful?' Josephine says, flicking her long blonde hair over her shoulder.

'It is,' Clara says, looking out over the lush green landscape. 'So what plans do you have for today?'

'I hadn't really thought about it.'

Clara sees the river winding its way through the estate, past the cattle pens and the orchard. 'What about a birthday picnic by the river? We could invite everyone.'

'I don't want too much fuss,' Josephine says, sitting on a garden seat. 'Besides, we'd be eaten alive by the flies.'

'Oh Jo, you've never had much sense of adventure.'

'Unlike you, Miss Pearson, I prefer to keep my

feet on the ground and my dress free of mud, thank you.'

Clara laughs as she sits next to her friend. 'Well at least let me organise a tea party here then. You can't have a birthday without a party and a cake and party games.'

Josephine rolls her eyes. 'Do I have a choice, dear friend?'

'I'm afraid not.'

A train whistle is carried on the warm breeze. Clara almost leaps from the seat.

'It's only been a few days, Clara. You shouldn't go jumping with excitement each time a train comes in.'

'You're right, Jo. But I simply can't stop thinking about him. I know I shouldn't. I expect you think it should be Walter I think about each day?'

'No one can tell you how to feel, Clara, me included.'

'I just can't see happiness with Walter. He's a nice man but...' Clara sighs and rests her head on Josephine's shoulder.

'He doesn't sweep you off your feet?'

'No, I'm afraid he doesn't.'

Mr Cole appears at the door to the house. The tall, fine figure of a man lights his pipe. He laughs at the two girls sitting in the garden – Josephine with her upright posture, and Clara slouched and daydreaming.

'I think I'll take a walk into town,' Clara says.

'I thought you might,' Josephine replies, with a smile.

'Well I'm sure there'll be something we need for the party in any case,' Clara says.

'Party?' Mr Cole enquires.

'Don't ask, darling.'

Clara fetches her basket and rushes to town.

**

By the time Clara reaches the railway bridge, the line is empty. At the station, the platform is deserted too. She drags her feet as she passes the ticket office. Clara sees a pretty bunch of flowers lying on a bench. She takes a seat. Looking around she doesn't see who they could belong to. *What a terrible shame – a lost present for someone special.*

**

3 December 2012

December breezes into my life much as Clara has. My daily thoughts are filled with her. In the past I've laughed at the idea that people can fall in love at first sight, but this bitterly cold winter I find I'm being warmly affected by someone I hardly know.

This all began as a quest for the origin of a photo, now it's much more than that. I keep catching myself smiling as I think of Clara and her playful ways. I'm experiencing cravings for the beautiful woman from the past – feelings I've never had for anyone else. I bring myself back to earth by thinking of the divide between us and the impossibility of a future together. But it doesn't stop me wanting her.

We've had a break from using the rig. Following my near miss with the fuel on my last crossover, I've built a tank twice as big as the old one. It's taken John a while to mix the gases to fill it. He's also recharged the old tank so it can be used as a reserve. I've fitted an automatic changeover valve so if the main tank should run dry, it will swap to the old one. We now have around seven hours running time.

I'd hoped to test it this week but John and Emily have been summoned to London to speak with an MI5 agent.

'Are you sure you don't want me to come with you?' I ask, dropping them off at Durham railway station.

'No, it's fine,' John says. 'I don't plan on giving much away anyway.'

'What are you going to say about the time travel?'

'I'm not. I'll just tell them it worked as an Aspect Scanner like it was designed.'

'What about Alan?' Emily asks.

'He won't be there,' John says. 'I'll just tell them we fed him the time travel story to keep our uni places.'

'Well, just be careful both of you.'

I pass John their bags. 'Let me know if you need me, it won't take me long to get down there.'

'I will. Thanks.'

I watch my friends walk into the station. I hope they'll be alright.

**

The next few days drag. I keep my mind occupied by doing my Christmas shopping. I even wrap everything and deliver it. John has phoned a couple of times and updated me on the MI5 situation. It seems they wanted the specifications for the design of the rig and all the chemical formulas John wrote. I'm assuming it's to prove we weren't building bombs.

I'm itching to return to Conley Hope. Every day that passes is another day I could be with Clara. I can't wait to use the rig again when my friends return. On Thursday lunchtime, John calls me.

'I think we're off the hook,' he says, after a brief catch up.

'Great. So, what did they say?'

'It was just a warning really. I gave them all the info they wanted but missed a few bits out so they couldn't recreate what we've built. If they copied the rig, it would show up a few hospital bugs and nothing else.'

'So, when are you coming home?'

'Well, Emily's never been here before so we might stay a few days and see the sights.'

'Oh, right. I was hoping we could carry on this weekend. You know, test the new tank.'

'It'll still be there when we get back.'

'I know. When will that be?'

'Monday, probably.'

'OK.'

'You alright, Si?'

'Yeah, I'm fine. You two have a nice time. I'll see you when you get back.'

'OK. See you later.'

I'm disappointed. I know I'm being selfish, but I really wanted to get back to Clara as soon as possible. I've almost put the rest of my life on hold since the university project hotted up. I have little else to do. *Maybe I could test the rig myself? That way I can have everything ready for when they get back.* It takes little thought. *I'll go to the church tonight – John and Emily won't mind.*

**

Not long after dark, I'm back in the little church. I take my time fitting the new fuel tank by the dim light of a gas lamp. I do the same with the reserve tank and check for leaks. I potter about doing routine maintenance on various components.

By eight o'clock, I'm bored of cleaning and oiling. *Maybe I should do a full test? It would save time later.* I switch on the laptop and power up the rig. I check the two truck batteries – I've doubled the battery power for the same reason I wanted larger gas tanks.

I've watched Emily programme the rig many times; it's only a case of starting the software and getting it talking to the scanner unit. I have a go. To my surprise, I manage it easily.

Green lights illuminate on the scanner. The gas tubes become rigid as they fill, and a faint crackling sound emanates from the rig. I also hear the whirring of small fans and the clicking of micro-switches. Everything seems more intense now I'm alone. All this would normally be drowned out by us chatting.

The crackling becomes louder. I make patterns on the gloomy stone walls as I pass back and forth across the light of the gas lamp. I'm nervous. I put on a face mask and watch the church interior change in the waves of gas. I alter the angle of the rig to search out something new.

After a few moments, I see the image of a funeral procession entering the church. I shudder. *This is creepy.*

I spin the rig to reveal the calendar on the back wall. The date must be 9 April as all the dates are scored through up to that point. That's before I first met Clara, so it's no use as an entry point. *Maybe I could scan every bit of energy in the church and note the dates?* If I only look for a few minutes, there'll be plenty of energy left for a crossover at that point later. I grab a scrap of paper and a pen from the van, and begin.

After an hour, I have four entry points written down - dates I can use to get back to Clara. That's assuming the calendar is correct. They're all from the summer of 1912. The energy left seems to be nicely concentrated around the time Clara lived in the valley. I don't actually know when she left, or what happened to her, but history says there wasn't much left of Conley Hope by the end of that year. I'm struggling to find any more energy, so I shut the equipment down.

Although it has no roof, the church is filling with gas. The gases we use are slightly heavier than air, so they linger – if they didn't, the rig just wouldn't work. I take a break and give the room a chance to clear. I don't want to be exposed for longer than I need to be.

I stand outside in the darkness. The sky is black and clear. Thousands of stars twinkle above me. The valley floor is as black as the night sky, although I catch sight of one faint light in the distance. *It looks like there's at least one building still here.*

I return to the ruin and find the room clear. I check the gas levels. I've not used much at all. I catch sight of the hydrogen input switch. *I wish Emily was here to press it.* I go to log out of the scanner software and turn off the laptop, but I can't bring myself to do it. I can't go home empty-handed. *I could just cross over for a few minutes, maybe an hour? John and Emily wouldn't mind.* I think I'd talked myself into it before I even left home. Otherwise I wouldn't have put my bag of 1912 clothes in the van. I go and get them.

Back in the church, I lock the door behind me. I don't want anyone to come in and shut the rig down while I'm on the other side. I change into my dark grey corduroy trousers, black boots, and a plain cream shirt. I'm cold without my warm hoodie and jacket; I can't wait for the sunshine of 1912. I've also brought an old watch, one with no strap so it fits neatly in my pocket.

I restart the equipment and watch the readings on

the laptop. The room starts filling with cloudy images. I check my notes; the first date on my list is 8 June 1912. I move the rig to find the energy I'd accessed while making my list. It's not long before all the dates on the handmade calendar are struck through up until Saturday 8 June.

My thumb hovers over the hydrogen input switch. My heart's pounding. I tease the button a few times before finally pressing it. The room becomes cloudier, darker. I get that drunken feeling.

There's a loud pop.

**

I'm startled by people singing. I was expecting an empty church, but the room is full. Luckily, I've appeared behind a pillar. I go to ground. Lying on the floor behind the last row of wooden pews, I realise I could be in trouble. I can't jump back through; I'd be seen. I can't run out. I'm hoping the congregation are too busy singing to notice me. The sun is blazing through the stained glass windows, as always. There's a line of wooden tables laid out under the side windows, right up to the rear exit. I slither under the first one. I think I'm unseen.

On all fours, I scramble along under the tables, making for the exit. The dazzling sunlight should blind any onlookers. I don't even get to see the cause of the energy that allowed me to access this moment. *Maybe it's a wedding?* I don't remember seeing a wedding when I experimented with the rig. *I hope I've got the right date.* I leave via the door at the base of the tower and burst into the early summer sunshine. It seems I've got away with it.

Before I go any further, I re-set my little watch to midday - I can use it as a timer.

I sneak around the side of the building. The

school grounds are quiet. At the lane, I catch my breath and brush dust from my trousers. I'm once again met with the scent of flowers and freshly cut grass that seems unique to Conley Hope. I hear a train whistle. In the distance, I see white smoke filtering through the trees. I head in that direction.

Rather than sticking to the lane, I explore a bit. I take a footpath trampled along the edge of a meadow. I pass through a boundary hedge, filled with wild flowers. I have an idea… I pick a handful of the flowers - yellow daffodils, purple spring crocuses, bluebells, and white snowdrops. I snap stalks as I walk, arranging them into a reasonable bouquet.

I leave the fields and follow a railway siding. I see the town in the distance. A bridge spans the railway. I pass under it. On the other side I chance upon a path that leads me to Conley Hope railway station. I head for the little sandstone building, with its slate roofs and tall clay chimney pots. I have to duck so not to bang my head on hanging baskets bursting with flowers. The platform is quiet. I only see one lady tending to two children.

'Come on girls, we must dash or we'll be late,' she says, ushering them away. One of the girls drops her doll. The woman retrieves it, but there's a red ribbon left on the floor; it must be from the doll's hair.

'Excuse me,' I shout, picking it up.

The woman doesn't hear me. She's rushing to catch a stagecoach that waits on the bridge.

I jog after them but by the time I reach the bridge they're in the coach. I realise I'd look stupid stopping a stagecoach just for a little girl's ribbon. I watch them leave then return to the platform and take a seat on a bench. The ribbon would actually make a perfect final touch to my bouquet of flowers. I tie it around them.

A man dressed in a dark suit – presumably the station porter – appears in a doorway. Sweat beads on his brow as he struggles to slide a heavy wooden box along the platform.

'Can I help?' I ask.

'That would be very kind of you, sir,' he replies.

I leave my flowers on the bench and help him carry his box to a storeroom at the back of the building.

After a firm handshake, I return to the platform. I'm amazed to find Clara Pearson sitting on the bench holding my bouquet of flowers. 'Hello, Clara.'

'Oh my! Hello Simon.' Her face lights up.

I feel like I've run into an old friend. 'Nice flowers,' I say.

'Oh, they're not mine. I just found them lying here.'

'They are yours,' I say.

'Whatever do you mean?'

'I brought them for you. I left them there for a moment while I helped the porter with something.'

'Oh, I see. That's very kind. But you shouldn't leave flowers lying around; you never know what manner of unsavoury character might pick them up,' Clara says, with a grin.

I laugh.

She pats the seat next to her.

I obey, sitting as close to her as seems appropriate.

Clara beams at me. There's a bright sunny glow surrounding her. Pollen blows across her face from the banks of the railway line. She looks so beautiful in the summer haze.

'What brings you to town today, Simon?'

'You do.'

Clara shuffles closer. The gentle breeze has her curly red locks tickling my face. 'Are you saying you came to visit me?'

'I did.'

Clara pierces me with those striking green eyes in a way that should have me feeling uncomfortable.

But I don't – instead, I feel at home. 'I hope you don't mind,' I add.

'No, not at all. I'm flattered. I didn't expect you to be here to see me. I thought you must visit town with your occupation.'

'No. And seeing you is far better than working any day.'

'I hope you don't mind me asking, Simon, but what is it you do for a living?'

'Well, I fix things.'

'I'm curious. You don't seem like a common blacksmith or boilermaker, and you seem to travel a great deal. You must be important. A railway engineer perhaps?'

I need to give a reasonable explanation for my new clothes and seemingly good education. 'Yes, I'm an engineer but not one you'd be familiar with.'

'Really? Do tell.'

I haven't thought through what I would say if asked further about my work. 'I fix machines.'

'What kind of machines?'

'Ones you wouldn't have seen, that's all.'

'Sorry, I shouldn't pry.'

'That's alright. I didn't mean to be rude; it's just difficult to explain. The machines I work on aren't publically available yet.' *I'm not lying.*

'That sounds awfully interesting.'

'It is. But it means I'm not allowed to talk about

it.'

'You're such a mystery, Simon. It seems the water gets deeper the further I paddle.'

'I'm sorry.'

'Don't be. I'm sure I'll discover you in time.'

I feel Clara draw away from me. *I'm making a mess of things again.* 'It's a shame I don't get to visit as often as I'd like,' I say.

'Well then, that must change.'

I'm hoping that's an indication that Clara wants to see more of me. 'Yes, you're right.'

A group of children arrive on the platform. They play with a wooden spinning top not far from us. They steal Clara's attention for a moment.

'I take it you live in town?' I ask.

'Yes, in a way. I'm lodging with friends until I can convince my father that I'm to stay. The position at the school comes with a little house and I'd like to take it soon.'

'Well, you should do whatever makes you happy. And maybe you'll let me see this little house one day; if it's anything like the rest of town, I'm sure it'll be lovely.'

Clara giggles. 'Actually I'm told it's rather awful, damp and draughty.'

'Well don't worry, Miss, fixing things is my speciality.'

'Yes, of course. I may need to call on you, Simon.'

I'm enjoying talking with Clara, but the children playing nearby are dampening my chances of the conversation becoming anything more than idle chat.

'Would you like to go for a walk or something?' I ask, feeling like a thirteen-year-old boy asking a girl on a date.

'I'd love to, but typically I have to go shortly. It's

my friend Jo's birthday today and I need to collect a few things for her tea party this afternoon.'

Great, I've blown it again. 'Oh, I see. Never mind. Maybe next time?'

'I'm sure we'll meet again.'

'Me too.'

Clara gets up and leaves. She pauses to talk to the children. They instantly respond to her – she definitely has a way with them.

Why am I watching this girl leave? I chase after her. 'Can I at least walk you into town?' I ask, catching Clara on the path to the bridge. 'I'm going that way anyway.'

She smiles. 'I don't see why not.'

Clara actually does most of the talking as we walk. *Maybe she wanted me to chase after her?* I don't care, I'm just glad of the extra time together. We stop at the general store. It's busier than on my last visit.

I wait outside; I think it best to avoid a possible repeat confrontation with the local shopkeeper. I watch the horse-drawn carts and people on bicycles pass by. It's like being on a movie set. Nearly every building has a painted sign of some sort decorating its gable or roof, carefully hand lettered onto tile or brick. I realise how much skill now escapes us.

Clara eventually emerges from the shop with another full basket.

I offer my hand.

She puts her soft hand in mine.

'I meant the basket,' I say.

'Oh, I'm sorry,' she says, quickly withdrawing her hand and passing me the basket. 'Thank you.'

'I'll gladly take your hand too if you want,' I say.

Clara skips ahead. 'You'll have to catch me first.'

**

After a brisk walk listening to tales of Clara's life so far, we arrive at the gate to her temporary home – on the same lane I'd dropped her off the second time we met. A cobbled path leads to a whitewashed house.

'Well, I'll be on my way.' I say, handing Clara her basket. 'I hope you have a nice party.'

'Goodbye. And thank you for the flowers, Simon.'

'You're welcome.'

Clara bites her lip.

I leave with that image burnt into my memory. I'm not twenty steps away when I hear Clara calling…

'Simon, please wait.' And then when she's caught up with me she says, 'Will you join us?'

'No. It wouldn't feel right...'

'Please. You'll be very welcome.'

'I'm not sure I should.'

Clara sticks out her bottom lip to make a sad face.

'I'd feel cheeky,' I say.

'Don't be silly. You'll be my guest.'

'Alright.' Common sense is telling me I shouldn't be doing this, my heart tells me I should.

The Cole residence seems traditional and basic, even though it's probably the largest and most lavishly furnished property in the whole of the valley. Clara leads me through a reception room and into a huge slate-flagged kitchen. There's an oak table big enough to seat ten or more, and a giant cast iron stove sitting in a chimney in the far wall.

I feel uncomfortable. There are several people buzzing around the table and all look upon me as I wait by the door.

Clara introduces me to the room. 'Everyone, this

is my friend, Simon Benson. He was kind enough to help me with my basket.'

Two young girls, possibly twins, run around me excitedly.

'This is Evelyn and Lillian,' Clara informs me.

'Hello girls,' I say.

A smartly dressed young man, about twenty years old, nods in my direction from the other side of the table.

'That's Harold,' Clara continues. 'And Mabel over there.'

An elderly woman in a rocking chair looks me up and down.

'And this is Josephine and Raymond Cole,' Clara says, presenting the couple. The woman has long blonde hair and a white apron covering her flowery summer dress. She and Clara exchange glances. The tall gentleman puffs away on his pipe. He offers his hand. We shake.

'Will you be staying for afternoon tea, Mr Benson?' Josephine asks, removing her apron.

'Yes. We're having a little celebration,' Mr Cole adds.

'I don't want to intrude,' I stutter. 'I just thought I'd say hello. I wanted to make sure Clara got home alright, now I'll be on my way.'

'Nonsense,' Mr Cole bellows. 'You've been of assistance to our friend so you shall stay for tea. I'll hear no more of it.'

I guess I don't have much choice. 'Thank you, that's very kind.'

'Take a seat young man,' Mr Cole says. Young is an interesting description of me considering that even the youngest in the room will be over seven decades older than me in reality. Two women flit back and forth between the stove and the parlour. They're both dressed in black and white and don't speak except quietly to each other, I assume they're maids. Josephine pulls a chair from the table and offers it to me.

I sit, stiffly.

Clara takes the chair next to me. 'Mary makes the most amazing cakes,' she whispers in my ear. 'By the end of this afternoon you'll be as fat as a house.' The maids overload the table with plates of sandwiches, potted meats, fish, fruit, and delicious looking cakes. The others sit and Mr Cole takes his place at the head of the table.

I still feel awkward, even when Clara secretly squeezes my hand.

'So, Mr Benson, whatever on God's earth brings you to my little town?' Mr Cole asks.

'Well, to be honest, I got here completely by accident,' I say, turning to Clara. 'But I'm glad I did.'

Josephine smiles.

'It's a lovely place. I think I'd like to settle somewhere like this in the future,' I say.

'Just somewhere *like* this?' Mr Cole asks.

'Erm... I meant here,' I say.

'You don't sound so sure,' Mr Cole says.

'I was just thinking how difficult it could be for me to move here if I wanted to, that's all.'

'Why would it be so difficult for you to move here if you don't mind me asking?' Clara says.

I don't like lying, but knowing the future of Conley Hope is rather short, I don't want to frighten anyone. 'I have a business in the city that's taken me some time to build up and I'm worried that if I move, I could lose all I've worked for,' I say. *I'm being honest.*

'That's a pity, we always need new business in town,' Mr Cole says. 'So what would bring you to a place like this?'

I look at Clara. 'Well I'd like to think I could settle down one day,' I say, being as truthful as I dare.

'Here?' Clara asks.

Those hypnotic green eyes have me saying anything. 'Yes. I guess money isn't everything and one day I want to enjoy the simple things... things that make us happy but come with no price.' My words couldn't be more truthful. 'One day I hope I could build a nice home and have a wife and even children.'

Clara's infectious smile develops before me. 'That sounds like a lovely idea,' she says.

For a moment I feel like everyone else around the table has vanished.

Josephine quickly passes me a plate of ham sandwiches. 'Stop asking the poor man so many questions and let him eat,' she says.

Clara and I break our stare and take a sandwich each.

'So what is it that you do?' Mr Cole asks.

'I'm an engineer of sorts... I repair broken machinery and make things.'

'That sounds very interesting,' says the young man sitting across the table.

'Harold likes to mend things too,' Clara explains.

Harold seems rather shy but I take an interest in him to give me some breathing space. 'What sorts of things do you mend then, Harold?' I ask.

'Well,' he says. 'I fixed Mr Wiseman's cash register, and helped my Uncle when they called him in to the broken printing press at the Durham Chronicle.'

I nod. 'Impressive. That must have been tricky work...'

I'm suddenly interrupted by a horrendous noise coming from the corner of the room; I hadn't even noticed the cot by the stove. Josephine gets up from the table and tends to the baby.

'And that's Molly,' Clara whispers. 'She's a lovely little thing but always cries at mealtimes.'

**

After some time, Clara eventually stands. 'Would anyone mind if I show our guest the estate?' No one objects.

I thank the Coles for their food and hospitality as Clara hastily leads me outside. We walk through a small yard onto a patch of open land where several animals are roaming. There are hens, chickens, and rabbits. We walk along a plush green hedgerow. Clara takes my hand firmly in hers as we head past a large red-brick barn. After the inquisition at lunch, I'm glad of some time alone with her.

'There's a lovely spot by the river on the other side of those trees over there,' Clara explains, tucking her fiery locks behind her ear. 'Shall we take a walk that way?'

'Why not,' I reply, with a smile. I see more of the valley in the distance. I recognise some landmarks like the large hill which the railway tunnel passes through, but the rest of the valley looks so different. The vegetation is younger; the spaces are so much greener; the air is sweeter. I'm not sure if it's the feel of the sun on my back or Clara's soft hand in mine that's making me so happy. This is a far cry from the harsh winter I should be feeling right now.

We enter a little orchard packed full of small apple and pear trees. We chat as we go. I do my best to impress Clara with humour, but I'm careful to keep it within the context of the time. We leave the shadow of the fruit trees and enter a beautiful sunny meadow. Clara lets go of my hand, picks up her dress, and skips away towards the river that winds its way through the wild flowers.

I purposely hang back to check my watch. I've been here for nearly three hours, but I still have plenty of time. I descend the hill towards Clara.

She glances back before running for the riverbank.

I've tried hard not to make comparisons, but I can't help thinking of how different she is to anyone I've known before. Rachel was good-looking but that didn't make her beautiful. I saw her as a career-minded, intelligent, and severely motivated young woman within an attractive but very hard shell. Clara I see as simply a beautiful person in a beautiful shell.

Clara stops at the water's edge.

I approach her. I notice the sunlight shining through her hair. The first thing that comes to mind is the shampoo adverts on the television. I want to tell her what I'm thinking to compliment her or even just raise a giggle, but realise she wouldn't understand. Sadly, I'm reminded of the void between us.

'Oh look, Simon, we should paddle,' Clara says. 'The water is so lovely and clear.' She suddenly loses her footing.

I try my best to grab the damsel and pull her into my arms, saving her from a wet fall. But I fail miserably. I catch hold of her dress but she still falls to the ground, landing in a heap on the riverbank. I then lose my footing and fall on top of her. I'm completely mortified by my failed attempt at chivalry. But before I can apologise, she wraps her arms around me and kisses me lengthily on the lips. It's a surprising, yet perfect end to my unfortunate blunder.

Eventually, our lips part and we just stare at each

other rather blankly, like we're waiting for something from the other. I'm trembling. The deadlock is broken as we laugh nervously at exactly the same moment. I forget all etiquette and kiss Clara again, this time for far longer.

**

Sometime later I find myself lying on my back in the long grass, staring at a clear blue sky. Clara lies beside me in a similar fashion with her head touching mine. The summer breeze blows her curly hair across my face. She giggles as it tickles me.

The sound of the river is soothing and calming as it bubbles and gurgles gently past. Not as soothing as the feel of Clara's soft lips on mine. I'm instantly addicted to her kiss. It's more special than I could have imagined. I'm left intoxicated by the taste of her, the feel of her hair between my fingers, the smell of her skin.

Time passes slowly as we whisper to each other over the sound of bubbling waters. It seems that for all our differences, the basic attraction of one person to another is no different with moments between us, or hundreds of years. I quickly become very comfortable in Clara's arms. I enjoy lying in the long grass overlooking a beautiful world travelling at a slow pace... travelling slowly enough for us to both fall asleep in the late afternoon sunshine.

ELEVEN

I'm not sure what wakes me – the constant birdsong from the nearby fruit trees, or the bubbling river gathering pace at my feet. I open my eyes and see a dark blue sky. The bright sunshine of earlier is absent.

It's only when I hear a murmur from the woman resting her head on my torso that I remember I'm not alone. I feel happier than I ever have. My dream of the last few weeks has become reality. I watch my companion sleep. Clara is stunningly beautiful. She has an innocent face – pale and pretty, its expression one of contentment.

After a while, she wakes. 'Oh my goodness, Simon, I'm so sorry. I've never fallen asleep so easily before.' She turns and lies facing me with her elbows resting on the grass, her big sleepy eyes looking into mine.

'Don't worry,' I say. 'I fell asleep too. It must have been the sun.'

'It's gone behind the hills now so it must be getting late.'

My heart sinks to my stomach. *How long has the rig been running?* I get to my feet and help the young lady up.

'Come on then. I'd better get you back or we'll be in trouble,' I say, trying not to look worried.

Clara giggles. 'Don't worry, Simon, we won't be in trouble. Besides, I don't care if we are.' She picks up her dress and runs up the grassy hill towards the orchard, laughing as she goes. 'I'll race you to the house.' Clara moves fast, I struggle to keep up. She disappears into the orchard.

I have a chance to glance at my watch - it reads eight thirty. I set it to midday when I crossed over, so regardless of what time it is; I've far exceeded my seven hour limit. I feel cold. I'm not sure if it's the temperature drop in the orchard, or the reality of my situation - I could be trapped in time.

Clara is waiting for me in the trees. 'It's rather spooky in here, Simon,' she says, playing with her hair. 'I need a lovely strong man close to keep me safe.'

'Where will you find one of those then?' I ask, trying not to show my anxiety.

Clara must sense something that gives away my real feelings. 'Are you alright my darling?'

'Yes, I'm fine.' I can tell she's not convinced. I'm flustered.

Clara eyes the watch in my hand. 'Oh dear, have I made you late?'

I don't want her to think my mind is on anything other than her. 'No, not at all. I was just wondering what time the last train was, that's all.'

'Oh dear, I have haven't I? Whatever will you do if you've missed the last train?'

I almost want to blurt out that missing a train is the least of my worries. Looking upon this gorgeous young woman in the middle of this lovely place, I'm calmed into a fitting response…

I take her hand. 'Don't worry, I'll be fine. And if I have to sleep out here in the cold woods for the night then it will be worth it just to have enjoyed some time with you.'

Clara is instantly in my arms and kissing me once again. The lovely warm feeling is soon interrupted by a voice calling across the fields. 'Clara! Simon!' It sounds like Harold.

'Come on, they'll be worried,' I say. We rush in the direction of the voice, leaving the fruit trees behind us. We still hold hands as we run through a paddock.

Harold stands by the gate to the next field. Clara lets go of my hand as we approach, giving the impression she doesn't want to advertise our union. I'm almost offended but then I'm not sure how the world works in this time. I know I must respect her.

'Wherever have you two been?' Harold asks, in a friendly manner. 'We were beginning to worry.'

Clara turns to me looking almost pleased that we share a secret. 'I'm sorry, Harold, we went for a long walk and completely lost track of time.'

Harold opens the gate and lets us through. 'I'll say you lost track. My goodness it must be almost supper time.'

When we return to the house, I don't want to go in – I need to get to the church as soon as possible. I stand in the courtyard and wait for Harold to disappear before reaching for Clara's hand.

'I'll have to leave now,' I say.

'Of course… your train,' Clara says, with a sigh.

'I'm sorry. I wish I could stay longer, but I must go.'

With a glance towards the house, she takes both my hands in hers. 'Will you take me with you one day? I'd love to see where you live,' she whispers. Her words are pleasing yet packed full of impossibility.

I can't lie. 'I'd absolutely love to, Clara, but for now I'll just hope I can get back to you as soon as possible.'

'I hope so too, I really do.' We kiss briefly.

I'm hoping I've left Clara feeling as happy as she's left me. I exit the estate through the kitchen garden, the taste of her lips lingering on mine. My concern now is getting back to the church, back to the portal. I run as fast as I can in the dusk light. I know my chances of getting home are slim. Luckily Conley Hope is quiet – so no one sees me rushing by.

**

Much to my relief, the church is open, but the candlelit hall gives me no hope at all. I find no swirling gas cloud. No Human Aspect Scanner. No sign of life from the other side. I feel sick as I leave the building in defeat. *What do I do now?*

The walk back to town gives me plenty of time to mull over my predicament. It's almost dark. I'll have to shelter somewhere for the night and reassess the situation in the morning. I enter the town park and head for the cast iron bandstand. It's surrounded by large shrubs. *This'll have to do.* Luckily, it's not a cold night. I lie on a bench looking up at the clear dark sky through gaps in the ornate roof. Somehow I nod off.

I'm shocked awake by someone leaning over me, a gentle tapping on my shoulder. I leap from the bench and find myself face to face with a policeman.

'Sorry to wake you, sir, but I don't think it's appropriate to be in the park at this hour.' The officer holds an oil lamp in one hand and a truncheon in the other.

I'm dazed. 'Sorry, I must have fallen asleep.'

The policeman gives me a lengthy look from top to toe. 'You don't look like you belong here Mr...?'

'Benson,' I reply. 'No, I don't suppose I do. I managed to miss the last train home and didn't bring any money with me. I'm in a predicament really.'

'Well, yes, we are in a muddle aren't we, sir? A bit of bad luck I expect.'

I nod.

'I'll escort you down to The Sun, Jack will put you up for the night and I'm sure he'll be flexible on payment terms. We can't have you hanging around here making the place look untidy.'

I don't really want to go; my goal has always been to avoid too much attention. *I don't think I have a choice.* I follow the officer.

After a short walk, we arrive at The Sun Inn on Conley Hope's main street. From the outside the place looks rather inviting; the frosted glazing in the sash windows is lit with a warm glow. Inside, the bar is busy, yet quiet. There's a foggy tense atmosphere. It's not like the kind of modern smoke-free gastro-pubs I'm used to. The policeman leads me past simple wooden tables and chairs to a large mahogany bar.

'Jack. You there?' the officer yells, as we reach the empty counter. Customers look up from their drinks. Two characters stir in the corner by the window. They seem agitated by the presence of a policeman. I notice they hide their faces with the rims of their cowboy-style hats.

A short bald man appears on the other side of the bar. 'Good evening, sergeant,' he says. 'What can I do for you this fine evening?'

'This is Mr Benson; he's had some terribly bad luck and needs a place to stay tonight. Can you help him out?'

The publican nods agreeably. 'Of course I can help him; I have my best room available, at the usual rate of course.'

The officer takes off his helmet and puts it on the bar. 'Well, here's the thing Jack. Mr Benson is in a fix.'

'I'm afraid I didn't bring any money with me and missed my train home,' I say.

A drunken man, sitting close by, sniggers. The policeman gives him a stern look.

Jack's welcoming face soon changes to one of displeasure. 'Not again, sergeant. I can't run a reputable business in this way, I'll be ruined.'

It's alright,' I say, 'I should go. I'll have a walk until the first train comes in tomorrow.'

The closest customer sniggers again.

'There aren't any trains tomorrow,' the policeman says.

Everyone in the room is now looking at me, except the two men by the window – they keep their heads down.

'I suppose I also can't be seen to turn a gentleman away,' Jack says, slapping his cloth on the bar top. 'Take a seat and I'll fix you a drink. Then we can discuss particulars.'

I'm still under the officer's watchful eye, so I do as I'm told.

'Whisky or beer?' the barman asks.

Christ, is this the Wild West? 'Beer, please,' I say, taking a seat at the nearest empty table. There's an increasing buzz coming from the room. I assume the customers are discussing me. I notice there are no women present.

The policeman puts on his helmet and tips it in my direction as he leaves. 'Goodnight, Mr Benson. Stay out of trouble.' He exits the building. The moment the officer has left, the atmosphere seems more hostile. All eyes are on me.

Jack brings me a glass of dark beer. 'There's only two ways to pay for this drink and the warm bed you'll sleep in tonight. With money or with hard labour,' he says. 'I'll be honest, mister, you don't look like you know much about hard labour so I'll be interested to see how you oblige me.'

'I'm no stranger to hard work,' I say. 'I'll do whatever it takes to pay.'

He looks me over. 'Very well. We also have a small holding,' he says, with a grin. 'I can't wait to see you there tomorrow, digging potatoes in those clothes.'

'That's fine with me, Jack.' I raise my glass and take a large gulp of the ale.

After a while, one of the men by the window gets up and strides to the bar. His weather-beaten mackintosh and cowboy-style wax hat seem unusual indoor attire.

Jack scurries back to his bar. 'What will it be, Mr Atkinson?' he asks.

'Whisky.'

This must be one of the Atkinson brothers. I notice Jack's hand shaking as he pours the alcohol.

'Is there something I can help you with?' the strange-looking character says to me. He must have noticed me watching.

'No,' I say.

'Please don't start trouble in my establishment, Mr Atkinson,' Jack says.

The guy takes his drink and removes his hat. He throws it on my table. 'Mind if I sit?' he asks.

My heart's pounding. 'Not at all.' The buzz in the room ceases immediately.

The stranger brushes the tails of his mackintosh away as he sits. His thick black hair has been flattened by his hat. The clothes under his coat seem good quality and clean – they don't match his unshaven face. He seems to be hiding them.

'You keep bad company by way of the police,' he says.

'I didn't have much choice,' I say.

'What brings you to town, mister?'

'I'm just visiting a friend.'

'I heard a railway engineer has been sniffing around town.'

News travels fast here – even the inaccurate stuff. 'Do I look like a railway engineer?' I ask.

'You don't look like you're not one.'

'Would it be a problem if I was?' I'm trying not to sound weak, but I don't want to wind this guy up either.

'Yes. The railway is taking my business.'

I catch a glimpse of his pistol.

'So I sincerely hope you don't work for the Newcastle and Darlington Junction Railway Company,' he says.

'No, I don't. I'm from the city. And like I said, I'm visiting a friend.'

'Without any money?'

'I made a mistake.'

'You're right there.'

Suddenly, the door to the inn is flung open. Clara rushes in. 'Oh, Mr Benson. There you are.' The man sitting with me recoils. All other eyes in the room swing my way again.

Once at the table, Clara lowers her voice. 'The Coles' farmhand said a stranger was brought here by the police, I thought it must be you.'

News travels even faster than I thought.

The man at my table stands then sits again. 'Good to see you, Miss Pearson.'

I'm surprised; the manners don't match the rest.

'Hello David,' Clara says.

'What are you doing here?' I whisper.

'I came to make sure you're alright. This place is known for its bar fights.'

'All the more reason for you not to be here,' I say.

Jack scurries over. 'You can't come in here, miss. This is a gentleman's only establishment.

'Well, I don't see many in here,' Clara says, glancing around the room.

'Go about your business,' David says, to the barman.

The little man edges away.

'I take it you two know each other?' David asks.

'Yes, Mr Benson is my friend,' Clara says.

'Does your friend work for the railway?'

Am I invisible?

'No, he doesn't.'

There's an instant change as David offers me his hand. 'My apologies,' he says. 'My name is David Atkinson, and that's my brother, James, sitting over there.' We shake, as James acknowledges me, from across the room, with a tip of his hat.

'I'm Simon Benson.'

'It seems you're in a bit of a predicament,' David says.

'You could say that.'

'Well you certainly don't look like a potato farmer.'

'I'm actually more practical than I look.'

Clara takes the remaining empty seat. 'It's true. Simon can fix anything,' she says.

'Is that so?' David asks.

'Yes,' I say, trying not to sound too arrogant.

'Simon knows an awful lot about everything,' Clara gushes.

'In that case, I may have some work for you. If you're interested, I'll meet you here at noon tomorrow.'

I nod. 'I might still be digging potatoes though.'

'No you won't.' David gets up and puts on his hat. 'Jack,' he shouts.

The publican reappears.

'Put Mr Benson's food and lodgings on my tab.'

'Yes, Mr Atkinson.'

'Thank you,' I say. I'm glad I won't be digging tomorrow, but I do worry what I might end up doing instead.

'I'd better walk you home,' I say, to Clara.

'No need,' David says. 'We'll be heading past the Coles', if you need a carriage, miss. No charge of course.'

Clara and I stand.

'Thank you, David,' Clara says. 'That's very kind.'

'Yes, thank you,' I add.

'I'll see you again, Mr Benson,' Clara says.

'Yes. Goodnight.'

Clara gives my hand a quick squeeze. I don't think anyone sees. She heads for the door. She's greeted by the other Atkinson brother.

'Hello, James,' Clara says.

'Evening, miss,' James says, tipping his hat.

I stand at the door and watch Clara climb into a

carriage waiting in the street. The brothers hop up front and steer the carriage away. Clara waves from the carriage window.

I return to the bar area. I manage to finish my drink but find it awful compared to what I'm used to. I expected everything to be more organic and better tasting in this time. Maybe that's the problem… I'm so used to preservatives and flavourings that I don't like what's natural. I place my empty glass on the bar.

'Your room and bath will be ready now,' Jack says, handing me a huge brass key. He waves his cloth at the ceiling. 'Up the stairs, along the hall. Room number three.'

**

In room three, I find a cosy bed with an oil lamp burning beside it. There's a fire in the hearth and a large tin bath full of water in front of the fireplace. The sash window is open making the thick net curtains blow in the breeze.

Lying in my uncomfortable bath, I hear distant birds singing even at this time of night. I wonder if they're in the trees of the Coles' orchard. Clara enters my mind once more. I think about our first kiss and how she wants to see me again. I'm smiling uncontrollably. *But what will the consequences be?* My thoughts become colder, mirroring the changing temperature of the bathwater. I think of Clara's father. The image of what happened in the attic back in Durham falls into mind. I remember her father's fury; I remember why he showed it.

I feel sick. I have to get out of this ridiculous tin tub. I dry myself on a rough towel. The air from the window has me feeling better. I think about the moment

Clara's father strikes her. *Has it happened yet or not? Is it because of someone Clara has already met, or because of someone she will? Could it be me?* I pace the room wrapped in my towel. I wonder if I've seen the aftermath of Clara telling her father about me. *No, that's impossible – I hadn't even met her yet when we first saw it.* My head hurts thinking about the rules of time travel. *Are there any rules?*

Even more unsettling is the possibility that Clara received that slap because she meets someone else. And from what we heard of that moment, Clara was already with, or supposedly planning to be with someone already. My heart sinks. *Is that why she didn't want Harold to see us holding hands? Is she spoken for?* Clara's kisses today could have just been for fun; a rebellious daughter with a point to prove.

I'm confused. Could I have caused Clara's problems or just become caught up in what would have happened anyway. I get into bed, close my eyes, and I find myself thinking of a night from a couple of years ago...

I'd been working on a new shopping centre in Newcastle and was invited on a night out with the other tradesmen. Sitting at a table with several other guys, I got chatting to a joiner named Will. Will was talking about fate. I listened intently as he told me he believed that no matter what decisions we make, we all have a path. I found myself agreeing with him to a certain degree.

Rachel picked me up that night and Will's theory was tested as I left the pub and got into Rachel's car. She pulled away from the side of the road not seeing a cyclist passing by. He swerved, fell off his bike, and went rolling along the tarmac. Rachel, in her usual way, got out and screamed abuse at the poor man lying in a heap in the road.

I intervened and checked the guy was OK.

Luckily for Rachel, it seemed the cyclist was riding home at the dead of night with no lights, and under the influence of alcohol. The cyclist admitted he was in the wrong and limped away with only a broken bike to worry about.

'I feel bad now,' I remember Rachel saying, sometime later. 'If I hadn't pulled out then he would have happily peddled home safely.'

I thought about what Will had said earlier. 'If you hadn't pulled out then someone else would have,' I said. 'Judging by the state of him he was guaranteed to fall off his bike at some point anyway, you just helped it along.'

**

I could easily apply similar principles to this current situation. Maybe Clara had met someone in Conley Hope, and the relationship blossomed. When I crossed over, I could have caused her to miss that original chance meeting replacing it with our own. Whatever causes her father to be so angry, I just hope I can find a way to eliminate their confrontation. But if I am changing history for this woman, I need to limit my influence as much as possible until I figure out what to do next. I don't know what damage I could be causing by being here.

I feel far more attached to Clara than I first thought, and more confused than ever. At least thinking about her takes my mind off being stuck in 1912. I hope tomorrow will bring answers. I wrap myself up in the itchy woollen blanket, and eventually, I fall asleep.

TWELVE

I wake late morning. I'm lucky David Atkinson asked me to meet him at noon. A night of interrupted sleep has kept me in bed longer than usual. With no alarm clock or mobile phone I have no way of waking myself. I dress and move to the window. The street looks busy. Horses and carts, and townspeople on foot and on bicycles drift past. I catch my first sight of a big yellow tram, accompanied by the sound of its bell getting louder as it nears. There's a knock on the door.

'Who is it?' I shout.

'The lady of the house.'

It feels creepy knowing someone is at the door the second I rise, as if they were listening for me getting up. I open the door to be greeted by a large woman with a bowl and steaming jug of water.

'Your hot water, sir. If you'd like to go next door to Alice's tea shop, it's late, but she'll still cook you a fine breakfast. There's no need to pay; it comes with the room.'

'Thank you.'

She wanders off down the landing.
I close the door, wash, and leave.

**

In Alice's tea shop, I'm met by Alice herself – an enthusiastic, but very lovely lady in her early fifties.

'Morning,' I say.

'You must be, Mr Benson? I've been wondering when you'll arrive. Take a seat; I'll bring you some tea.'

I enjoy a fantastic cooked breakfast. While finishing my pot of tea, I have time to reflect on the last twenty-four hours. I think my first kiss with Clara masked the pretty horrible predicament I'm in. Out of the window, I notice a boy in a little suit and cloth cap shovelling horse manure from the road. I also catch sight of a newspaper seller; the headline chalked on his stand reads "War breaks out in the Balkans, Europe could be next." *Jesus, it must mean The First World War. I don't fancy being stuck here during that.*

I hope John and Emily realise I'm missing and come looking for me. I need to find a way to get a message to the future. *Is the clock even still ticking for them?* So far, every time I've returned, it's been to the same moment. I could spend years here then cross back to exactly the point I left – I'd return much older than I'm supposed to be. *I don't fancy that either.*

My brain gets a rest as Alice clears my table and makes small talk. I'm no expert on the science of time travel but I'm fast becoming one in its practical application – I'll find a way out of this.

I thank Alice for the breakfast and enter the street. It's another glorious sunny day. I've never seen rain here. I've always believed the past to be dark and depressing, but that couldn't be further from the truth. In my experience, it's our future that's dark.

The clock above the bank reads noon. I worry about David Atkinson's offer of work. On one hand it might keep me out of harm's way – the last thing I want to do is interfere with more lives. On the other hand I could get caught up in things I shouldn't and send shock waves through time.

My thoughts are suspended by the thunder of horse hooves on the cobbled street. People dash for the safety of the pavements and shop doorways as the dark blue stagecoach rounds the bend at speed, pulled by its four brown horses. The powerful beasts come to rest before me, twitching and straining on their tack. They tower over me slavering as they chomp.

The driver lifts his hat; it's David. 'Hop up on the back, Mr Benson.'

I reluctantly climb the wooden steps to a platform at the rear of the carriage.

'Hold on to something,' David shouts, yanking on his leather reins.

I grab a rail that runs along the back of the carriage. I feel a sudden jolt as the coach sets off. The horses canter along the main street. I look over the roof to see where we're going. We leave the main street and the road turns to a bumpy track. The coach speeds up as we travel a narrow gap between two brick buildings and enter open ground. We join the railway line and follow it away from town. I wonder where David's taking me.

After a few minutes we bump over a crossing to the other side of the railway tracks. We round a small hill and enter a large meadow. Although it's uncomfortable at times, I'm actually enjoying the ride.

Eventually, a cluster of buildings come into view

through the grassy haze. The nearest of the buildings look like new railway sheds, the sun glares off their red barrel shaped roofs. They look deserted. We pass the sheds and come upon a group of run-down structures nestled in the centre of a parched patch of meadow. One looks like an old stone farmhouse, and the others are old sheds or barns.

David guides the stagecoach to the largest of the barns. A figure appears in the open doorway – I recognise David's brother from the night before. The carriage stops just short of the barn. David and I climb down.

My legs feel like jelly.

James approaches and wipes his hands on his tatty corduroy trousers before introducing himself. 'I'm James,' he says, opening his collarless cotton shirt. 'It's a fine day.'

'It is. I'm Simon, but most people call me Si.'

James is wearing a gun belt and pistol; the sight of the gun does nothing for my nerves. David takes off his hat and coat. Like yesterday, he reveals smart clothing. The pressed shirt and trousers are in stark contrast to the scruffy mackintosh. He looks younger than I first thought – my age. James seems younger still.

I also catch sight of David's pistol. 'I hope you don't want me to shoot anyone,' I say, with a hollow laugh.

'Not yet,' David says, with a smirk.

I wait in the sun with a lump in my throat.

'This was once the fastest thorough-brace stagecoach in the north of England,' James explains, pointing to the carriage. Everyone wanted to travel in her. Then the railway came.'

David uncouples two horses and disappears around the side of the barn with them.

'Our father, Michael Atkinson, founded this company and worked every day his whole life to make it the best independent stagecoach company this side of the Pennines,' James explains. 'He was always one step ahead until he had to endure the insult of the Newcastle and Darlington Junction Railway Company building a siding right next to his house.' He nods in the direction of the shiny new buildings across the meadow.

I'm beginning to see where the hatred for the railway comes from.

'Now if it was up to our Dave, he'd go right over there and burn them buildings down, but he knows our father was better than that.'

What happened to your father?' I ask.

David returns for the other two horses.

James doesn't answer my question. 'Let me show you something,' he says.

We leave David and I follow James into the huge barn. It takes a while for my eyes to adjust to the dim light inside. Concentrated rays of sunlight pierce the roof at regular intervals, showing where holes have appeared. I feel cobbles under my feet.

James leads me past an impressive collection of horse tack hanging from the walls. Further in, I find a comprehensive workshop with a fireplace. There's also a mezzanine level above it with what looks like an office of sorts. James guides me to something at the back of the barn. It's a large object covered with a hessian tarpaulin. James pulls the tarpaulin revealing a magnificent coach carriage. The black paint finish on the timber is matt. All the fittings and hand rails are silver rather than brass. The main carriage body is shaped quite sleekly with a narrower top and front, and the windows are dark.

I wonder how many men in sacks have been bundled into

the back of this thing? I'm no expert on coach carriages but this is far from standard. It's almost like a modern interpretation of a stagecoach. It looks like something out of a sci-fi movie; it's far too sleek and well poised to be old. On closer inspection, I notice it's damaged – severely.

'The timber frame is badly twisted,' James explains. 'The axles are broken and she's all lopsided.'

'How did this happen?' I ask.

'That doesn't matter.' David says, joining us. 'The point is... can you fix it?'

'Erm... I'm not sure.'

David stands with arms folded. 'Well you can stay the night while you decide if you can.' James nods in agreement.

'If you can, we'll pay you more than the going rate,' David says. 'If you can't, then there'll be a train on Monday morning to take you home.'

'What about what I owe you?' I ask.

'I'll be expecting you to return with the money,' David says. With that, he leaves.

'Excuse my brother,' James says. 'He's like that with everyone.'

'Why me?' I ask.

'You needed work, didn't you?' James says. 'And David tells me you can fix anything.'

'Well, I...'

'And I'm sure you'll have noticed that we're not very popular,' he adds.

I shake my head. 'Not really.'

James laughs. 'You're polite, I'll give you that. In our line of work, we don't have much time to spare. And we can't be soft or we'll lose everything to the competition. So we've exhausted our stock of friends and hired help.'

I nod. 'I see.'

'You help us, we'll help you.' James strokes the side of the beaten carriage. 'Take a look at her, see what you can do.' The silhouette of David appears in the barn doorway. 'I've got things to do,' James says. 'I'll show you to your room.'

We leave the barn floor and I'm guided up a wooden staircase to the upper level. James leads me into an office; it's a good-sized room with a stove in the corner. It's lightly furnished and has a single bed at one end. It's better than where I stayed last night. *This might be the perfect place to hide out for a while.*

'What do you think?' James asks.

'Looks good to me.'

'I'll get you some fresh bedding, you can eat with us. Supper is at eight, over in the farmhouse.'

'Do you mind if I pop out later to see Miss Pearson?' I ask.

'You're a free man. You can do as you please. A word of warning though,' he adds. 'Be respectful where that young lady is concerned.'

'Of course.'

'Good. She's the kindest girl in this valley and if you abuse that, you'll have us to answer to.'

James leaves. 'Eight sharp,' he shouts, as he descends the staircase.

I explore the barn. I also get a closer look at the carriage. It's impressive. This could be the luxury supercar of the 1900s. It's a shame it's so badly damaged. I wonder if it's stolen. Most of the things I'd need to repair it are already lying around. I stumble across framework parts, nuts and bolts, steel plate, straps, all the rigging for the horses, and much more. The more I see, the more confident I am that I can repair the carriage – and with my modern mechanical background, maybe even improve it.

Not long after James leaves the building, I see him take a couple of horses from a paddock behind the barn. He and his brother ride off in the direction of the town. In their absence, I spend the rest of the afternoon exploring the farm. The other sheds dotted around the barn are mostly empty. Apart from the odd stack of firewood, there isn't much else of interest.

At the far end of the land I find a broken old boundary fence leading to the edge of a river. It must be the same river I visited with Clara yesterday, just further upstream. I sit on a rock by a large pool and think of her. I'm enjoying the warmth, it's still only early summer here but I'm sure it's warmer than any British summer I've known in my time.

I can't resist a dip. I leave my clothes on the bank and jump into the cool clear water. The pool is deep and the water refreshing. Luckily, I don't think anyone sees me. I climb out and dry instantly in the warm sun. I dress and lie on the warm rock for a while. I almost fall asleep.

Eventually, I head back to the barn. Walking along the riverbank, I chance upon a group of mounds in the grass. I see the crooked wooden crosses that accompany them. *A family graveyard maybe?* I hope it is, and not a burial ground for the renegade's past victims. On my way to the barn I pass the paddock. At least eight strong looking horses roam in the late afternoon sun. I don't know much about horses but I'm guessing these are good ones. I'd love to know the full story of this place.

The brothers still aren't home, so I stroll into town. It doesn't take long to cross the meadow and follow the railway line to Conley Hope. I walk through the park and along the main street, all is quiet. I carry on until I find myself at the lane that leads to the Coles' estate. I wonder where Clara is right now. I can't resist calling in on her, so I head down the lane towards the house.

I stop at the gates but don't see anyone around. I idle for a while, but there's still no sign of life. I've come a long way just to turn back. I approach the house and knock.

A lady answers the door. I recognise her – she's one of the maids from the tea party yesterday.

'Can I help you?' she asks.

'I was just wondering if Miss Pearson was at home.'

'Who is it?' I hear a voice bellow.

'Erm... Mr Benson,' the maid says.

Mr Cole appears. 'I don't think it's appropriate to be calling on a lady, especially on a Sunday. What's the matter with you, man?'

'I'm sorry. I err... just forgot to ask her something yesterday and I was passing so...'

'She isn't here,' he says. The maid has her head down.

'Like I said, I was just...'

'Look, Mr Benson. You're a fine chap, but I worry about your intentions towards Miss Pearson.'

'My intentions are perfectly good, I promise you.'

'I'm sure they are, but others might not agree.'

'What do you mean?' I ask.

'I don't think my doorstep is the place to discuss such matters, and not on a Sunday evening when I should be sitting in my chair, smoking my pipe.'

I get the message. 'I apologise for disturbing you, Mr Cole. I'll be on my way.'

'Good man.' The door is slammed shut.

I walk away feeling embarrassed – ashamed almost. There's a lot I don't understand about how people live in this time. It seems so easy to offend someone. I'm guessing Mr Cole is a friend of Clara's father. *Could he know Clara is spoken for?* I drag my feet back to the farm.

**

At the run-down farmhouse, David is standing on the step, surveying his pastures. 'Hungry?' he asks.

'Yeah, all this walking around builds up an appetite.'

'Do city folk not walk anymore?'

I laugh. 'Yes, we still walk, maybe just not enough.'

David waves me into the house.

I wash up and join the brothers in a humble farmhouse kitchen. James stands at a cast iron stove preparing a meal. 'Take a seat,' he says, waving a ladle at a small table in the centre of the room where David's already sitting.

James serves the food. It's only a simple looking combination of meat and potatoes but I'm so hungry that I'm glad of anything.

'What about the carriage then, Si?' David asks, as we tuck in.

'I'll see what I can do,' I say.

'So, you'll try and fix her?' James asks.

'I'll do my best.'

'That's good enough for me,' he says.

'I don't mean to be nosey,' I say. 'But I need to know what happened to it so I can check for any unseen damage.'

James glances at his brother. David nods.

'A few years ago, as a last attempt at keeping us afloat, our father teamed up with Phillip Walker,' James explains. 'He was a good friend of our father, and widely known throughout the industry as the best coach builder in the country. They created a work of genius. Your room is where Phillip stayed; he didn't leave that barn for nearly a year.'

'I'm guessing you're referring to the carriage you showed me.' I say.

'Yes. They built the fastest stagecoach to ever raise dust in this country. But my father didn't realise that by doing so, he would become so hated.'

'Why?'

'My father and Phillip built a fast, safe, and comfortable coach,' James says. 'One to rival any other. It could be pulled by up to ten horses.'

'No coach has ever been pulled by more than six horses,' David explains, dunking bread.

'I take it the competition didn't like that,' I say.

'Definitely not,' James says. 'The coach was completed and entered into one of the last great carriage trials in Weybridge. This was before motor carriage racing became popular.'

'How did it do?'

'It won hands down and everyone who witnessed it was amazed by what they saw. My father was approached by two wealthy London businessmen and they offered to buy the carriage. They also wanted him to build four more just for their coach company.'

'Did he?'

'No. Being proud and independent, he refused.'

'Good for him,' I say. 'So what happened next?'

'He returned to Conley Hope and ran the new coach for a while setting new standards. The railway was becoming popular, but he could still reach all the remote little villages.'

'So, why did people hate him?'

James sighs. 'Well, the public loved it. But as you can imagine, the competition got jealous, especially the southerners.'

'Yeah, so they resorted to dirty tricks,' David adds.

'What kind of tricks?'

'They threatened Phillip with his life if he didn't betray our father and give away the construction secrets of the carriage,' James explains.

'How did it get so damaged then?'

'Well, Phillip disappeared,' David recalls.

'Did he betray your father?'

'No. Phillip was an honourable man,' James says. 'My father suspected the southerners killed him after he refused to work for them.'

'Christ.'

'Father was furious,' David adds. 'Instead of just selling them the coach, the silly old fool carried on rubbing their noses in it by making runs to London. It...'

James interrupts. 'Father wasn't a fool Dave; don't call him that.' The brothers glare at each other across the table.

'Anyway, it wasn't long before father was held up one night on the road back from York. It took half a dozen horsemen on the strongest steeds to even have a chance of catching him.'

'Father was a great coachman,' James adds.

I'm only halfway through my meal but I've almost forgot to eat as I'm so engrossed in the tale. 'So, that's how the coach got damaged?' I ask.

'Yes. He managed to keep her on the road, and would have got away had it not been for the river Tees,' David explains. 'He tried to cross at high speed. As the coach hit the deep water the horses just ripped the wheels from under her.'

'Oh my God,' I say. 'Was your father alright?'

'He was thrown from the carriage and broke both his legs,' James says. 'He died a few weeks later.' Both brothers hang their heads.

I wish I hadn't pressed them for the story now. 'Did they find out who did it?' I ask, quietly.

'No, the police are useless,' David says. 'We know they weren't common highwayman. The coach was empty, so there was nothing to steal. They must have been sent by the southerners.'

'How long ago did this happen?'

'Two years ago,' David says.

My eyes fall upon a shotgun propped up against the stove. 'So, why all the guns? Is there still a threat from them?'

'After father died, local coach companies thought they could muscle in on our trade,' James explains. 'Some thought they might even get the chance to buy, copy, or steal the carriage, which by then had become rather famous in certain circles.'

'So we had to up our game,' David adds. 'But thanks to the railway, and those stupid new motor carriages, we're fighting a losing battle.'

'Unfortunately, a shotgun is the only thing some folk understand,' James says.

I can see why these men are the way they are. 'And may I ask what happened to your mother?' I ask. The table falls silent.

David glares at me. 'We'll respect your privacy, Si. All we ask is that you respect ours.'

'Sorry, I will.' *Wrong question, Si.*

David clears the empty plates and leaves the room.

'I apologise for my brother,' James says.

'That's alright. I hope I haven't annoyed him.'

'He's still very bitter about the whole thing.'

I feel I shouldn't ask anything else, but I want to know more about my curious hosts. 'So when you say you're unpopular, is that because of the things you've had to do to keep the rivals away?' I ask, glancing at the gun again.

'We've had to appear rather ruthless in order to warn people off our business, but it's not all bad as it's also given us a reputation for being safe people to travel with.'

I note the word 'appear' in his explanation. It gives me hope that these two aren't as dangerous as first thought. I don't want to test the theory. 'Do you like it that way?' I ask.

'Well, the railway is seen as a great place for thieves to apply their trade. So, when it comes to moving valuables, we usually get the contract. But I must admit, being looked upon with suspicion all day gets me down.'

'What made you want to repair the coach after all this time?'

'Stir up some interest again. I want us to be known for something other than being a couple of thugs.'

I nod. 'Maybe I can help you with that too.'

'How can you help?'

'Well, I'm fairly good with people so I can tell stories of how I've seen you doing heroic things on your travels. It might clean up your image a bit.'

'Image?' James asks.

'You know, make you look better.'

'Can you really help with that?'

I puff out my chest. 'Of course I can.'

'I like the sound of that, Si.' James offers his hand and we shake. David enters the room with three bottles and passes one to me and one to James.

James removes a cork and takes a big gulp. 'David's ale is the best in town,' he says. 'Did you hear that Dave? Si said he could help us look better.'

'Yeah, I heard. Let's just concentrate on the carriage first.' He removes the cork from his bottle with his teeth and spits in on the table. The cork bounces and hits him right back in the face.

James howls laughing. A grin creeps across David's face. I hold my breath, trying not to laugh. Eventually I crack and so does David. Our laughter can probably be heard halfway across the Conley Valley.

THIRTEEN

21 December 2012

'Still nothing,' John says, throwing his mobile phone on the dashboard. 'He must have gone back.'

'We don't know that,' Emily says, staring out the windscreen at the little church covered with snow. She checks the laptop charging cable is plugged into the cigarette lighter. The computer on her knee comes to life.

'Anything?' John asks.

'It's just booting up.'

'That muppet's gone back; I know it.'

'Right,' Emily says, frantically pressing keys. 'The last time the rig was used was... two weeks ago.'

Jesus. 'That's when we were away. No wonder we've heard nothing from him.'

'He could have been stuck there for two weeks,' Emily asks.

'Technically, he could have been stuck there for over a hundred years,' John adds.

'Oh my God.'

'He could have died of old age by now,' John says, shaking his head.

'He must have left a note, or a clue, or something.'

'Nothing,' John says. 'I've turned that church upside down.'

Emily slams the laptop lid shut. 'The data can tell us how but it can't tell us where he went.'

'I know that, babe,' John snaps. 'We need to get out of here before this snow gets any deeper.' He gets out of the car and trudges back to the church to collect the two empty gas tanks. He covers the rig with a plastic sheet. The stainless steel containers clunk together as John locks up and staggers back to the car. He struggles to stay on his feet on the snow-covered grass.

As John drops the tanks into the car boot, he sees the plastic storage box filled with all his notes and plans for the Human Aspect Scanner. *It's a good job MI5 didn't keep everything.* Tucked down the side of the notes are the two black and white photos he'd snatched back from Alan. He takes them and gets back in the car.

'What's that?' Emily asks, putting the laptop on the back seat.

'Just those old photos,' John says, looking at the first – it's the one of Clara kissing Simon on the cheek by the lemonade stand. 'I wonder if he got his kiss.'

'He must have.'

John looks at the second. 'Hang on a minute...'

'What's wrong?' Emily asks.

'Look at this.' He shows her the photo Alan found of Clara standing in a doorway with a dog. The photo has changed. It's now an image of Simon and Clara holding hands. They stand together in the same doorway. Clara has a daffodil in her hand and they're both laughing together. There's even the same dog but it's at Simon's feet, not Clara's as before.

'Oh my God, it's different,' Emily says.

'What's that?' John asks, pointing to something in Simon's free hand.

Emily strains to see the object. 'It's a piece of paper, and there's something written on it.'

'What does it say?'

'I don't know – it's too small. We need a magnifying glass.'

John starts the engine. 'Let's get home and find one then.'

**

12 July 1912

I've been living in Conley Hope for over a month now and I'm still waking to a glorious day every morning. Some days I wake forgetting what a crazy situation I'm in, others I wake in a cold sweat longing for home. Today is an important day; the town of Conley Hope is ten years old. I open the curtains of my little bedsit in the barn. As always, the early morning sun is making the river sparkle. I miss my friends and family, but looking upon this quiet plush valley, I don't miss the hectic life I left behind.

The Atkinson brothers have taken me under their wing, in return I've worked hard on their carriage. I think I'll have it finished in another week or two. I've tried to keep a low profile to limit any damage I may cause by being here. But because I've been seeing a lot of Clara, I've had to venture out in public from time to time. Some of the town's folk are getting to know my face, and some even remember my name. I just hope I don't leave too big an impression. I could be changing history enough just by me being here.

When I have been to town, I've spoken highly of the Atkinson brothers. I don't think anyone is entirely sure what my relationship is to them, but we probably all prefer it that way. I'm hoping my tales are helping to bridge the gap between the two renegades and the people they share the valley with.

I've been on many dates with Clara, both public and not. I've spent a lot of time with my new girl. There's definitely no sign of another man and I trust her implicitly. I've told her the Atkinson brothers have employed me to repair their famous carriage, and that's no lie. She hasn't pressed me much about anything else in my life so I've remained truthful. I've often thought about telling her everything, but I don't want to frighten her. She wouldn't believe me anyway, and I don't want to lose her.

Clara's helped me through my ordeal without even knowing it. I've fallen head over heels, and I like the feeling. I've become good friends with the brothers too, especially James. He's even teaching me to ride a horse. I've thought of ways to get a message to John and Emily about my predicament. I have some ideas; it's just a case of waiting for the right opportunity. I need to keep my head down and bide my time.

Today however, is not a day for lying low. There are big celebrations taking place in town; Clara tells me it'll be bigger than the annual fete. I've already asked if I can accompany her, and she's accepted. Even the Atkinson brothers will be making an appearance, although probably only in The Sun Inn.

Fed, washed, and dressed in my best 1912 clothes, I meet David and James outside the house. Their existing blue stagecoach stands on the parched meadow. Thanks to me it's polished within an inch of its life and has the brothers' four best steeds providing the power. David and James are dressed to impress too. No scruffy mackintoshes today – and much to my relief, no guns.

We all climb up front.

'Shame our father's famous coach couldn't be ready for today,' David says, setting the horses off at a slow canter to town. James and I nod.

The main street is packed with people already, and it's only mid-morning. Two trams pass us draped with flowers and colourful decorations. The sky is alive with red, white, and blue bunting.

'This is my stop guys,' I say, spying a beautiful redhead waiting by the park gates. I leap from the coach and jog to meet Clara.

The coach carries on along the street.

'Good morning, miss,' I say, taking Clara's hand and kissing it.

Her bright green eyes flash in the sun. 'Hello darling. One day you'll fall off that coach and land flat on your face.'

'How do you know I haven't already?'

Clara giggles.

'Shall we take a walk?' I ask.

'Why not?'

I walk tall along Conley Hope's main street with my girl's soft hand in mine. My head couldn't feel any bigger. I don't think I've ever seen so many people here. Gentlemen politely tip their hats at us as we pass, although their eyes are fixed on Clara.

Market stalls line the pavement and all the shops have tables set up outside. I even see Doris and Margaret selling their home-made lemonade again. They wave as they see us. We catch up to David and James who have parked the stagecoach outside the general store. David stands talking to a family at the roadside. James is helping a child up onto one of the horses. In front of the coach is a car – the first I've seen in Conley Hope. It looks like an early Ford. Its cream paintwork and brass fittings are gleaming in the morning sunshine. The black folding roof is down, and the owner sits proudly in the driver's seat. Clara and I cross the road to look.

'It's Mr Cole in his new motor carriage,' Clara says.

I let go of her hand at the mention of his name, not wanting to create a stir, but she grabs mine again.

I nod towards James as we pass. I never thought I'd see the brothers displaying their carriage alongside a motor car. I'm surprised David hasn't dug out his shotgun and blown holes in it by now.

'Hello, Mr Cole,' Clara says.

I nod and smile.

'Hello Clara,' he says.

'That's a fine machine you have there,' I say.

'It's not a machine, Mr Benson,' he says. 'It's a combustion-engine-powered carriage.'

'Sorry, my mistake.'

A young boy rushes over, wide-eyed. He skips around the car under the watchful eye of his mother. 'Will you take me for a ride, mister?' he asks.

I see Mr Cole grinning from ear to ear. 'Of course, he says.'

The boy looks at his mother. 'Can I, Mother, can I?' The lady nods agreeably. The boy leaps into the car.

Mr Cole gets out and inserts the starter handle. With one turn the engine starts, but before the big fellow can get back in, the engine stalls. 'Nothing to worry about,' he says. 'She's a stubborn girl when people are watching.' He returns to the handle.

I peer inside the car. I notice the choke is pulled right out. 'Is the engine warm?' I ask.

'It's supposed to get hot,' Mr Cole bellows, turning the handle again and again.

'I know, but it's flooded,' I say.

Mr Cole stops winding. 'What ever do you mean, man?'

'Too much fuel's gone into the combustion chamber. Lift the bonnet.'

After hesitating for a moment, Mr Cole unties the leather straps holding the polished cream hood down. Once open, he peers inside. 'I'm not happy with this,' he says. 'The salesman insisted this was the most reliable model on the market.'

'It's nothing to worry about,' I say.

Clara looks on as I tinker with the engine.

'I'm not sure you should be doing that, Mr Benson,' Mr Cole says. 'We need a trained expert in such matters.' He wanders around the car anxiously rubbing his forehead.

'All done,' I say, closing the hood. I reach into the car and push the choke in.

Mr Cole joins me.

'Only use the choke when the engine's cold,' I say. 'Pull it right out in winter, and only halfway in summer. Don't leave it out.' I go to the front of the car and turn the starting handle.

The engine starts. Mr Cole stares at me. The boy in the car looks like he has ants in his pants.

'You'd better go,' I say. 'You have an impatient passenger.'

Mr Cole offers his hand and we shake. 'Thank

you,' he says. 'Would you like a ride in my motor carriage later?'

'It's alright,' I say. 'I have one at home.'

Mr Cole laughs and gets into his pride and joy. He drives away. The car noisily chugs down the street spewing black smoke.

I return to Clara with oil on my hands.

'You big fibber,' Clara says.

I grin.

'You're amazing, Simon.'

I shrug. 'No I'm not.'

'Yes, you are,' she says. 'I love you.' I think the world stops spinning for a moment. It's the first time she's said that to me.

'I love you too,' I say, moving in close.

Those hypnotic eyes stare right at my soul. 'Kiss me,' she says.

'I can't kiss you here. We'd be the talk of the town.'

'Does it matter?'

'No it doesn't, but I fear you'll end up with oily hand prints on your bottom.'

Clara giggles and blushes. 'We'd better get you cleaned up then hadn't we? Come on, I'm told the bank has a water closet.' We cross the street and pass a photographer setting up outside the bank. I leave Clara and enter the grand stone building, seeking out the customer toilet.

Back outside, I find Clara talking to the photographer. 'He'd like to take another photograph of us, Simon.'

'Alright.' I stand with Clara in the doorway to the bank and wait for the photographer to finish setting up his camera. I see a little girl sitting with a couple of women at a table outside the cafe next door. On the table is a bunch of daffodils.

'I'll be back in a minute,' I say.

At the table I find the girl drawing. May I buy a flower for my beautiful friend?' I say, to the little girl.

She nods.

'Do you mind?' I say, to the ladies.

'Not at all, mister.'

I give the young girl a half penny from my pocket and take a daffodil. I also spy blank sheets of paper and pencils. 'May I write a little message for her too?' I say.

The little girl grins and hands me a pencil.

As I fold a sheet of paper, I try to remember the four possible crossover dates I'd put on my list back in the little church of 2012. *What was the last date?*

Got it. I scribble... 'I'll be in the church at dusk on 27 July 1912.'

I hand the pencil back. 'Thank you.' I return to Clara keeping the note concealed.

'Whatever are you doing, Simon?' she asks.

'Buying you a gift,' I say, handing her the flower.

She gifts me a gorgeous smile. She takes my hand.

'May I take the photo now, sir?' the photographer asks.

'Yes, of course.'

He holds aloft his tray of flash powder.

I make sure the note in my other hand can be seen by the camera. A small dog appears at my feet.

'Great, this thing's going to wee on me,' I say.

Clara begins laughing - I laugh with her. There's a flash.

**

We spend a while wondering the town of Conley Hope enjoying the tenth anniversary celebrations. We eat at Alice's tea shop and take an open-top tram ride.

'What should we do now?' Clara asks, as we get off the tram near the railway station.

'I think it's time I gave you that kiss,' I say.

'That sounds like a lovely idea. Take me somewhere nice.'

'My pleasure, miss. I know just the place.'

**

After a leisurely walk beside the railway line, we arrive on the Atkinson brothers' land. I lead Clara to the rock pool I found the first day I came here.

'Oh how wonderful,' she says, running to the water's edge. 'Let's paddle.'

We sit together on the large rock. Clara sits between my legs with her back to me and her bare feet dangling in the water – she has such delicate little feet. I love them. I have one arm around her waist with my hand flat on her tummy. I gently hold up her hair with the other. I slowly explore every inch of the back of her neck with my lips. It isn't long before Clara turns and takes her overdue kiss. That kiss continues until the sun goes down.

**

The rest of July follows a similar pattern. I see Clara nearly every day and we get plenty of time alone to fuel our friendship and love for each other. She visits her family in Durham from time to time but I'm encouraged by her speedy returns. As the month nears its expiry, I feel I'm working to a deadline with the stagecoach carriage repairs. I'm hoping the photo of Clara and me is seen in the future by John or Emily. I pray they see my note. Before long 27 July is just one day away.

On the twenty-sixth, I wake early. I wash, dress, and make my way down the staircase to the workshop floor. I cross the cobbles and catch sight of a familiar silhouette in the open barn doorway. It's Clara. She's surrounded by a sunny morning glow.

'Hello, beautiful,' I say, greeting her at the door. 'I didn't expect you this early?'

She presses her soft cheek against mine then kisses me lengthily on the lips. She gazes at me with those big green eyes. I tingle all over every time she does that.

'I thought I'd bring you some breakfast, darling,' she says.

'Well you do look good enough to eat,' I say.

Clara giggles. 'No, not me, silly. I have a basket outside. I thought we could have an early morning picnic before I leave for work.' She bites her lip. 'Although I wouldn't complain if you'd prefer me, Mr Benson.'

My heart skips three beats. I respect Clara immensely and I've remained the perfect gentleman. Although it's difficult at times, I intend to stay that way. I kiss her again. 'A breakfast picnic sounds perfect.'

Clara skips off into the sun grabbing her basket on the way to the meadow.

I run after her.

David and James have already left to deliver packages to the docks in Newcastle, so Clara and I have the meadow to ourselves. She takes a blanket from her basket and lays it out under a tree.

I peer into the basket to see what else Clara's brought. There's bread, jam, honey, cheese, and lemonade to drink. 'This looks nearly as scrummy as you,' I say, cuddling up to her.

'What am I going to do with you, Simon? You always know just how to charm me.' She spreads honey on a slice of crusty bread and feeds it to me. I take a bite and she does the same.

We share the rest of the contents of the basket and the shade from the tree. There's a nice cool breeze blowing down the valley. I'm glad of the break from the heat; it's been a hot dry month.

'I'll be going home first thing in the morning, Simon.' Clara says, hanging her head.

I've not seen that look before. 'Is everything alright?' I ask.

'My mother's not well.'

'I'm sorry to hear that.'

'I never like going home anyway. I much prefer to stay here with you. I also expect this visit to be a rather unpleasant one.'

I'm now bolt upright. 'Why?' I ask.

'I need to have a very serious talk with my father.'

My heart starts thumping.

'Ever since I was a little girl, I had a friend named Walter Clarke.'

On hearing the name I know what to expect next.

'Walter and I grew up together and he has always liked me. He's now working his way up in my father's constabulary and my father expects us to be together one day.'

I go cold. 'Do you think you should do as your father expects?' I ask.

'No I don't.' She takes my hand. 'I have no intention of it.'

I feel the blood pumping around me again.

'I want to be with you forever, Simon.'

'I want that too.' We kiss and cuddle for a while.

I hear a loud whistle as the eight thirty train steams past the nearby sidings on its way to Conley Hope station. It's Clara's cue to head off to work. I help my sweetheart pack her basket and wait for a goodbye kiss.

She pulls me to her. 'Come to me tonight,' she whispers. 'I'll be at the Coles' barn just before dusk.'

'I will.'

Clara kisses me and leaves. I watch her hurry off towards town.

I think tomorrow will be the day John, Emily, and I have seen with the Human Aspect Scanner in the house on North Bailey. I can't believe the time has come. I was hoping it might never happen. And now I know it's because of me. I feel sick thinking of Clara being struck by her father. Typically, tomorrow is also the day I'm hoping John and Emily will be firing up the rig. I'm praying they got my message. I retreat to the barn to make last-minute adjustments to the carriage. I don't stop thinking about Clara all day.

**

In the late afternoon I hear the sound of hooves and wheels coming along the dirt track towards the farm. David's distinctive yell brings the beasts to a stop outside the barn. He and James jump from their carriage.

I walk out to greet them. 'Hey up, gentlemen,' I say.

'How's she coming along?' James asks.

'She's all done.'

'Really?' David asks, excitedly. 'That's great news.'

'Can we take a look?' James asks.

'Definitely not,' I say. 'I need to polish her up

first.'

The boys look disappointed.

'Well I think that calls for a drink,' James says.

I shake my head. 'Not for me, thanks.'

'Oh, I see. Is my brew not good enough for you anymore then, sir?' David says, with a grin.

'I'm meeting my girl this evening.'

'Yet another evening with Miss Pearson, Si?' James asks.

I nod.

You're a lucky man, Si,' David says. 'She's definitely special that one.'

'I know she is.'

'You're a perfect match,' James adds.

'Do you really think so?' I ask.

Both brothers nod vigorously. 'She doesn't belong here anymore than you,' James says.

I haven't let on about my situation so I'm intrigued. 'What do you mean?'

James pats me on the back. 'We may be just a couple of coach runners, but we've met everyone worth meeting on our travels, Si. You learn a lot on the road.'

'Yes,' David adds. 'And no one could have repaired the coach that quickly. Not even Phillip Walker.'

'I just...'

James holds his hand up to stop me. 'I think you'd better get in the house and draw a bath if you're going to be dating the prettiest girl in Conley Hope this evening.'

I nod. 'Thank you.'

**

At dusk, I enter the lane to the Coles' estate. I see the sun setting over the hills on the other side of the river. I wonder if the sun could be setting on my time here. Even though I hope I have a chance of getting home tomorrow, I'm sad at the thought of leaving. I avoid the house and take a shortcut across the fields to the red-brick barn. I wander around the outside and find no sign of Clara. Then I hear her voice. I look up at the open hay loft doors and see Clara's face alight in the warmth from the sunset.

'Is everything alright?' I shout.

'Shhh. Come inside,' she whispers.

This kind of behaviour is nothing unusual. It always leads to a prank or planned intimate kiss out of sight of others. I prepare myself for a spider down the shirt or bucket of water over the head.

I enter the dark barn and negotiate items of farm machinery. I climb a ladder leading to the hay loft. The loft is half-full with loose hay concentrated in a great pile in the centre. The whole space is flooded with deep orange sunlight from the open loft doors. I don't see Clara.

I walk around the hay and stop to admire the view. I can see the whole of the valley from here – the river, the rolling fields, the woods, and the town in the distance. All is covered with a golden blanket of dusk light. I hear someone breathing behind me. I turn to find a collection of blankets in a hollow in the hay. Nestled amongst them is Clara.

I approach. 'Hello,' I say.

I'm met by the most seductive look I've ever encountered. Those bright green eyes look hungry.

'What are you doing up here?' I ask, as I kneel in the hay beside her.

She puts a finger on my lips. 'Shhh...' She wears a delicate nightdress. It shows every curve, every crease.

My heart thumps against my ribs. Just when I thought Clara couldn't be any more attractive, I'm simply overwhelmed by her.

She puts her arms around my neck and pulls me in until I'm hovering over her, my weight on my arms.

Our lips meet and we kiss lovingly – lengthily.

I'm breathless as our lips part for a moment.

'Make me yours, Simon,' she says, in a husky whisper.

I'm trembling.

Clara turns onto her belly, offering me the buttons on the back of her dress. I slowly undo them. We gently undress each other until we're both naked. We lie together, our warm bodies touching. Our hearts are thumping against one another's chests.

I see Clara's hands are shaking.

'Are you alright,' I ask, softly.

'Yes, my darling.'

I take a hand and kiss her palm – nibble the back of her wrist. My lips travel the length of her arm until they fall upon her collarbone. I linger there a while.

Clara draws a deep breath as I descend her body. She arches her back bringing her breasts to my lips, inviting me to taste her skin. I explore every goose bump with my tongue. I feel her hands gripping my lower back – they're no longer shaking. I explore further. My journey takes my lips past her belly button, along the crease of her hip to her inner thigh. I linger there a while too.

Clara whimpers. She pulls me back to her lips and wraps her legs around me. Her eyes alone tell me everything she wants.

Our bodies become one. We move as one. I feel everything she feels. For a moment I could swear my soul leaves me to be with hers. I struggle to breathe – like I'm underwater. I'm drowning and burning in the same moment. I'm fighting the fire that courses through every nerve in me. Clara's strangled groans tease my ears. We inhale each other's breath as we kiss. We grip each other tight as our bodies become rigid in mutual release.

We lie together naked, bathed in dusk light. Our lips barely leave one another. I run my fingers through her hair and stroke her neck. The moments fill with silent gazes and feelings reserved only for us. We cuddle together, wrapped up in each other under the blankets until moonlight replaces the dusk.

'Do you have to go home tomorrow?' I ask.

'Yes, I must see my mother. Don't worry darling, I'll return to you as soon as I can.'

I smile. 'Can I ask you to do something for me?'

'Of course. I'll do anything for you, Simon.'

'Please don't upset your father.'

Clara draws away from me. 'Do you not want my family to know about us?'

I pull her close again. 'I want everyone to know about us,' I say, staring into those beautiful eyes. 'I'm just worried what he might do.'

'He wouldn't hurt you, Simon.'

'I don't care about me. I'm worried about you.'

'Don't worry for me, my darling. I can look after myself. I'll be alright... I promise.'

'Promise you'll come back to me,' I demand.

'With all my heart.'

A roll of thunder clatters the distant hills, making Clara jump. 'Oh dear, Simon. I don't like thunder and lightning.'

'I'd better get you back to the house before it gets any worse.' No sooner have I made an attempt to move, the barn roof is battered by heavy rain. The moon disappears and we're left in darkness. There's a flash of lightning outside.

'I'm frightened,' Clara says.

I make sure she's well wrapped up in blankets and hold her tight. 'You're safe with me,' I say.

'I know I am.' She buries her head in my chest as the thunder grows louder and travels nearer.

Through the open hay loft doors, I see the valley floor flash white, over and over again. I feel Clara shaking. 'There's nothing to be scared of, Clara.' I lift her head and kiss her. 'Watch the storm with me.'

'I can't.'

'You can... look.'

She rests her head against mine and watches. There are more rumbles and flashes.

'Thunder and lightning is only energy,' I say.

'Energy?'

'Yes. The same thing that makes light bulbs light up, makes motor carriages move, makes you and me fall in love.'

'What do you mean, darling?'

'Energy is good. We're all full of it. It's what makes us happy, sad, what makes us passionate and angry. That's all that's going on out there. The sky's just angry.'

'I don't like the sky when it's angry.'

'It's also in all nice things too, it's what makes rivers flow, birds sing, grass grow. All the things you love are made of the same things as thunder and lightning. Energy is what makes you special, Clara. It's what makes you so beautiful. It's what brought me here and made me fall in love with you. Thunder and lightning is energy – so thunder and lightning is good.'

Clara squeezes me tightly. 'You never stop

surprising me.' She's stopped shaking. We watch the storm together.

After an hour or so, the weather has calmed. The rain has stopped and the storm subsided. Clara is fast asleep. I don't want to wake her. I get up leaving her wrapped in a blanket. I dress in the returning moonlight, hardly able to take my eyes off her. Clara's face is illuminated – she looks stunning.

I gather her clothes and place them beside her. Gathering her in the warmth of the blankets, I pick her up and carry her out of the loft. The staircase and lower barn are tricky but I manage to negotiate them. I carry her through the field to the house. The whole time she doesn't stir.

On the back step, I gently wake her. She looks confused staring up at me with those big sleepy eyes. I set her on her feet. She stands smiling wrapped in the blanket. A pile of clothes falls out of the bottom.

She giggles. 'I love you,' she whispers.

'I love you too,' I say, stroking her cheek. 'I'll see you very soon.'

'I hope so.' She kisses me.

As I walk the lane heading back to the farm, the sky changes again. The moon retreats back to cloud and an unfamiliar cold breeze blows up the valley. My journey home will be more difficult without moonlight. But I imagine my journey back to the barn will be nothing compared with finding my way home to 2012 tomorrow.

FOURTEEN

27 July 1912

I wake with a jolt and check my pocket watch – I've slept in. I dress and leave the workshop office. Descending the staircase, I hear a train whistle. I rush out into the paddock. There's white smoke on the horizon. That'll be the morning train carrying my sweetheart to Durham. I have no control over what happens now.

Shergar approaches – he's one of the fine creatures that pull the stagecoaches. I recognise the white flash on his brown belly. I pat him and he rubs his chin on the top of my head. I realise he's wet. *So am I.* It's raining. For the first time in Conley Hope, I feel no sun on my back.

Hazy from sleep I trudge back to the barn. I make a hot drink and wander the cobbled floor drinking it. I feel kind of empty, but can't work out why. *Maybe I'm just worried about Clara, maybe it's the thought that I might be going home today.* Even though I don't belong here, I'm going to miss this place. I'll miss seeing Clara every day.

After breakfast I set to work polishing the repaired stagecoach ready for a test run. My thoughts are filled with Clara and our time in the barn. I smile uncontrollably as I remember how special she made me feel. Sadly, my warm thoughts are marred by the cold possibility of her returning home to trouble.

By mid-afternoon the coach is ready. I open the large barn doors. Thick mist clings to the distant hills and the meadow looks grey and uninviting. That empty feeling is growing. I feel guilty for not doing more to protect Clara from what I suspect might happen today. I can't just hang around waiting for the inevitable. For the first time since all this began, I actually want to change history.

David and James appear from the house, interrupting my thoughts.

'How's she looking, Si?' David asks.

'All done.'

'Can we take her out and stretch some legs?' James asks.

'She's all yours... but can I make a request?'

James nods. 'By all means.'

'Can we run her to Durham and back?'

'Any particular reason you'd like to run to Durham?' James asks.

If John and Emily got my message, they could be here within hours. But Clara comes first, and it's time to save her from her father's wrath. *Can I get to Clara, and return in time?* 'I think Clara might be in trouble and I need to get to her father's house to see her.'

James raises his eyebrows. 'You mean Clara's father as in Captain Pearson of the Durham police?'

'Yes,' I say. 'But you don't have to take me all the way... just get me near.'

David laughs and slaps his brother hard, on the back. 'Well I don't know about you brother, but I'm all for it. It's been a while since we ruffled some feathers in the Durham constabulary.'

James grins back at us both. 'Yeah, why the hell not?'

I show them inside the barn for the first time since I began my repairs.

David and James inspect the carriage, taking in its renewed majestic presence. I've worked harder over the last few weeks than at any time in my life, taking my modern knowledge and mixing it as best I can with the traditional.

I point out my improvements. 'I've removed the old leather suspension straps and replaced them with a torsion bar system,' I explain. 'I've restored the chassis and strengthened the timber frame with iron. I've also replaced the axles.'

The brothers gaze wide-eyed. 'Will she go faster?' David asks.

'She sure will.' My confidence is bolstered by the fact the suspension on this carriage is now forty years ahead of its time. 'You can push her as hard as you want now, this beauty is so rigid you can put her under a lot more stress.'

'What do you mean?' David asks.

'Well, you can go around corners far quicker than with any other coach and she won't tip over.'

David grins from ear to ear. 'I can't wait to frighten the public with this.'

James shakes his head. 'You've frightened the public enough over the years.'

'Right,' David says, rubbing his hands together. 'You grab the horses, James, I'll get the tack.'

'How many animals, Dave?' James asks.

'Let's put eight on.'

James runs to the paddock chuckling to himself.

I'm left to tidy a few tools away and prepare for the trip to Durham, mentally more than anything. I'm just desperate to get to Clara. I wash and change while David and James prepare the stagecoach. I leave the workshop office to find eight huge twitching beasts on the cobbles below. The stagecoach is ready. The sound in the barn is unbelievable. Thirty-two hooves pounding the cobbled floor coupled with panting and snorting echo around the timber structure.

I watch David pat Shergar at the lead. He's whispering something in the horse's ear. I see Shergar's heart thumping through his glossy brown coat – it's as if he knows what he's about to pull. At the bottom of the stairs, James hands me a mackintosh and hat similar to his.

'Well you might as well look the part,' he says, with a grin.

'Thank you.' I put them on.

David throws a shotgun and pistol into the carriage.

I haven't seen those in a while. I climb onto the rear platform.

The brothers climb up front. I see David take a deep breath before gripping the reins.

I take a tight hold of the steel rail in front of me.

'Yar.' We lunge forward with the horses' power. We leave the barn and canter across the misty meadow.

We arrive in town and enter the main street. People line the pavements, shocked at the sight of eight horses pulling the magnificent stagecoach through their streets. The sound of hooves echoes between the buildings. Outside The Sun Inn several miners stand and watch. A couple of them wave as we pass. We turn a corner and canter past the lane leading to the Coles' estate.

I want to get a better view before David speeds up. 'Hey, James,' I shout.

A face peers over the carriage. 'You alright, Si?'

'Yeah. Can I join you up there?'

'Of course. Can you climb round?'

I look down at the cobbled road flashing beneath the carriage. Normally I'd think it far too dangerous to attempt climbing to the front while moving, but today I fear nothing. I slide onto a metal rail that runs the length of the stagecoach. Clinging to the roof by my fingertips, I shuffle along to the driver's platform.

'Welcome sir,' James says, with a grin.

I join the brothers on the leather driver's bench.

'Let them go Dave,' James says.

With a flick of his reins, the horses surge forward. The carriage thumps us in the back as we accelerate. I feel like I'm in a powerful car and the driver just put his foot to the floor. My heart pounds as the stagecoach gains speed. The wind fills my open mackintosh and almost takes my hat. We leave town and travel the road to Durham at speed.

Grinning from ear to ear, David becomes braver with every turn of the road. Where he would normally slow down, he speeds up. James cheers as the coach hugs tight bends. The horses, although running at full stretch at times, don't seem to tire. Onlookers wave as the horses pound the road through small villages. We wave back.

I feel the anticipation building as we pass the mid-point in our journey. I can't stop thinking of Clara. I hope we can get there in time. I hope I can be back by dusk.

At one point, we travel a long straight lane with overhanging trees on each side. The horses are running at full tilt. I don't even feel the leaves whipping my face and neck as we dodge low-hanging branches. My only concern is getting to Durham, and to Clara.

On arrival at Durham, David avoids the main road. He guides us down a track that runs alongside the railway line. We slow as we pass a large railway siding and workshop. I recognise the building – it's the repair shed, the workshops owned by the university in the future.

We cross a small bridge over the river and come closer to the centre of town. David's route has brought us to the rear of the cathedral, an area dominated by small quiet lanes where the stagecoach will be hidden by trees. The two great towers of the cathedral are licking the misty sky on the hill above us. *It'll be getting dark soon.* We eventually come to a stop by an inn.

David pulls the horses into its yard and we all climb down. He takes the guns from the carriage and hands me a pistol.

'I don't want a gun,' I say.

'You don't know what's going to happen, Si. Take the pistol.'

I hesitate.

'You want to protect your girl don't you?' he says.

I take the pistol and slip it inside my mackintosh.

A man emerges from a nearby building. 'Can I help you, gentlemen?'

David loads his shotgun and starts walking towards the man.

I grab his arm to stop him. 'I'll handle this,' I say.

David stops but doesn't hide his gun.

I'm met by the well-built, rugged guy. He's dressed in outdoor clothing so I assume he's a stable hand.

'Do you work here?' I ask, tipping my hat.

'Yes I do. What do you want?'

'We've been sent from York Minster with important documents for delivery to the cathedral. It's important that our visit remains a secret. Can I entrust you to water and watch over these animals until we return?' I'm taking a complete gamble. In my time this guy would probably just tell me to get lost, but I have more faith in the people here.

The man peers over at the magnificent stagecoach. 'That looks like it could be the coach of the archbishop himself.'

I raise my eyebrows.

'Oh my goodness,' he says, his eyes widening. 'I'd be honoured.'

'God bless you,' I say. 'Your deed will not be forgotten.' I tip my hat at him again and re-join the brothers.

It looks like David's about to wet himself.

'Well, what else could I say?' I whisper.

We leave the inn and rush along the network of cobbled alleyways. The weather's deteriorating as we cross the grounds of the cathedral. The beautiful summer I've been used to over the last few weeks is well and truly absent today. A swirling mist clings to almost everything. On the other side of the square, the university comes and goes in waves as the wind blows. It reminds me of the gas clouds created by the rig.

We cut down an alleyway onto North Bailey. The street is gloomy, it's not dusk yet but lamps are already lit. We duck into a tiny churchyard not far from number twenty-six. We crouch behind the low wall.

A small stagecoach is pulling away. I hope that

isn't Clara – I hope I'm not too late.

'How do you know Clara's in trouble then, Si?' James asks.

'Just something I heard.'

David points out a tall figure in a trench coat standing close to Clara's house. 'That could be a guard.'

We'll attract far too much attention if we all troop over. 'You lads stay here,' I say. 'I'll go over alone.'

'Are you sure, Si?' David says.

'Yeah, thanks for the backup, but this is my problem. You two stay here.'

David nods.

'If it all goes wrong, get away from here,' I say, stepping out from the shadow of the church yard wall.

'If you need us we'll be right behind you,' James says.

I walk casually along the pavement towards the town house with a lump in my throat. It feels strange visiting the house I've seen all those years in the future. It looks so much newer.

'Can I help you?' the man outside says, as I reach Clara's door. I notice a pistol under his coat, it shines in the lamplight.

'Good evening. I have a message for a Miss Pearson,' I say, making out I don't even know Clara. 'It's from Conley Hope and it's very important.'

The guy runs his eyes over me. 'I'll take the message,' he says, holding out his hand.

'It's a verbal message and I've been instructed to deliver it in person.'

He whips his hand away and looks over me again with a crumpled brow. 'Who sent this message?'

'I've been sent by the town council. Unfortunately, I can't discuss the matter with you any further.'

'On a Saturday? I find that very unusual,' he remarks. 'May I have your name, sir?'

'John Hartley,' I blurt out.

'Wait here.'

He knocks and enters the house, closing the door behind him.

It begins to rain, heavily. I hug the house wall and watch the rain blow sideways in the orange of the nearest street lamp. From the corner of my eye I see David and James moving in the distance. They leap over the yard wall and disappear down an alley.

Clara's door opens and two men step out. It's the tall guy plus a second who's much larger.

My heart starts pounding.

'Miss Pearson is not at home. The message will have to wait,' the big man says.

He's lying. 'I was told she would be here,' I say.

Both men look like they have little patience. 'Miss Pearson stepped out not that long ago, I'm afraid you've missed her.'

The tall guy tickles his pistol. 'Your message will have to wait for another day. Now be on your way.'

I remember the stagecoach pulling away earlier. *Maybe she has left? She might be on her way back to Coney Hope, and hopefully to me.* 'Where did Miss Pearson go?' I ask. 'I can deliver the message to her there.'

The big guy flashes his eyes at me. 'I told you to be on your way. That's your final warning.'

I'm glad to see David and James creeping up the alley beside the town house. They must have sneaked through the back gardens.

'Look, I'm only doing my job,' I say. 'I really need to get this message to Clara.'

The tall man draws his pistol.

I raise my hands and back off.

'Clara? I don't think you're who you say you are,' he says, pointing the pistol at me.

'Yes I am,' I stutter. 'I don't think that's necessary.'

The larger man also pulls a pistol from his coat. He grabs me. 'Come with me. I'm taking you to see the captain.'

James steps out from the alleyway and presses his pistol barrel against the back of the tall guy's head. 'He's not going anywhere.'

David springs from the shadows and points his shotgun in the face of the larger man. 'Yes, let go of him.'

Wide-eyed, my captor lets go.

I pull out my pistol and wave it around.

David pushes his shotgun barrels closer. 'If you don't stand down, I'm going to let this off in your face.'

Both men lower their pistols. James takes their weapons.

'Where's Miss Pearson?' I growl.

'We're not at liberty to tell you that.'

'Tell me where she is or I'll use this,' I say, pointing my pistol at the tall man.

He sniggers.

James takes his pistol from the man's head and points it at his testicles. 'If you want to keep those I suggest you answer my friend.'

I ask again. 'Where's she gone?'

'Her father will have you all hung for this.'

'I only want to get a message to her you ignorant bastard. What the hell do you think this is?' I'm shaking. 'Where did she go?' I scream.

'I'm afraid I don't have that information.'

I hear high-pitched whistles. Two uniformed policemen come running.

'I think we'd better go,' David says, lowering his shotgun.

Shit. I don't believe this. We tear down an alley across the street. There's shouting behind us. The murky day makes our escape easier. We soon put some distance between us and our pursuers by making use of the labyrinth of alleyways. Between us we know enough about the old town of Durham to navigate our way to the river. There's muffled shouting on the wind, and dogs barking. We run along the riverbank towards the inn where we left the stagecoach.

'Do you think they recognised us, Dave?' James splutters.

'No, if they recognised us they'd have shot us,' David says, laughing.

'I'm sorry I dragged you into this, gents,' I say, struggling for breath.

'Don't worry about us, Si,' James says, giving me a friendly punch on the arm. 'We've been doing this for years.'

By the time we reach the inn, the distant shouts and dog barking is fading.

'I think we sent them the wrong way,' David says.

We catch our breath before entering the yard. The stable hand has kept true to his word – the horses are fed and watered.

'Hello gentlemen, she's all ready to go,' he says, with a smile.

'Thank you,' I say. I offer him some coins. 'A little for your trouble.'

It isn't much but his face lights up. 'Oh thank you, sir. That is one very fine stagecoach and it's been an honour to serve you.'

I shake his hand and join James and David as they check the horses and tack.

'Which direction do you think Clara will have gone then, Si?' David asks. James stands shoulder to shoulder with his brother.

'I'm hoping she's gone back to Conley Hope. That's if she's left at all.'

'Well if she has gone back, we'll soon catch up. James says, climbing onto the driver's platform. I join him.

'I'd better keep an eye out behind us,' David says climbing onto the rear platform, shotgun in hand.

The coach jolts as James flicks reins. This is the first time I've seen him drive. We canter the bridge and along the railway line. James doesn't seem as gung-ho as his brother. The ride home takes longer as he keeps the horses at a steady speed without pushing them too hard.

We chat to pass the time. 'You look worried, Si.'

'I am.'

'You care for her greatly don't you?'

'I do. I'm just not sure if we can be together.'

'Do you worry about the class divide?' he asks. 'Because you shouldn't. I've seen the way she looks at you, Si. There's no divide between you two.'

'I know, but it's a little more complicated than that.'

'You're not already married are you? Because that's not right if you are,' James adds.

'Oh no, definitely not. I just need to find a way to keep her, that's all.'

'There's always a way, Si. And I know you won't give up on her.'

'You're right; I won't – ever.' My head feels heavy.

'It's just difficult.'

'How difficult can it be? You love her don't you?'

'Yes, I do.'

'Then you'll be fine. You might have finished this coach, but your job in Conley Hope isn't done.'

'You're right.' Can two people one hundred years apart really make a life together? Where would we do it - here, or in 2012? I recall the disintegrating hymn book from my first crossover. I've thought about that book and what happened to it a lot. If I take Clara home with me, she could also age a hundred years in a second. *I don't fancy testing the theory.*

If I want to be with Clara, I'll have to stay here. If I don't get back soon, I'll be stuck here forever anyway. 'I'm not sure what I'm going to do yet,' I say. 'Obviously I'll get out of your hair now my work's finished.'

'You can stay with us as long as you want Si. You'll always be welcome.'

'Thanks James.' I see the darkening sky ahead. 'Is there any chance we can speed up a bit?'

'Of course. Sorry, I was forgetting you're keen to find Clara.' James flicks the reins and the carriage accelerates. The rain stops and stars appear as night falls over the north-east.

**

It's dark as we ride into the Conley Valley. My stomach's doing summersaults as we approach town. The streetlamps are lit, the mist has lifted and the rooftops are bathed in moonlight. The message I tried to get to John and Emily said to meet me at dusk. That's long past. *Would they have waited for me?* We arrive at the farm.

I dive from the carriage. 'Can I borrow a horse?' I

ask.

'Of course,' David says. 'Will you be alright alone?'

'Yeah, I'll be fine.'

James leaps from the driver's platform. 'I'm coming with you. I've seen you ride.'

'You really don't have to…'

'I'll get two fresh horses,' he says, running for the paddock.

I rush up to the office and collect a few personal items. I stuff them in my mackintosh pockets as I leave.

Back outside, David hands me another pistol. 'In case you run into trouble.'

'Thanks Dave.'

'Can I give you a piece of advice?' he says.

I nod and tuck the pistol in the front of my trousers.

'Next time you stick a loaded pistol in a policemen's face... cock it first.'

I grin. 'Never thought of that.'

David laughs.

James arrives with two saddled beasts. We mount and head out across the moonlit meadow.

'We'll follow the river,' James shouts. 'It'll be quicker.' He rides up front, following the river towards the Coles' estate.

I'm close behind, just trying not to fall off. Luckily, my horse seems to know where he's going.

**

At the Coles' estate we find a dark, empty-looking house. There's no answer at the door.

'Where is she?' I say, banging my fists on the gate.

'Maybe it's best waiting till morning?' James says.

As much as I hate the technology-riddled nature of the future, this is just frustrating. I pace the driveway, what I'd give for a text message from Clara right now.

'Is there anywhere else she would go?' James asks.

'No, I don't think so.' *Damn, it must be at least two hours past dusk.*

'There's just one place I can check,' I say.

'Where?'

'The church.'

'Let's go,' James says, setting off up the lane.

I clamber onto my horse and catch up.

**

I pull my horse up at the top of Schoolhouse Lane. The damp green slate of the church spire is shining back at the moon.

James halts a little way ahead. 'You alright, Si?'

I dismount and walk my horse over. I offer him the reins. 'I'll go alone from here,' I say. 'You've helped me enough.'

James cocks his head. 'You don't want me to come with you?'

I hand him my pistol. 'I'm just going to sneak in; I don't want to make a fuss.'

'Alright, if that's what you want,' he says, taking the gun.

'I really appreciate what you did today. I couldn't have done it without you,' I say, offering my hand. 'Thank you for everything; you've been a good friend.'

He takes my hand and shakes it firmly. 'You're welcome, but that sounds like a goodbye.'

'Just in case anything happens,' I say.

James sighs. 'Be careful.'

'I will.' I take off along the lane and jog into the church yard. At the doorway, I glance back.

James has gone.

Inside I find a few candles splitting the darkness. I look around the room but see no one.

A voice startles me. 'Where the hell have you been?'

I'm not sure where it came from. I hear a rustle from the gallery. 'Who's there?' I say.

The reply is comfortingly familiar. 'Don't shout; you'll wake the hillbillies.' John appears from the shadows above me.

'Thank God it's you,' I say, collapsing onto a pew. 'You got my message then?'

John descends the staircase. 'Yeah, one hundred or so years later.'

'I can't believe you're here.'

'I can't believe you are. What the hell were you thinking of, Si?'

'I don't know. I just thought I'd do a quick test and pop over for a few minutes.'

'You're a bleeding idiot. How long have you been here?'

'Over two months. You wouldn't believe the things that have happened.'

'Yeah well never mind that,' he says. 'We need to get back and quick. I've been waiting hours and I don't want to get stuck here too.'

I hesitate.

John crumples his forehead at me. 'What's wrong?'

'I can't just drop everything and leave.'

'What? You're having a laugh. Do you realise

what we've been through to get me here to this point in time to pick you up?'

'Look, I know how stupid this must sound but...'

'I don't give a shit, Si. You're coming home now.'

'I just need to know Clara's safe.'

'Well, you won't find out by getting us both stuck here and leaving Emily to try and find us. She'll be going out of her mind on the other side.'

I can't argue. 'Sorry. Thank you for coming to get me, John. I never thought I'd get home.'

'Well if you don't get a move on you never will.'

I hesitate again.

'Look, she's not here,' John says.

'How do you know?'

'She just isn't.'

'What do you mean?' I ask.

'I've done my research, OK? She's not in Conley Hope tonight, so you might as well come home.'

'Damn. Where is she then?'

'We have to go. I'll answer your questions on the other side.'

'Alright.'

John pretty much drags me over to a chair at the back of the room. Directly above the chair is a swirling cloud of gas, just visible. It looks more spectacular than I remember – the candles make the cloud twinkle.

'Promise me we can come back,' I say.

'What? Why?'

'Because I'll be leaving a lot here, John. If I can't get back here again I'm not going anywhere.'

He looks at me blankly. 'You'd better be joking, Si, you left a lot behind at home too when you sodded off on your little adventure. Be grateful someone came to get you.'

'I'm sorry,' I say. 'My head's a mess at the minute.'

'I'll say it is.'

I accept it's time to go home. I have a time machine after all – I'll just come back. I'm happy to leave, but I'm not happy I'm leaving the woman I love behind, possibly hurt and upset.

John points to the chair. 'Up you go then.'

'No, you go first,' I say.

'No chance. I promised I'd find you and take you back so get up there and jump.'

I get the message. I climb onto the chair as instructed. I take a deep breath and leap.

FIFTEEN

2 August 1912

James Atkinson and his brother David take a pew at the back of Durham Cathedral. He's hoping they won't be noticed. The nave is full of mourners. A wash of black covers the great hall. The bishop addresses a solemn crowd.

James notices Captain Pearson at the front. 'That man's just cold,' James whispers, to his brother. David nods.

The captain shows no emotion, not in front of his men. Near on thirty police officers are seated behind him. The rest of the congregation is made up mostly of children. The lady on the captain's arm weeps. Others cry too.

James sees the coffin being carried out and placed before the altar. A couple of police officers, sitting not far away, keep eying the brothers. The congregation stands and sings.

'I think we'd better leave,' David whispers. James

nods. The two slip away.

Out in the square, David and James stand shoulder to shoulder by their stagecoach. They wait. Their mackintoshes blow in a strong summer breeze. James looks up at a grey sky. David hangs his head.

The cathedral bells capture their attention. A flock of blackbirds give flight from a cluster of trees nearby.

James sees people appear from the cathedral entrance. The coffin is carried gracefully across the grassy graveyard, a sea of black figures follow. Even from this distance he can hear the sobbing. David sighs, wearily. James squeezes his brother's shoulder, and climbs onto the coach.

**

28 December 2012

I hit the ground hard. It hurts. *I'm out of practice.* The biting cold hits me next. I attempt to get up, but I'm flattened - John's fallen through and landed in a heap on top of me.

I brush him off and get up. 'You alright?' I ask.

'Yeah, I'm OK.' He looks shaken.

'Oh my God... Simon!'

I recognise the face rushing towards me. 'Hi, Em.'

She gives me a hug. John peels himself off the floor. Emily hugs him too. 'I thought you'd both got stuck there, I've been worried sick.'

'I'm sorry, Em. That was my fault,' I say.

John stands shivering, he looks at me with a vacant expression.

'You'd better grab him a jacket,' I say. 'I think he's in shock.'

Emily hands us both a coat. She tries to comfort John.

I realise I'm draped in a moth-eaten rag. I brush the remains of the one-hundred-year-old mackintosh from my shoulders and put on the coat Emily gave me. I'm relieved to be back with my friends. 'It seems you got my message.'

'We did,' Emily says. 'She takes a photo from her pocket and hands it to me. It's the photo of Clara and me at the ten-year celebrations.

'Where did you find this then?' I ask.

'We already had it. You saw it, remember?' she says. 'The original was just of Clara on her own. She looked so sad.'

I remember. 'Wow. I went back and changed it from just a photo of her, to one of both of us. That's nuts.'

'She doesn't look sad now,' Emily says, with a smile.

John's still shaking.

'Will he be OK?' Emily asks.

'Yeah, but we need to get him warm. The first couple of times you cross over you get really cold.'

Emily shuts the rig down and closes the laptop. We leave the church quickly and sit inside John's car with the engine running and the heaters on. Emily takes the driver's seat.

From the back seat, I look around at the icy scene. There's no snow but the grass and trees are almost white with frost. I'd forgotten how big the trees were behind the church, they were only a few feet tall back in 1912. I see the lumpy fields rolling along the valley. The houses along Schoolhouse Lane are all gone – the families I remember living there have vanished. The school is nothing but a mound in the grass.

'How did you know Clara wasn't at Conley Hope, John?' I ask.

John and Emily glance at each other.

I wait patiently for my answer.

John comes to life. 'I don't know.'

'You must know.'

'We're tired,' Emily says. 'It's been difficult, Si. We had a hell of a job finding the date you asked for.'

'I can imagine, and I'm grateful, but that's no reason to go all quiet on me. What's going on?'

'Do you realise the damage you could have caused?' John says.

'I didn't do it on purpose, John. I've said I'm sorry.'

'We all make mistakes, babe,' Emily says.

'I just thought I'd help you out,' I say. 'You know, do all the donkey work before you got home.'

'No, Si. You just thought you'd go gallivanting off, chasing that girl.'

'OK, so I was stupid,' I say. 'But if it was the difference between you and Emily being together or not then you'd have done the same thing.'

Emily looks at John.

He looks back. 'What?'

'Would you have done that for me?' she asks.

'Done what?'

'Gone travelling through time to be with me, regardless of the risk.'

'Who's side are you on?' he splutters.

I step in. 'Hey, this isn't about you two.'

'No, it's about you and a dead girl. Emily and I are from the same time and space, Si. It's a bit different don't you think?'

I slump in my seat. 'You don't understand. And she's not dead.'

John and Emily look at one another again, in a way that makes me nervous.

'I need to know what happened to Clara, if you know, tell me.'

'I just don't think you should be going back,' John says.

'You're kidding, right? I know I messed up last time but I have to see her again. I can't let her think I've just left her... that's bloody awful.'

'Why?' Emily asks. 'What happened?'

'Don't ask.'

'You can't demand we tell you everything then not tell us anything,' John spits.

'Fine, what do you want to know?' I say.

'How serious has it got with you and Clara?' he asks.

'Serious enough to not abandon her,' I say, bluntly. 'She's in trouble at the moment and I need to make sure she's alright.'

'She was in more trouble than you think,' John says.

Emily thumps him on the arm. The car engine is the only thing breaking the silence.

'Is there anything I should know?' I ask, eventually.

After a long pause, Emily obliges me. 'We're better off showing you.' She puts the car in gear and the church gets smaller in the rear window.

'Is it something I've done?' I ask, as we drive the track back to the railway tunnel.

'It's nothing that wasn't already done anyway,' John says.

I don't like the sound of this. 'Come on, is it serious?'

'No, it's nothing to worry about. You'll see when we get home.'

'So, how long were you there?' Emily asks.

I sense a change in conversation being pushed on me. 'I don't know exactly, nine weeks, maybe more.'

'Blimey.'

I realise John's cast has gone. 'That's a point. What date is it here?' I ask.

'It's December twenty-eighth,' John says.

My heart sinks. 'Shit. I've missed Christmas. What on earth am I going to say to my mum?'

'Don't worry about that,' John says.

What have I done? 'I haven't erased them or something by being in the past, have I?'

'No, nothing like that,' he replies. 'I hacked your email again.'

'What do you mean?'

'I sent your mum and dad an email posing as you. I said you were going away for Christmas and that you'd be in touch soon.'

'You promised not to do that again.'

'You didn't leave me much choice.'

'Guess not. Thanks, John. I owe you one.'

'You owe us more than one, mate. We've spent all Christmas trying to find you.'

'I'm sorry.'

'We know.'

For the rest of the journey home, I tell my friends as much as I can remember about my time in 1912. I hadn't realised just how much I'd done. The further we travel, the more tired I become. The stuffy car isn't helping. I nod off.

**

I wake to find us parking in the square by Durham Cathedral.

John opens his door.

The cold air soon brings me around. Everywhere is crispy and glistening. Still sleepy I don't even question why we're here.

John leads us into the cathedral grounds. We walk an icy path towards a cluster of graves. There's a real chill in the wind. Emily holds my hand. We stop beside a large gravestone nestled under a tree.

John retreats leaving Emily taking a tighter grip on my hand.

'What's the matter?' I ask.

Emily points to the gravestone in front of us.

I look over the frosty object. I read the words carved on its stone face...

IN LOVING MEMORY OF

CLARA MARY PEARSON

DIED 27 JULY 1912

A sickness washes over me. I always knew that Clara would be dead in my time but seeing this is a shock. It takes a minute for the penny to drop... 'That's the date I just left her, isn't it?'

Emily nods.

It's as if I've been hit by a steam locomotive. I feel dizzy. I'm sick on the grass. *I have to sit down.*

Emily grips my arm and guides me inside the nearest building.

**

John hands me a bottle of water. 'Here, get that down you.'

I take a drink. My hand is shaking. I look around at the cathedral interior not really seeing anything. I'm still cold. I feel... empty.

'Are you alright?' Emily asks.

'I'm sorry.' I'm not sure what else to say. I just sit and watch the images of Clara buzz around in my head. She's smiling at me, waving, taking my hand, kissing me. Then she disappears, leaving me numb.

Emily takes the water from me.

'I'm sorry,' I say again. I keep apologising but I don't know what for. *This is embarrassing.* I stand.

John and Emily keep their distance as I wander a while.

I'm not sure what to do. I stroll along the centre aisle running my fingers along the tops of the pews. At the front of the hall I see a hymn book left on a pew. I pick it up. The tatty pages of faith remind me of how delicate we all are.

'May I help you, son?' A gentle voice asks.

An elderly bishop appears beside me. 'It looks like you need the help of the Lord, my child.'

I'm almost offended. 'No imaginary guy on a cross can help me,' I say.

'I'm sorry you don't believe,' he says.

'Oh, I believe,' I say. 'But what I believe in is real... well, it was.' I look at the book in my hand. 'Why do people come here and sing from these books week in and week out? What do they gain from it?'

The bishop sighs. 'It reminds them that there's hope, and working together to find hope is what makes us human.'

I hand him the book and walk back to my friends. The nearer I get to them, the quicker I move, and the higher I lift my head. 'Come on you two, we've got work to do.' I pass them and stroll straight out of the door and into the cold day beyond. I ignore Clara's grave and walk briskly along the path to the road.

'Where are you going, Si?' John shouts.

'Conley Hope,' I reply.

My friends have to run to catch up with me.

I'm determined and prepared to do whatever it takes to put this right... I don't even care what happened to Clara. I just assume this is something I can repair, like a leaking air-conditioning unit or a broken stagecoach.

John grabs me and spins me around. 'Wait, Si. Just hang on.'

'What the hell?'

'Just stop and listen,' he says, almost shaking me. 'Whatever you're thinking of doing, it won't work.'

I push him off as Emily arrives. 'What do you mean it won't work? What the hell do you know, John? I know what I'm doing. I can travel through time.'

'No, you can't.'

'What? I spent months in 1912 with a woman I've fallen in love with and I've promised to look after. She's now six foot under over there by that tree. Don't tell me what I can and can't do, John, because you don't know anything.'

He grabs me again. 'I know you're being a bloody idiot. Look at the state of you. What on earth were you thinking going back there and chasing that lass anyway? You're crazy, Si.'

I glare at him.

Emily steps in. 'Babe, I don't think this is the

time...'

John takes a step back. 'Fine, if that's how you want to play it then go ahead, mate. Knock yourself out, but you're wasting your time.' He walks away towards the road.

Emily takes my hand. 'Si, will you let me talk to you please?'

No matter how angry or frustrated I am, I always have time for little Emily. I nod.

'There's more we need to tell you before you go running off trying to change anything,' she says, firmly.

'Go on.'

'We found that Clara died in a stagecoach accident the night you must have left her, she...'

I jump in. 'That's the point, Em... I left her. I should have stopped her, but I didn't. I just left her to get hurt.'

'Look, calm down. We think Clara might have died in an accident travelling back to Conley Hope, she must have been going back to see you. That's a good thing, right?'

'A good thing?' I roll my eyes. 'Great, that makes me feel a whole lot better. So, you're saying she died because of me?'

'No, Si, I'm not saying that at all. That came out wrong.'

'I'll say. I'm going back to put this right.' I stomp towards the road. 'If you're not going to help me, just leave me to it.'

Emily chases after me. 'You can't go back, Si.'

'Why the hell not?'

'There's nothing left.'

'What do you mean, there's nothing left?'

Emily hangs her head.

John returns. 'There's no energy left in the church, mate, none at all,' he says.

I don't understand. 'What do you mean there's none left? There's plenty of energy. I have a list and...'

'We used it all up, Si,' John adds.

'When we were looking for your date we accessed loads of different points before we found you,' Emily explains. 'We used all the energy up. John crossed over on the last attempt.'

I don't believe this. 'I told you I didn't want to come home unless I could return!'

'You don't belong there, Si,' John says.

'You could have at least told me.'

'Would you have still come back? We got you home, Si.'

I'm grateful for what my friends did, but the only way I can get back to save Clara has been exhausted by them in the process. I can't be angry with them. I'm only angry with myself for not doing more to stop her going home that day. It feels so long ago.

'You two are right,' I say, leaning on the boundary wall and cradling my head - it feels so heavy. 'I'm sorry.'

'Let's get you home,' Emily says, taking my arm and directing me towards the car.

**

I can't believe how luxurious my house seems. The bed is firm, the carpets feel so thick underfoot, and the instant hot water is just fantastic. I stand opening and closing my refrigerator. 'You wouldn't believe how hard it is to live without one of these,' I say.

John and Emily sit at my kitchen table with a cuppa.

'Do you think he'll be OK on his own,' I hear Emily ask.

'He'll be fine. He's not a kid.'

'I'm still here,' I say.

'Sorry, Si,' Emily says. 'I'm just worried about you. You've been there a long time; you don't know what it's done to you.'

'I know what it's done to me,' I say. 'It's left me feeling guilty as hell, that's what.'

'Do you want us to stay over?' John asks. 'I don't fancy coming round tomorrow to find you hanging in the garage.'

'Thanks mate,' I say, with sarcastic flavour.

'Well, I don't know, do I?'

'Look, don't worry about me. I'll be fine,' I say, shutting the refrigerator.

'Maybe you should accept what happened and move on, Si,' John says.

'No chance. I'm going to put this right.'

'But how?'

'I don't know. I feel like it's all been a weird dream and I've woken up with a huge hole in me.'

'We all lose people we love,' Emily says.

'Yes, but not of our own doing. And we don't all have a time machine, do we?'

'You really did love her didn't you?'

'You'll think I'm crazy if I answer that truthfully.'

'Tell me,' Emily says.

'She made me want to be better than I'll ever be,' I say. 'That's the only way I can describe it.'

John rolls his eyes.

'Don't, John. I'm not in the mood.'

'I'm not stone cold, Si. I know we can't always control what we feel but don't you think this is completely stupid?'

'Did you think it was stupid the moment you realised you just couldn't go another day without kissing Emily?'

Emily smiles at him. She takes his hand.

'See, that's what I've always wanted,' I say. 'And now I've got it, I want to keep it. I thought it was crazy too, but I... well... no one expects to fall in love do they?'

'No they don't,' Emily says.

'I can't let her die because of me.'

John shakes his head. 'If you can find a way to get back, I'll help you. But I'm warning you, you could make things far worse.'

'I know that. I'll be more careful this time. Anyway, it's time you two went home,' I say. 'I'm knackered and I want to get in the shower.'

My friends nod and I show them out.

'Thanks again,' I say, as the couple walk my path.

'Don't do anything stupid,' John says, getting in the car.

'I won't, I promise.' I close the door.

**

Although comfortable, my home feels cold and uninviting. Maybe it's because I've spent so little time here recently – maybe it's because my real home isn't a building at all, but a person – Clara.

I keep grappling with the feelings of helplessness. I imagine everyone who ever lost a loved one would feel the same, but it doesn't help me. I have the added frustration of my previous ability to travel through time. In any other situation a person would have to accept the one they grieve for has gone forever, I have the added turmoil of knowing there's always a possibility of bringing her back. It's tearing me apart not knowing what happened to my sweetheart.

I make phone calls to my parents and sister. I don't like lying to them but I have little choice. I think they all believe John's story. I put the two black and white photos of Clara and me on my bedside table. We look so happy. I mull over what to do next. *There must be something I can access: a moment at her father's house, or somewhere else in town maybe... Surely I can find one?* The moment of her death comes to mind. *Can I scan that moment? No, I couldn't possibly watch that.* The thought of Clara mangled under the wheels of a stagecoach just cripples me. I head for the shower.

The hot water feels so good; it's something I missed living in 1912. As I cover myself in soap I see a few fading marks on my body – they must be from lying on the straw in the barn. It was only a couple of days ago I was making love to Clara; and now she's gone. *I have to get back there; I can't leave it like this.* Flooded with emotion, I rest my forehead on the tiles and let the water run down my back.

Hang on. Why do I have to look for a moment in her history? I turn off the water. *Why not scan a moment in our history?* I loiter in the steam, my mind rolling over the possibilities. I realise I might have more control over this than first thought. I leap out of the shower and quickly dry myself – my sadness quashed by energy and enthusiasm. I pace back and forth across my bedroom, planning my next move.

I spend the next few hours on the Internet looking for any trace of the Coles' residence and the barn they once owned. I go to bed but hardly sleep; I'm too determined to let something like sleep distract me from my goal.

SIXTEEN

13 August 1912

Two years before the beginning of the First World War, the town of Conley Hope is in chaos. James and David Atkinson are the last to leave the mine, ferrying survivors pulled from the pit engine house. The fastest stagecoach in all of England tears through the wood towards Conley Parish Church. David struggles to keep her steady with all the extra weight. They carry ten shell-shocked men. Two are on the rear platform with James clinging onto them to stop them from falling. The rest are inside peering out of the window at the carnage.

James watches in horror as the ground behind them is swallowed up by the earth. David drives the horses harder as they round the bend into Schoolhouse Lane. A great fountain of water shoots skyward from behind the trees as the mine floods with water, forcing air out of the pit shaft.

'Faster, Dave, faster!' James shouts.

Water and soil rain down. Farmland collapses into

the mine tunnels. Even buildings don't escape as houses across the lane disappear. People are running in all directions.

James scans the horizon for the school, he can't see it.

After a few minutes, they arrive safely at the muster point, outside the town bank. The brothers help the injured off the stagecoach. There's quite a gathering. Friends and families of the brave men, who've been caught up in the pit disaster, wait patiently for news of their loved ones.

Two ladies grab James. 'Did you find anyone at the school?' One woman asks. 'We're missing someone.'

James shakes his head. 'I'm sorry, ma'am, we could only get to the pit. The school's already been lost.'

'Anything I can do to help you boys?' Mr Cole shouts, as David and James climb back onto their coach.

'You need to get everyone out of town,' David says. 'The water's heading this way.'

**

29 December 2012

John and Emily sit on my sofa. They must be wondering why I've dragged them around so early on a Saturday morning. I'm excited as I hand out mugs of tea and slices of toast. I can't even sit down as I pour out my plan.

'I've found a place we can scan to get me back to 1912,' I say.

'Where is it?' Emily asks.

'The Conley Valley. Not far from the church.'

'I thought there was nothing left,' she says.

'I did too. But there is one building. The night I got stuck in 1912 I went outside the church to get some fresh air, and I saw a light.'

'That could have been anything,' John says.

I've looked on satellite images online, it's a building alright. In fact there are two.'

'That doesn't mean they'll be any use,' John adds.

'One will be.'

'How do you know there's enough emotion left there to scan?' Emily asks.

'Trust me, I know.'

'Why, what happened there?' she presses.

'That's not important, what's important is that it's the perfect time to go back. The moment I'm thinking of is not long before Clara is... well, you know.'

'Killed,' John says.

'Yes. Thanks, John.'

'How come you didn't think of this before?' Emily asks.

'Well, it's not really an old moment.'

'It must be,' she says. 'It must be from 1912 or... oh, I see.'

'Yeah, it actually only happened two days ago. The problem is; I'll be there.'

'What do you mean, you'll be there?' John asks.

'Si means it's a moment he spent with Clara,' Emily explains.

'Oh right. What makes you think there'll be good emotional energy there?'

I feel my face flushing. I raise my eyebrows at John.

'You didn't... Did you?'

I nod.

'Jesus, Si.'

'That's the moment we could access,' I say.

'It must have been good then?'

'Don't even go there, John.'

Emily glares at him.

'This is crazy... by far the craziest thing yet,' he adds, shaking his head.

'It's not. All I need to do is use that point to access the past, and tell Clara not to take the stagecoach.'

'And what about the other you?' John asks.

'I'll avoid him.'

John laughs. 'I'm gonna end up in a mental hospital. I thought we agreed not to alter the course of history?'

'I wouldn't be. I'm just altering it back to how it should be. I can access the past using that moment and hide until the original me leaves, then I'll catch up with Clara and warn her of her fate.'

'This is nuts, she'll know it's not you,' John says.

'How can I not be me, John? If I dress the same and time it right she'll just think it's the original me returning a few moments later.'

'Is that fair to her?' Emily asks.

'Yes, if it saves her life. I just want to make sure that whatever happens to Clara isn't because of me.'

'As much as that's how you'll see it in your mind,' John says. 'What you're really doing is changing history to suit yourself.'

'That's not true.'

'And then what?' he asks. 'Are you going to leave it after that? Will you let her life take its natural course or will you be jumping backwards and forwards every time she dies?'

I hesitate. 'Alright, I'll make you a deal,' I say. 'If we find a way to go back, I will. But just to make sure that

Clara doesn't die because of me or what I've done... plus I get to say goodbye. Anything that happens after that is history and I have to accept it.'

'And what if it makes things worse?' Emily asks.

'I'll go back in time to a moment long before all this started and leave a message for us warning us not to ever use the rig, that way none of this will ever happen.'

John looks shocked. 'Great plan, Si, but I'm not letting you go back and erase four months of my life.'

'I don't want to…'

Emily steps in. 'Look guys, there's no point in arguing about it when we don't even know if we can go back yet.'

She's right.

'Where did you sleep with Clara?' Emily asks.

'In a barn.' My reply raises eyebrows. 'It was 1912; you couldn't just go online and book a Premier Inn.'

'Are you sure it's the same building?' she asks.

'I'm ninety per cent certain.'

Emily looks at John. 'Well, if you're up for it, I'll help.'

'I can't believe we're doing this,' John says.

'Just one run, I promise.' *I'm tired of talking.* 'Can we crack on with this or what?'

**

Back in what was the Conley Valley, we go in search of what used to be the Coles' residence. A heavy grey sky threatens us. *I hope it doesn't snow.*

'You're miles out,' Emily shouts, from the path. 'It was over that way somewhere on the satellite image.' She points to some trees close by.

'Are you sure?' I say, stumbling through the

brambles.

John slips and disappears behind some shrubs.

I laugh.

'Not funny, Si. Jesus, what have I stood in?'

'I can't even see the river,' I say. *This is annoying.* I don't recognise anything. Everywhere is so overgrown.

'What's this?' John says.

I struggle over to John who's standing in a little clearing, surrounded by dense shrubs. I see why nothing's growing here. He's standing on a concrete base. It's round with steps leading onto it at each end.

'I know what this is,' I say.

'What?'

'A bandstand.' I check where we are in relation to the little church further up the hill.

'Have you found something?' Emily shouts over.

'I think so.' I get my bearings. 'You're right, Em. It's over there.' I point to some trees less than half a mile away. John and I battle the undergrowth until we join Emily on a footpath leading across the valley.

'What's that?' Emily asks, pointing to a gravel track weaving its way around a nearby hill. 'Any house still here will need a road to it. Won't it?' she says.

'You're right. The old road used to come by the mine but that's under the lake now,' I say. 'That must be a newer road to the farm.'

We cross a boggy field and pick up part of the track. The further we walk along it, the more I recognise. We pass a stone wall that looks familiar, and then I hear something... the gentle bubbling of a river. *I know that sound.* The track takes us through a small wood. I see apples and pears hanging from the mature fruit trees. In the distance, I see a chimney through the branches. I pick up the pace.

On the other side of the wood we find the Coles' old residence. The whole place looks overgrown and neglected. There's a car in the driveway with flat tyres. The gates are missing.

'Is this the place then, Si?' John asks.

I take it all in. 'Yep. The last time I stood here I was with Clara in 1912.' I enter the property and knock on the door.

After a long wait, a woman answers. She's dressed in a dark blue district nurse's uniform.

'Hello, I'm sorry to bother you,' I say. 'Do you live here?'

The nurse looks us up and down. 'May I ask why?'

'My name's Simon and these are my colleagues from Durham University. We're doing some research on the Conley Valley and the people who lived here years ago. We'd like permission to take some photos, if that's possible.'

'Well, this isn't my house,' she explains. 'Mrs Shields is the owner. I'm her carer. You'd better come in.'

We follow the nurse inside. I instantly recognise the place as we make our way to the large flagged kitchen. An elderly lady is sitting in a chair by the stove; she has a blanket draped over her knees and cradles a cup of tea. She looks frail.

'Molly, there are some people here to see you,' the nurse says.

I realise who this is. It's Molly – the baby in the cot from 1912. She's in almost exactly the same place as the last time I saw her. *At least she's not crying this time.* It feels strange seeing someone at the beginning and then almost the end of their life, without me changing at all.

'Hello,' I say, with a smile.

'You'll have to speak up,' the nurse says.

'Hello. My name's Simon,' I add, much louder.

'Oh, hello,' Molly says.

'We're from Durham University,' I say. 'We're learning about the beautiful valley you live in and we'd like to ask a few questions, and take some photographs from your property, if you don't mind.'

'There's not much exciting happened recently, I'm afraid,' Molly says. 'I doubt I'd be able to tell you much.'

'Anything would be good,' I say. 'Even old tales.'

'You'll have already heard about the pit collapse, I expect?'

'That's the thing, Mrs Shields. We don't really know much at all,' I reply.

'Why don't you all take a seat and I'll tell you,' Molly says.

We remove our coats and sit at the table.

'Many years ago, when my parents owned this house, my father had a coal mine on the other side of the valley. There was a lovely little town between here and there and my father had a hand in building most of it.

I nod.

'In the summer of 1912 they made the mistake of tunnelling under the river. It would have cost too much money to dig a new shaft on the other side so a tunnel was extended from the existing shaft under the river. As there was hardly any rain that summer it was seen as perfectly safe.'

I remember that hot summer very well.

Molly continues. 'Luckily there was only a light shift working that day, all the miners were either in the main shaft or in the engine house. The river tunnel caved in and filled with water from the river, the water surged through the mine filling all the tunnels until the pressure became too much and the land above the mine collapsed.'

We listen intently as the shocking tale unfolds.

'Lots of land around the mine was lost including land where the school and the village hall once stood. Many other houses were lost in the flood water that followed. It's a miracle the church remained standing.'

'Were many people killed?' I ask.

'Yes, nearly forty in total,' Molly replies. 'It was the beginning of the end for Conley Hope. The death toll would have been far higher if it wasn't for two brave local men who were passing by that day. They rescued many from the pit buildings before they were swallowed up by the earth.'

This explains a lot about the land around the little church, why the schoolhouse is gone and why the lake is now so big.

'So what happened to the rest of the town, Mrs Shields? Was that destroyed by water too?' I ask.

'Some of it survived,' she explains. 'But after the mine closed the town went into decline. My father and a few others stayed and farmed for a while but eventually everything turned to ruins. It's very sad really.'

Molly begins shuffling about in her chair. The nurse looks concerned.

'So what is it you'd like to do here?' The nurse asks.

'We'd just like to take some photographs of the valley but using a large camera that can look over the entire landscape. Do you have a barn, or out building here?'

'Yes, we have a barn,' Molly says. 'It's in a bad state though I'm afraid.'

'Does it have a hay loft or somewhere we can get a good view of the valley?'

'Oh yes, it does,' Molly replies. 'There's a fantastic view of the valley from up there. You'll have to be careful though, the floor is very old.'

I remember the last time I looked upon that view. 'Don't worry, Mrs Shields, we'll be careful,' I say. 'Thank you for your help. We won't stay long.'

'Stay as long as you like.'

'Do you mind if I drive my van along your track?' I ask.

'Not at all. You can get to it from the main road from Highfield. Go about three miles past the picnic area and you'll see a right turn bringing you this side of the valley. You can't miss it.'

'Thank you.' With that, we leave.

**

I rush back to the little church as fast as I can with a new fire in my belly. John and Emily lag behind. I find my van still buried in the shrubs where I left it three weeks ago. Luckily it starts.

John and Emily help load the rig into the back. We erase all trace of us ever being here and remove our lock from the rear door. I feel sad leaving the place unwanted again.

The cold day becomes brighter as we enter the afternoon. We leave John's car at the picnic area and take my van to the Coles' farm via the route Molly gave us. The dust cloud my van generates reminds me of my days riding the Atkinson brothers' stagecoach. The track continues past the house through where the beautiful walled garden once was. I manage to get the van all the way to the barn. I see what Molly meant - the once pretty red-brick building looks overrun with ivy and has a badly damaged roof. It's in a similar state to the little church.

Before unloading any equipment, I make my way inside to inspect the upper floor while John and Emily check the rig. I pass through the opening where the side door would have been. I remember passing through here with equal uncertainty the last time. At least I had the warmth of Clara to look forward to – today all I have is the cold December air biting at my fingers. The wooden staircase hasn't survived, but a modern aluminium ladder stands in its place. I climb it and pause at the top. I reacquaint myself with the emotions I left here.

'You in here, Si?' John shouts, from below.

I see John and Emily carrying the rig in.

'How the hell are we going to get this up there?' John asks.

I look around me. *He has a point.* It will be difficult, and I doubt the floor will take the weight. Many boards are missing and the ones left behind look rotten.

'Do you think we could scan from down there?' I ask.

'No chance. There's too much space and the gas won't drift that far.'

'Damn.'

'What if we set the rig off down here but funnel the gases up there?' Emily asks, pointing to a coil of large diameter flexible hose at the other end of the barn.

'Don't see why not,' John says.

'Let's do it,' I say, leaping from the ladder. 'I'll get changed in the van and get some tools.'

**

After thirty minutes or so, we're ready to go. The rig is set up on the ground floor with the foot-wide flexible hose attached. I've poked it up through the missing floorboards and tied it to a beam close to where Clara and I made love.

'Do you think it'll work?' I ask Emily.

'Yeah, I think so.'

I hope we find something. Clara and I may have spent a very emotional and happy few hours here, but what we did could have left nothing more than a nice memory for us both.

'You might get a delayed reaction when we change the mix before the crossover,' Emily explains. 'It'll take a while for it to work up the hose.'

I give her a hug.

John stands watch by the barn door. 'Just don't get stuck again, Si. Remember, you've only got seven hours.'

'I know.' I set my strapless watch to midday.

'So, you're sure those are the clothes you were wearing on the night, Si?' Emily asks.

'Yes, don't worry. There's not much I'd forget about that night,' I say. 'Thank you for helping make this happen guys.'

'Nothing's happened yet, mate,' John says.

'Well, thanks anyway,' I add. I make for the ladder. Halfway up I glance back. 'If I'm not back soon I've run off with Clara.'

'You won't, Si,' Emily shouts. 'Because I'll come through and drag you back myself.'

I climb onto the old hay loft floor and negotiate the missing boards. It creaks and moves under my weight. *This feels lovely and safe*. 'Don't worry, Em,' I joke. 'If this floor goes I'll be back quicker than you think.'

She taps keys on the laptop.

I move away from the edge and lose sight of my

friends. I'm glad the rig is downstairs as I may be about to relive a rather intimate moment in mine and Clara's history. I certainly wouldn't want anyone else to see.

Crackling noises echo around the lower barn.

'Anything happening yet, Si?' Emily shouts.

'No, nothing yet.' I smell gas venting from the hose sticking out of the floor. I'm soon surrounded by swirling clouds, the loft becomes blurry. Images begin to appear.

'Something's happening now,' I shout, seeing the loft transform.

'Do you want me to come up?' John shouts.

'No I don't.' I can hear John laughing below. The crackling sound gets louder.

A naked Clara, partly covered by blankets, comes into view. My world goes quiet. I also see myself cuddling the beautiful woman I miss so much. *This is weird.* I fill up as I watch her beam at me while in my arms. I remember the overwhelming feelings I had while holding her. I'm so close to Clara I could almost reach out and touch her.

'You alright, Si?' John shouts, interrupting the moment.

'Yes, I'm fine,' I snap. I've seen and done some strange things over the last few months, but this gets first prize. *It's time to go back and put things right.* 'Mix in the hydrogen, Emily,' I shout.

I move to the edge of the loft where the old staircase used to be. I don't want to appear right in front of them, and frighten myself to death. I'd be hidden behind the hay pile here. I wait for the crossover reaction to begin.

I feel the change in the gas as it becomes rich with hydrogen. I manage to glance over the side of the loft floor and give my friends the thumbs up. I get that familiar drunk feeling. They disappear.

**

It's the day before Clara is tragically killed and I'm sitting behind a pile of hay on the upper floor of Raymond Cole's barn. I hear the two of us talking, exactly as I remember it.

'Do you have to go home tomorrow?' I hear myself ask.

'Yes, I must see my mother,' Clara replies. 'Don't worry darling, I'll return to you as soon as I can.'

'Can I ask you to do something for me?'

'Of course. I'll do anything for you, Simon.'

'Please don't upset your father.'

'Do you not want my family to know about us?' I hear Clara say.

'I want everyone to know about us. I'm just worried what he might do.'

'He wouldn't hurt you, Simon.'

'I don't care about me. I'm worried about you.'

'Don't worry for me, my darling. I can look after myself. I'll be alright... I promise.'

'Promise you'll come back to me.'

'I promise with all my heart.'

A roll of thunder clatters the distant hills.

Idiot. Why didn't I make her stay? I edge away and creep down the wooden staircase leaving the two lovers to talk and cuddle. I move slowly so not to make the steps creak.

I know we spent at least another hour here watching the thunder storm; I'll have to wait it out. I find a dark corner of the lower barn and get comfy on a pile of empty sacks. I listen to the thunder and the rain. I think of the past version of me up there in the loft with the girl I love. I want to be with her. I'm jealous... of myself.

**

I'm startled by the creaking of the wooden staircase. I see a shadow move down them and across the barn. It's me carrying Clara. I wait. After fifteen minutes or so, I sneak out into the night.

At the house, there's a light still shining from the kitchen window. Through it I see Clara is dressed and making herself a hot drink.

I'm shaking. I watch the beautiful redhead for a moment before gently tapping on the window.

Clara comes to the kitchen door. She opens it and floods me with a big smile. I love the way she always looks delighted to see me. It's weird to think I'd have only left her a few minutes ago.

'Is everything alright, Simon?' she asks. 'You're back so soon.'

I want to speak but nothing comes out.

'You look like you've seen a ghost,' she says, pulling me inside.

It feels strange having this woman standing before me, when only yesterday I was looking upon her grave. I finally stop staring into those gorgeous sleepy eyes and open my mouth. 'I'm sorry, Clara. I didn't mean to disturb you again.'

'That's alright. Whatever's the matter?'

'I've come back because there's something important I need to tell you.'

'There's something important I need to tell you too, Simon.' She wraps her arms around my neck and kisses me.

I have goose bumps.

'I need to tell you I've fallen deeply in love with you, Mr Benson,' she whispers. She has her usual playful look.

I manage a weak smile.

Clara pulls away. 'Something's wrong. What is it, Simon? Please tell me.'

'Let's sit down,' I say. We sit together at the table. I take both her hands in mine. I've rehearsed every word I need to say but now I'm faced with the task, my brain turns to jelly. 'Please don't go home tomorrow.'

'Oh, Simon. We've already talked about this.'

'I know, but this is very important. I have a horrible feeling something bad might happen to you.'

Clara sits back on her chair. 'Don't be silly, nothing bad will happen... I promise.'

I'm struggling to find the words I'd put together so perfectly in my head. 'Please Clara, just trust me. I want to keep you safe and this is the only way I can do it.'

'You're worrying me, darling. Keep me safe from what?'

'I think that tomorrow you'll be upset and want to leave your father's house in a hurry...'

Clara interrupts me. 'This is about my father again isn't it? What are you so frightened of?'

'I'm not frightened. I just don't want you to tell him about us, not yet anyway.'

'Why ever not?'

'I just, well...'

Clara lets go of my hands. 'Is there something you're not telling me?'

I feel her eyes on me – desperately searching my face for reassurance. She can break down my every barrier with no effort. I hesitate.

'I see,' she says with a sigh.

'If I tell you the truth I'm afraid I'll lose you, Clara.'

'You're asking me to trust you, but you don't trust me.'

I shake my head. 'I didn't mean that.'

'Why don't you want me to tell him? Have you got another woman or something? Are you afraid I'll...?' I see Clara's eyes change; they suddenly match her fiery curls. She leaps from her seat. 'Oh my dear Lord! That's it, isn't it? No wonder you only visit me here and never take me with you. No wonder you're such a mystery.'

'No Clara, that's not it at all.'

'You've had your way with me tonight and now you're afraid I'll advertise it to the world. Well maybe I shall.' She's trembling.

This isn't going well. I stand and try to take hold of her.

She backs away.

'I don't have another woman, Clara. You're overreacting.'

'I'm what? Now you sound like my father, Simon. I suppose I'm an emotional, irrational, silly little girl am I?'

'Of course not.' *Jesus, I've hit a nerve*. 'I just know that if you tell your father he'll be angry and it'll lead to you getting hurt.'

'I don't need you to warn me about my father. I'm a big girl, Simon. I can handle him.'

For the first time since we met, there's an awkward silence. I can see Clara analysing me. That unconditional trust in me has vanished in a second.

A tear rolls down her cheek. 'You know I love

you deeply, Simon. You're hurting me now, especially after we've spent such a lovely evening together.'

I try to comfort her, but she won't let me. 'Alright, listen to me,' I say. 'Tell your father if you want, tell everyone including the cat, I don't care, but I'm coming with you.'

'I appreciate the offer, but I don't think that's necessary.'

'Fine. At least let me pick you up and bring you back here then.'

'Why?'

'It's a long story.'

'See, you don't trust me,' she says, hands on hips.

At every turn there's a brick wall; I'm struggling to keep a grip on the conversation. I get as close as I dare. 'Do you want the truth no matter how frightening or unbelievable it might be?' I ask.

'Yes. If you love me then you would tell me.'

'I do love you, Clara, with all my heart. That's why I came back tonight. I told you I'm an engineer, right?'

Clara nods.

'Well I'm lucky enough to have a couple of friends that invented a machine that lets me see through time. I helped them test it. I met you by accident because the machine sent me here unexpectedly.'

'Sent you from where?' she asks.

'From the future,' I reply.

Clara laughs. 'If you don't want to be with me, Simon, then please have the decency to tell me. Don't play with my heart like this.' Her laughter turns to further tears.

'It's the truth. I've seen something bad happen tomorrow so that's why I'm here... to warn you.'

Clara shakes her head. 'So, I've fallen in love with

someone who supposedly loves me, yet chooses the happiest night of my life to tell me this tale and upset me.'

I try to touch her.

She edges further away. 'Well I don't believe you, Simon. And I don't believe you ever loved me or you would have just told me that you didn't want me before I gave myself to you.'

I don't believe this. 'Everything I've told you about me and the way I feel about you is true,' I say. 'I just don't belong here, I was stuck here for a while but now I've found my way home again.'

'Well that's definitely the worst excuse to abandon a lady I've ever heard, Mr Benson. I think it's time you left my home.' She opens the kitchen door.

'I'm not abandoning you, Clara. You won't believe what I went through to get back here to see you.'

'You only left five minutes ago.'

I roll my eyes. 'I want to be with you forever, Clara. But I know something bad will happen tomorrow and I have to protect you or I'll never forgive myself.'

'Will you forgive yourself for breaking my heart?'

'Clara, I just...'

'Please leave.'

'Just promise me one thing, please.'

'Promise you what?'

'No matter how you feel about me, don't travel in any stagecoach for a while.'

'Why?'

'Promise me, Clara.'

She sighs. 'Alright, I promise.'

I feel a coldness I could never have imagined would come from the woman I adore so much. I feel sick. She slams the door shut as I step out. Through the window I see her run from the room.

I jog back to the barn stumbling in the darkness. I reach the barn and climb the wooden staircase to the hay loft. The swirling gas cloud hovers above me. I stop to compose myself. I can't believe how bad tonight has gone. But Clara has promised not to take a stagecoach, so my task is done – I've done what I can to save her life.

I'm suddenly startled by something flying past my head; it's a black bat. I wave my arms to see the creature off. Then I jump and catch a roof beam, swing and leap through the cloud.

**

I hit the cold wooden floor. I roll onto my back and look up at a great hole in the modern-day ruined barn roof. I've made it back and I feel the usual relief. I'm about to get up, when I hear the squeaking of a bat. I see the bat from 1912 fly out of the roof to freedom.

How did it manage to travel through with me? My thoughts are suspended by a loud creaking sound.

There's a sudden snap and I fall.

SEVENTEEN

I come around feeling really stiff. I expect to open my eyes and find John and Emily looking down on me. Instead I find my mum standing there. I'm confused. I realise I'm in a hospital bed.

'Mum. What on earth's going on?'

'You had an accident.'

I don't remember anything.

'Rachel's here,' my mother adds.

'Rachel?' I assume my girlfriend is waiting outside. My head hurts. Scraps of my memories return as my mum straightens my bed sheets and adjusts my pillows. I think most things come back but I'm not sure which order they should be in. *Hang on, Rachel left me.* 'Why's she here?' I ask.

'Rachel heard about your accident and was worried.'

That's a first. 'Does she think she's still on my life insurance or something?' I sit up and feel a sharp pain in my head. *Jesus, that hurts.* 'What have I done, mum?'

'Luckily, not too much. John said you fell helping

him take some photos in a barn somewhere. You're always getting into bother, you two.'

I'm still not assured of my sanity when I remember why I was there. *Have I dreamt half of this?*

'You've got a few cuts and bruises and a severe concussion. The doctor said you'll have a headache for a few days but that's about all.'

I feel lucky. There's no way my mum would know the full story. 'Has John said anything else?'

'He said he'd pop in and see you. Shall I send Rachel in?'

It's nice that she came, but there'll be an ulterior motive. I don't want to see her. She'd only play the perfect girl in front of my mum, then turn back into the perfect bitch the minute my mum leaves.

'No Mum, I don't want to see her. But tell her thank you.'

My mother nods. 'OK, Simon, I understand. John will be here soon so I'll shoot off. I'll see Rachel on my way out.'

'Thanks, Mum.'

With a kiss to my cheek, she leaves.

I stare at the discoloured ceiling tiles thinking of what happened. I remember my last conversation with Clara. It sickens me. *She must hate me now.* I hope she kept her promise and has lived a full and happy life, but the thought of her spending it with someone else upsets me even more. I drift off.

**

I'm woken by a nurse. 'You have a visitor, Simon,' she says. 'Do you feel up to seeing anyone?'

I assume it must be John. I don't feel too good

but I want to know what happened in the barn. 'I'm fine. Send him in.'

'Hey, Si,' he says, taking a seat next to my bed. 'How you feeling?'

I point to my head. 'I'm a bit sore but apparently I'll live. So, what on earth happened?'

'Well you came back from your visit to the past and fell straight through the floor. You ended up in a heap in the barn. Out cold. You scared the life out of us.'

Oh no, what an idiot. 'How did I get here?'

'Ambulance.'

'Oh God, I'm sorry, John. All I seem to do is make a right mess of things, don't I?'

'Don't worry, mate. We're used to it by now.'

'Thank you for getting me here. I wonder if my trip did the trick.'

John shakes his head. 'Afraid not.'

'You're joking? What did I do this time?' I expect my friend to tell me I'd made things far worse than they already were.

'Nothing,' he replies. 'I've just come from the cathedral now. The grave's still there and it's exactly the same.'

'How can it be the same, John? She promised she wouldn't take the stagecoach.'

'I've no idea, mate. Maybe she didn't believe you. From what you were mumbling in the ambulance, it sounds like you made a right mess of it.'

'Yeah I did, so surely she wouldn't have even told her dad about me after that. And she wouldn't have got slapped, left in a hurry, and got herself killed. Oh for Christ's sake.'

'Maybe what's done is done, Si. You said it yourself, we're all on a path and maybe nothing can lead us from it.'

'I know, but I've changed Clara's path just by being there. If her life continued in a happy way after I'd left then I'd accept it, but she dies, and I don't know if that's because of me or not. Until I find out, I'm not walking away.'

John sighs. 'This is tiring, Si. It's like watching you throw a bouncy ball at the wall in the hope that one day it won't bounce back… but it always will, mate.'

'I'm not giving up.'

'You're chasing a ghost.'

'She wasn't a ghost until I meddled in her life. I've got to put it right, John.'

'You don't know that. I understand, honestly I do. I'm just not sure if you can straighten this out.'

'She was so upset, John. I can't believe how much I messed it up.'

'You tried. Don't beat yourself up about it.'

'I didn't try hard enough.'

John slumps in his seat. 'Well, I think Clara's number's up, and whatever you do won't change that. But I can see why you'll want to make things right between you.'

'What does Emily think?'

John laughs. 'She's being a good friend to you.'

'What do you mean?'

'She's spent the last two days trying to convince me to keep going with this.'

I'm amazed. ''Did it work?'

John rolls his eyes. 'One last chance, Si, absolutely no more.'

I lean out of bed just enough to shake his hand. 'I'll get it right next time, I promise.'

'You don't need to promise me anything, Si. Just

don't get yourself, or anyone else killed over this.'

I won't. As soon as I'm out of here we'll get back to the barn and I'll go back and sort it all out.'

'We might have a problem with that. After you fell through the bloody floor, we forgot about the rig. It was left running and used up all the energy in there.'

'How do you know it's all used up?'

'I had to pack the rig away before the ambulance arrived. I left Em looking after you and went in the loft to untie the hose. The place was still filled with gas but the images had just greyed out, like in Clara's bedroom, and the church.'

'Great!'

'Yeah, I know. Now all the energy's gone, there's nothing to access.'

'So, we need more, again?'

'Yep, exactly.'

'I've been thinking though, this could be far more flexible than we think,' I say. 'We don't have to use moments in Clara's life to get back there. Any moment in anyone's life will do.'

'As long as we have the right date?'

'Yeah, and as long as we're near enough to her so we can get to her and back within seven hours.'

'Well, I guess there's only one way to test the theory.'

'I just need to find some energy from before the twenty-seventh of July, 1912. Anything will do.'

'You just work on getting better; I'll work on getting you back there. You can make up with the missus and save her skin at the same time. But then we're done.'

I can't argue with that. 'It's a deal.'

**

After being discharged from hospital, I spend the New Year with my parents while John and Emily hunt for my way back to 1912. After a few days, John calls and tells me to meet him at Durham railway station – he says they've found an energy hot spot like the little church at Highfield.

I drive under the imposing railway viaduct and up the hill to the station, filled with excitement and trepidation. I get out of my van and greet John and Emily in the main car park.

Emily gives me a hug. 'Nice to have you back,' she says. 'Again.'

'Thanks, Em. So, why are we here, John?'

'Come with me and I'll show you.' I follow my friends into the station building. We leave the main lobby and head for the platforms.

'Where did you find the energy then?' I ask, as we reach the middle of platform one.

John spreads his arms theatrically. 'Here.'

'You're having a laugh? Why on earth would we want to scan here?'

'Because my friend...' John says, still waving his arms about. 'There's more energy here than you could possibly imagine.'

'Really?'

'Yeah, think about it… all the sad goodbyes, and happy moments when people are reunited after long periods apart. There must be something we can use.'

I look around me. Today is Sunday and the station is still fairly busy. 'But how can we scan here?' I ask.

'Well, see that platform over there,' John says, pointing to a smaller station building and platform on the other side of the tracks. 'That's the oldest, the one that was used in Clara's day.'

'Yeah, but we can't go leaping backwards and forwards in time right in front of everyone though, John.'

'Course we can… that platform used to be far longer to take the big steam trains. See that over there…?' John points to a fenced off area. 'That's just a bike park now but it used to be part of the platform. And it's closed off at the minute – the roof's knackered or something.'

'You've done your homework. So, what are you suggesting?'

'We scan there at night. We pose as a maintenance team looking at the roof, scan, then get the hell out of here before anyone can check up on us.'

'I admire the plan, John, but it's a bit risky.'

'It's not. I've been here every night this week and after the last train at eleven o'clock, I didn't see a single person in that building or on platform two. There's hardly any staff working at night and they never leave the main building over here.'

'I appreciate you doing all this for me, John. What do you think, Em?'

Emily nods. 'I think it's doable, we can even get your van right up to the fence so no one will see the rig. But you can't be gone long.'

'Well, in theory I should only be gone a few seconds.'

'That's settled then,' John says. 'But this is the last time we do this. As soon as you've done what you need to do, I'm dismantling that thing for real.'

The thought is saddening, yet sensible. 'When should we do it?' I ask.

'Tomorrow night,' he says. 'Let's get this over with.'

'OK.' After a final glance around the station, we leave.

**

It's been over two weeks since I went back to Conley Hope. I've thought non-stop about my conversation with Clara, and how she'd have felt about me when she died. Now I'm fully fit, I'm chomping at the bit to get back and put things right.

I visit Clara's grave at the cathedral, to see for myself that nothing has changed. I wonder if the grave was there, with the same name and date on it, even before we started using the rig. *John could be right – am I trying to change the unchangeable?* I'm even considering going back in time to before our experiments, just to see.

I meet John and Emily at eleven o'clock outside the station bike park. It's encouraging seeing our vehicles are the only ones here. The smaller building, alongside platform two, is in darkness. My friends are wearing overalls and hi-visibility vests.

'Wow, you've really gone all out this time,' I say.

John hands me overalls and a jacket. 'Here, suit up.'

'Where did you get these from?' I ask.

'I borrowed them off my dad,' Emily says. Her pant legs are rolled up and her jacket looks three sizes too big. She looks funny.

I slip on my contractor clothing over my 1912 outfit. Only half of the station lights are on, and a freezing fog lingers in their dull blanket of light. The bike park is the furthest point from the main building, so we have no trouble carrying the rig inside unnoticed. We unpack our equipment and set it up behind the high fence. While John and Emily do their thing with the rig, I keep warm by patrolling the space behind our fence. I keep an eye on the figures moving in the station office window. We're so far away; I doubt they'd see us in the dark.

'So how do we know what date we're accessing?' I ask.

Emily hands me a couple of old photos, they show the station platform back in the early 1900s. 'There used to be a ticket office over there,' she says, pointing to a wall close by. 'A train timetable was put up outside it every day. It has the date on it.'

'That's handy.'

'Yeah, all we need to do is keep scanning until we see the date you want.'

I notice John still has the hose from back in the barn. He's attaching it to the rig.

'What did you keep that for?' I ask.

'We can use it to concentrate the gas in the direction of the old ticket office,' John explains. 'So we don't have to flood the whole platform and waste loads of gas.'

Good thinking. I'm lucky I have these two.

While Emily punches keys on the laptop, John briefs me. 'Right, Si. We might have a problem with the running time. We'll lose gas fast here. I reckon we can keep the rig going for two to three hours tops.'

'That doesn't give me much time to play with.'

'Exactly. When you get to the other side you'll have a twenty-minute train ride to Conley Hope. According to the 1912 timetable there's a return train within thirty minutes, so you'll only have about an hour to find Clara and put things right. Don't risk any longer.'

I nod. 'No problem, boss. Do you not want to

come with me now your ankles better?

'No, thanks, mate.'

I'm surprised at the prompt response. 'You sure?'

'Yeah, I'm better off here in case anything goes wrong.'

I pop my head over the fence to make sure we're still alone, I don't see anyone around. As I wait for my friends to start the rig, I see a bat flutter above us. Its elegant flight is captured by the dim lights hanging from the platform roof.

'Hey, John, I've just remembered... The last time I crossed over, a bat flew through with me.'

'And?'

'Well, everything that I've brought back so far just disintegrated, but the bat didn't.'

'Maybe organic things don't age the same,' Emily says.

She could be right. I've always believed anything from the past ages instantly the second it crosses over; the bat in the barn has proved my theory wrong. *I wonder what other organic things could pass through unscathed?*

John must see the cogs turning in my mind. 'Don't even think of bringing her back,' he says.'

'I won't.'

I hear a familiar crackling sound. I watch as John sprays the bike park with gas from the hose. It's barely noticeable in the thin evening mist. I'm nothing more than a lookout as he and Emily work their magic. The station's been quiet all night and remains that way as we approach midnight.

As John flicks the hose around, the fence, the bike park, and the modern day platform disappear. We see flashes of people kissing or crying and embracing each other on the same platform long ago. Steam trains come and go. It's strange to watch, as is the faint colourful light patterns swirling in the freezing mist. Each time we see something, John points the hose back at the wall beside me to reveal the normally invisible ticket office timetable.

I wait patiently for a date close to the time I last saw Clara. I'm just starting to worry we won't find what we need, when two lovers appear close to us. They're kissing. John flicks the hose back to the wall to reveal the timetable. The date on it reads 20 July 1912.

I jump with excitement. 'That'll do,' I shout. 'Keep it there.'

John holds the hose steady, showing the kissing couple in the waves of gases.

I stumble around in a panic, shedding my contractor clothing. 'Stick the hydrogen in,' I shout, leaping into the cloud. In seconds I feel weak and intoxicated.

**

Suddenly I feel a shove in my back and I fall onto the station platform.

'I'm very sorry, sir. I didn't see you there.'

I turn and see a station porter with a trolley loaded so high that he wouldn't have seen me even if I hadn't jumped in front of him from 2012. Night turns to day and the temperature rises in an instant. It seems I've timed this perfectly. Apart from a little embarrassment on the part of the porter, my crossover went unnoticed. I get to my feet.

The two lovers part as one boards the huge green locomotive, standing at the platform beside me.

'I'm so very sorry, sir. Is there anything I can do to help?' the porter asks.

'Oh no, don't worry I'm fine,' I say. 'It's my fault for being in the way.' I take in the sweet smoky atmosphere of the station. It's far smaller than the modern version, yet much nicer. Everything is brightly painted, clean, and well kept.

'When's the next train to Conley Hope?' I ask.

'The Conley Valley, sir? You'll need the Newcastle train which happens to be this very one.' He points to the green locomotive close by. The name plate on the side reads *Emerald Princess.*

'Better hurry, sir; she'll be leaving in a moment.'

I climb onto the nearest carriage. Inside I find the train rather luxurious in its fitments and less crowded than expected. I take a window seat at an empty table. I set my watch to twelve thirty rather than the usual time of midday - to compensate for the thirty minutes or so of gas we'd used back in the station. If I do make it to Clara then my visit will have to be brief.

A young gentleman approaches my table. 'Do you mind if I sit?' he asks.

'Not at all.'

He's well dressed in a brown suit and tie. He places a bunch of flowers on the table. The train jolts forward and we pull away from the station. I'm reminded of how polite people are here as I overhear two ladies near us talking about the weather.

'Yes, it was indeed…' one lady says, 'a very cold night last night, for August. I nearly lit a fire, I did.'

August? 'What date is it?' I ask the man sharing my table.

'It's the sixth of August,' he replies.

I bang my fist on the table. 'Damn.' I think I startle him. 'Sorry,' I say. 'The timetable in the station had a different date on it. I shouldn't be on this train.'

'Those timetables are always blowing away when the trains come into the station,' he says. 'It's a common problem; an old one is often left behind.'

'I see.' I peer out of the window at the hedgerows flashing by; I can't even get off now.

'Are you alright?' The man asks.

Do I look like I'm alright? I'm too late to make a difference to Clara's fate and now have to endure a pointless train journey. I'm also wasting precious gas back in the future. 'Yes, I'm fine.' I sit wearily taking in the beautiful unspoilt scenery as we steam towards the valley I've grown so fond of.

'You seem agitated, sir.'

'I was just hoping to meet someone I haven't seen in a while and miss very much, that's all.'

I offer my hand. 'My name's Simon.'

The man crumples his brow as he sheepishly shakes my hand. 'I've only ever heard that name once before,' he replies. 'I'm Walter. Walter Clark.'

Jesus, this is the copper that was keen on Clara. Judging by the flowers on the table, he must have moved on quickly. *I wonder if he knows what happened to her.*

'I believe I've heard of you from my companion in Conley Hope,' I say.

'Really?' he asks. 'You'll have heard good things, I imagine?'

'I was told you'd be the captain of the Durham police one day.'

Walter blushes. 'Probably so. Who is your friend you mention?'

'Unfortunately she died,' I say.

'I must have known her though surely? What was her name?'

I puff out my chest. 'Clara Pearson.'

Walter crumples his brow again. 'I doubt that. Mrs Pearson was married to my captain,' he says.

I'm confused. 'No, Miss Pearson,' I reply. 'Miss Clara Pearson, you know pretty young lady... red hair. Have you forgotten her already?'

Walter folds his arms and grins. 'No I haven't forgotten her. If Miss Pearson was your friend then you'd know her real name is Elizabeth. Clara is her middle name. And she certainly isn't dead.'

I think my chin hits the table.

EIGHTEEN

I can feel my face burning. Although, any embarrassment is soon engulfed by the thought of Clara being alive and well. 'So Clara's alive?'

Walter remains silent with only a cheeky smile showing his advantageous position.

'Look, I just want to know if she's safe,' I say, leaning over the table. I've spent so long thinking I wouldn't set eyes on that wonderful girl again, now I know I can it's like someone's lit a fire in me.

'You need to brush up on your names, Simon. Clara Mary Pearson, Clara's mother, died a couple of weeks ago. Her daughter, Elizabeth Clara Pearson, is still very much alive.'

I don't believe it. 'What an idiot I am.'

Walter shows his dirty teeth again. 'No, you're not an idiot, Mr Benson, you're a wanted fugitive. It is, Mr Benson, I presume?' He produces a clumsy looking pair of hand cuffs.

This is the last thing I need. 'What am I wanted for?'

'You're a horse thief.'

'A what? I can't even ride a horse, never could.'

'Well you can now,' he adds, still grinning. 'I'm going to make sure you never get to see Clara again and then I'll marry her and you'll rot in jail, or better still, hang on the common.'

This guy's unbelievable. 'And what if Clara doesn't want to marry you?' I ask, glaring at him. 'She can make up her own mind...'

'And what do you know of her mind, Mr Benson? You didn't even know her real name until I told you of it.'

He has a point. I can't believe I've spent all this time feeling so guilty about something that hasn't even happened. What a mess I've made of all this. My eyes revisit the flowers on the table. 'So I guess you're on your way to see her then?' I ask.

'Yes I am,' Walter replies. 'She's taking the schoolchildren to the railway station today to learn about trains. However, I plan to arrest that idea and take her for a picnic.'

'Has she agreed to that?'

'Not yet, but that won't matter.'

My face is burning again. 'So what Clara actually wants to do doesn't matter to you?'

'I'm the only eligible bachelor she knows,' Walter adds, sticking his nose in the air. 'And with my reputation she won't be able to resist.'

The carriage goes dark as we pass through the Conley Valley railway tunnel. I don't have much time to get out of this. 'You can't visit Clara and arrest me at the same time,' I say.

He shakes his hand cuffs at me. 'Yes, I can.'

I think it's time I shook off the gentleman act. I lean across the table. 'Right you ignorant bastard, listen carefully,' I say.

He looks at me wide-eyed, as do the other passengers sitting close by. 'Excuse me, but you can't talk to me like...'

I interrupt. 'Shut it, Walter, and listen. Clara and I are in love and she knows I'm no horse thief. If you put me in jail she'll hate you.'

'No she will not. I'll be a hero.'

'Maybe to others, but Clara will hate you. And you'll humiliate her.'

'Whatever do you mean?' he asks, his facial expression deflating rapidly.

'Because there'll be a trial and everyone will know that Clara courted a fugitive.'

Walter slaps the table. 'Nonsense.'

I remain calm. 'No it's not. And I have some rather unsavoury friends who'll come here looking for me if I don't return home today. They'll hunt you down, Walter.

'But I'm the law.'

'I don't care,' I say, 'and neither will they.'

Walter points a shaky finger. 'That's ridiculous. I've never heard...'

I cut him off. 'The girl of your dreams hating you and a pack of outlaws chasing you. I don't fancy being in your shoes, sunshine.' I see distinct anguish on Walter's face. I also feel the train come to a stop; we've arrived at Conley Hope. 'But it doesn't have to be like that,' I say. 'Let me go free and I promise you'll never see me around here again. And who knows, with me gone maybe Clara will see that you're the most eligible bachelor around. But arresting me won't help you.'

He looks vacant. A station porter is waving a flag on the platform below.

I can't wait any longer. 'Sorry, Walter, but I'm

getting off, you either arrest me now or leave me be.' I glare at him.

He puts his hand cuffs back in his pocket.

'Wise choice.' I leave the carriage. Walter doesn't follow me.

**

I step off the train, hearing the whistle from the engine. I watch the train pull away. I guess I'll never know what's going through Walter's head right now. I find it odd that he gave in so easily, but I don't care why. I'd almost forgotten I could be face to face with my sweetheart again in a few moments. As I walk the platform my heart pounds furiously. I'm delighted I don't have to warn Clara of her fate, but I'm nervous, nervous and excited. Unfortunately, I also remember our last meeting. If I hadn't gone back to change anything, that day would have still ended perfectly with us both deeply in love and Clara believing I'm a good man. Instead, there's a chance she won't even want to speak to me.

As people disperse to go about their daily business, I spot the stationmaster orating to a group of schoolchildren at the end of the platform. I head that way, passing the station building with its many hanging baskets overflowing with colour. Everything about this place seems so beautiful, but then its beauty becomes meaningless and everything around me simply vanishes as Clara steps out from the crowd of children and looks straight at me.

Her reaction isn't what I was expecting. She runs towards me. She moves at such a pace that I spin around with her momentum as she crashes into me. She throws her arms around me and wraps me up in her warm embrace.

I tingle all over as my body remembers hers. We've become the centre of attention, anyone passing stops to admire our spontaneous magnetism. I'm still not sure what to say, I doubt that if I tried to speak anything would come out anyway. We hold each other tightly and don't let go. This feels far too good.

'I'm so sorry, Clara,' I say, eventually.

Clara puts her lips to mine; she kisses me for an immeasurable length of time. Neither of us care that the people of Conley Hope are whispering around us. I'd forgotten how sweet and soft her lips were. We stop kissing and hold each other. I feel I just can't get close enough to her. I kiss her neck and whisper in her ear.

'I never wanted to hurt you, Clara, I really didn't...'

She presses a finger against my lips to silence me. She takes my hand and leads me into the quaint sandstone station. We enter an empty waiting room. We move to the far corner of the sunny little space and sit on a bench facing each other.

'I know you never meant to hurt me, Simon, I know that now. You were only trying to protect me, and I'm sorry that I didn't believe you.'

I'm surprised by her words. I was certain I'd face another enormous task convincing Clara that I had the best of intentions the last time we met. 'You had every right to be upset,' I say. 'I couldn't have picked a worse time to upset you. I really loved being with you in the barn. It was the best night of my life.'

Clara presses her forehead against mine. I can smell her soapy skin. I close my eyes; I'm intoxicated by her.

'I know that now, Simon. I'm sorry I thought

badly of you.' She cradles my face with a gentle hand and presses her cheek against mine.

Here in Clara's embrace, I feel at home. I'm so happy I'm breathless. It's like I'm falling but with nowhere to land.

'You thought I was going to die that very next day didn't you?' Clara asks, quietly.

I open my eyes. 'Yes I did.'

'I'm so sorry, Simon.'

'I'm sorry you lost your mother that day,' I say.

'We knew it would happen soon. My mother was very ill you see; which is why I always made sure I visited her when I could. Otherwise I would never have left this place...' she melts me with those eyes, 'and never would have left you.'

We kiss again.

'She was very ill then?'

'Yes, she had been for some years.'

I'm puzzled. 'I thought it was a stagecoach accident?'

'No…' Clara replies, 'although there was a tragic coach accident in Durham that night. A young lady was killed.'

I roll my eyes. *John and Emily must have got their wires crossed.*

'Oh my goodness,' Clara exclaims. Those beautiful green eyes glaze over. 'You thought it was me in the coach didn't you?' She puts her arms around me and presses her face against mine once more. I feel a tear run from her face to mine; it tickles as it rolls down my cheek, cooling as it goes.

'I'm sorry you had to go through that, Simon, I really am.'

'You've nothing to be sorry for, Clara. It was all

just a stupid mix up.' I taste the sweet tear as it rolls over my lips.

'I can't believe you came back for me,' she says.

'Of course I came back for you. I couldn't just leave you.'

'Do you want to be with me, Simon? Forever?'

No hesitation. 'Yes I do. The laws of physics won't allow it but laws are made to be broken. I learnt that from a couple of good friends of mine in your time.'

'Are you really from another time, Simon?'

'Yes I am, as unbelievable as I know that is. But it's nothing to be frightened of.'

'Just when I thought you couldn't excite me any more than you already do,' Clara adds.

I feel my face burning once more, but for a very different reason this time. 'So what changed?' I ask. 'You must have realised at some point that what I said could be true, even though it's so crazy.'

Clara giggles. 'Yes, well it's certainly a good job I didn't tell anyone about our conversation or people really would think I'm quite mad. You owe my trust to your good friends.'

'My good friends?'

'Yes, David and James. When you left me for the last time I was sure you had spun me a yarn, and that I would never see you again.'

I hang my head as I think of our conversation.

Clara gently lifts my chin. 'But a little part of me didn't want to believe that the perfect man I'd met could be anything other than just that. I visited my father and told him I'd fallen in love with you, I suppose I still hoped you would come back and I would discover I was wrong about you. The death of my mother meant that I couldn't return here until after the funeral so I didn't know if you were here or not.'

That's why I couldn't find her.

Clara continues. 'After the funeral, I defied you and took the stagecoach instead of the train, even though you told me not to.'

I smile, thinking of Clara's mischievous streak. It only fuels my attraction to her.

'It was very silly of me, I know, but I can be a bit like that at times,' she says.

I grin and nod.

She gently slaps my hand. 'Anyway, cheeky, I took the Atkinsons' coach and had a long journey to realise that you knew something bad was going to happen that day. Then I remembered I hadn't told you that I use my middle name and not my first, so you could have thought it was me that passed that day. I'm so sorry, Simon.'

'Don't worry,' I say. 'I don't expect you to tell me everything about you straight away.'

'But I want you to know everything about me,' Clara replies. 'You are my life now. When you gave me your name I didn't think to give you anything other than the name my closest friends use. I completely forgot to tell you any different. How positively silly of me.' Clara bites her lip in that irresistible fashion.

We sit in the station waiting room completely mirroring each other, holding hands and smiling uncontrollably.

Clara continues her tale. 'When we arrived back in town I asked the boys about you. James told me about your heroics on that very night, I can't believe you were on my father's doorstep with a pistol pointed at you.'

I shrug. 'I just wanted to check you were safe.'

'James also said you disappeared that night, after looking for me. You left him outside the church but he followed you thinking you were in trouble.'

'He followed me?'

'Yes. And he saw you and another man disappear into thin air. When he told me that, I realised you were telling the truth.'

'That must have been frightening to watch.'

Clara laughs. 'Nothing frightens the brothers.'

'Does it frighten you?' I ask.

'It did at first, but then I remembered that I always feel so safe when I'm with you.'

I kiss Clara's hand. 'I'll never hurt you again,' I say lovingly.

'I know that.'

'I guess I owe David and James an explanation?' I ask.

'No you don't, I told them enough to stop them from asking too many questions.' Clara giggles. 'And besides, they know you're odd anyway. After all you must be to fall in love with me.'

I feel so comfortable talking with Clara. We chat about everything that's happened and what the future may hold for us. I paint Clara a picture of my other life but I'm careful not to say too much about the future. I don't want to scare her. I'm still not sure how I'll do it, but I can't spend my life without this woman. Would the others allow me to continue moving backwards and forwards in time? Could I live here? Could Clara come home with me?

A butterfly enters the waiting room on the summer breeze.

'Oh, how beautiful,' Clara says, watching it flutter around the sunny room.

'Nowhere near as beautiful as you,' I say, in return.

Clara blushes.

As I watch my girl, enchanted by the butterfly, I think of the bat in the barn loft again. *I need to test that theory.*

'You must know everything that's going to happen to us all,' Clara says.

In reality I don't know anything of what happens to her as she left no history that we could find. 'Clara, I have something I need to tell you. I don't want to frighten you but it's important.'

'What is it, my love?'

'Something's going to happen in this valley that will change the place forever, something terrible. And I don't want you to be caught up in it.'

'Oh dear. Whatever is going to happen?'

'Most of what you love here will soon be gone,' I say.

Clara glances out of the waiting room window. My eyes follow hers over the rolling green fields beyond the hanging baskets of the station platform.

'Will I still be able to teach at the school?'

'No, I'm afraid you won't.'

'Have you seen anything of our future?' she asks.

'Not a thing.'

'Then my future is with you,' she says. 'No one should know what lies ahead.'

'With me… here?'

'With you anywhere, Simon. You'll always tell me the truth won't you, no matter how frightening it may be?'

'Of course I will. I have nothing to hide from you now and never will again. I promise.'

'I have nothing left in Durham now that my mother has gone. My only future is here,' she says, pointing to my heart.

'I wouldn't expect you to stay here, Simon. But you could take me with you.' She grabs me tightly. 'I don't want us to be apart any longer.'

'I know,' I say. 'I don't want us to be apart either. But I might not be able to take you with me,' I say, stroking her hair.

'But you could try, couldn't you?'

I don't see it as fair to expect Clara to come home with me, but I couldn't leave her here to witness the destruction of the town she loves and be left alone either. 'Yes, I could try,' I say.

'What will I need to do?'

I stand and pace the waiting room pondering the possibilities.

Clara sits watching me. It doesn't make me uncomfortable, I just find it harder to concentrate – but then she always has that effect on me anyhow. I quickly muddle over everything I've learnt about time travel.

'If we're to do this then I can't take you with me straight away. It's too risky. I need to try something first.' I'm still pacing. 'You won't be able to take anything with you either, and may not even have time to say goodbye to anyone. Could you cope with that?'

'If you are at my side, Simon, I can cope with anything.' Clara grasps at a pretty locket hanging from her neck. 'Oh dear,' she says, showing me the item. 'This was my mother's. She gave it to me before she died. Will I have to leave it behind?'

I think about the disintegrating hymn book from the day I first crossed over. 'Yes, unfortunately.' I then have a thought… 'There may be a way you can still have it in the future.'

'How?'

'If I can find a way to take you with me, would you be returning to Durham to say goodbye to your father?'

'Yes, I would. I owe him that.'

'Then don't worry, I have an idea.'

Clara stands. 'Tell me Simon.'

'When you return to Durham, wrap up your locket and leave it somewhere safe in your room. Somewhere no one will ever find it, even if the house was emptied. Like under a floorboard.'

Clara nods. 'I will. Then what shall I do?'

I hear a whistle. The two thirty-five from Newcastle to Durham rolls into Conley Hope station right on time.

'Wait for me.'

'I will, Simon.'

'I'll come back for you.' I say, holding my girl tightly. 'I'll find us somewhere beautiful to live. Somewhere just like here, if not better. I'll look after you, Clara.'

She looks at me with those bright green eyes. 'No, I'll look after you,' she says.

I give her a lasting kiss goodbye and leave the waiting room. As I board the train, I watch my lover go back to the schoolchildren. She almost floats like an angel, glancing back occasionally. She's glowing again, partly from the summer sunshine blazing through her hair, and partly, I hope, because of how she feels about me.

**

The journey home is far improved from the one taking me to my sweetheart. I can't believe how much my outlook has changed from only an hour ago. I think about my discussion with Clara and what I'll need to do before I can risk trying to take her with me. I also have the task of getting back to her, but I'm confident I can, otherwise I would never have left. I hope I can fulfil my promise.

On arrival at Durham, I wait until the platform has cleared of people and then look around for the familiar swirl of gas. I see it hovering above some stairs by the ticket office. Luckily the view from the main station building is obstructed by a cart loaded with wooden boxes. There's a stray cat sitting by the cart. *That cat could be a quick way to test my theory.* I grab it and head for the stairs.

The cat isn't impressed. It's even less amused when I climb the steps and leap.

**

I roll out of the gas cloud and across the cold, dark platform two of Durham railway station, still clinging to a very unhappy moggy. 'Hello you two,' I say, landing on my feet in acrobatic style, the cat still under my arm.

John and Emily stare from the bike park.

'What the hell's that?' John asks, still peering over the fence.

'It's a cat,' I say. I check the creature is fully intact. It is, if a little put out.

'I can see that. But what are you doing with it?'

'Do you want it?' I ask.

They continue to stare in disbelief.

'Fine, suit yourselves,' I say, letting the poor thing go and watching it run off down the platform. 'I just needed to prove a point that's all.'

John shakes his head.

My spirits are high. I feel a spring in my step and a fire in my belly. Nothing can distract me from my goal. I leap over the fence and join my friends.

'So, what happened?' Emily asks.

'No time to explain. How much gas have we got left?'

'Oh for God's sake, Si. Why?' John asks, hands on hips.

'Did you not find Clara?' Emily asks.

'I did.'

'Did you save her?' Emily asks.

'I didn't need to.'

'So why do you need to go back?' John asks.

'Because there's one last thing I need to do.'

'But I thought this was going to be the last time?' he adds.

'I know, and I'm sorry but I have to do this.' I guess I'm just being selfish and want this to end my way, but if I tell my friends what I plan to do I doubt they'd back me up this time. Not only am I thinking of bringing Clara back with me, but I should also warn Mr Cole of the end of Conley Hope.

John and Emily look at each other.

'I just need to do one more thing to make everything as it should be. That's all I can say as it'll take me forever to explain and I'm wasting precious time.'

'Why couldn't you do it while you were there?' John asks.

'I didn't have time.'

Emily stands arms folded, her pleasant expression unusually absent. 'I'm not sure I like the sound of this.'

'Please guys, I'll never ask anything of you ever

again. I promise.' There's a draughty silence.

Eventually, Emily throws her hands up and turns to her partner. 'It's up to you, John.'

'No. We've done enough damage,' John says. 'If she's alive and well, then we leave it at that. That was the deal.'

'Are you sure you don't want to come?' I ask.

'Not after that first go when I came looking for you. I felt like crap for days. I don't know how you do it.'

'But you've never seen the other side properly, only a dark church in the middle of the night. You'll never know what your invention can do.'

'Don't try bribing me, Si.'

'I'm not bribing you. I need one last visit, and you'll always wonder what it was like back there if you don't see for yourself.'

'You should go,' Emily says, to my surprise.

'Come on, John,' I say. 'You'll regret it.'

'Alright,' he says. 'There's another full gas tank in the van. But that's the last of it.'

I give John a friendly punch on the arm. 'You're a star. I'll never forget this.'

'Damn right you won't. What do I do about my clothes?'

'It doesn't matter. We won't be there long.'

**

I hadn't planned to take John with me, but I doubt he'd have let me go back otherwise. *I wonder how he'll react when I tell him I plan to bring Clara back with us?* Everyone is quiet as we fit the other tank and set up the equipment to carry out another run.

'Promise me you won't do anything stupid,' Emily

whispers, out of range of John. 'And make sure you bring my boyfriend back.'

'Don't worry, Em; I know what I'm doing.'

'You will be coming back too won't you?'

I smile. 'Yes, I will. Come on, I've got things I need to do.'

'We'll only have about three hours tops,' John says, starting the rig.

Emily guides the hose this time. 'What date do you want?' she asks, glancing at the wall where the ticket office should be.

'Early August, please.'

Only a few minutes later, she's found something. 'Thirteenth of August, Si. Is that any good?'

That's seven days after I last saw Clara... that's if the timetable is correct. *It's not as close as I'd like, but it'll do.*

'That's great, Em. We're off. See you in a bit.'

I open the hydrogen input valve and pull John into the gas cloud.

Emily and the rig disappear.

NINETEEN

My return to 1912 is less dramatic than previously. I reappear by the ticket office and find the station empty and quiet.

John appears next to me.

'Are you OK,' I ask?

He looks a little shaken, but nothing like last time. 'Yeah, I'll be alright in a minute.'

I sit him on a bench and wait. After ten minutes or so I'm getting worried, there's no station activity at all. I don't even know what caused the crossover, but that's not important – getting to Clara is. Suddenly a porter comes into view.

'Excuse me,' I shout. 'Are there any trains running to Newcastle?'

'Yes, sir. I think the next one will be in about an hour or so,' he says, looking curiously at John's denim jeans.

Damn. That won't leave us enough time to get to Conley Hope, find Clara, and bring her back. 'Sorry to bother you again,' I shout. 'What date is it?'

'Thirteenth of August, sir.'

At least we have the right date this time. 'Is there any other way to get to the Conley Valley from here?' I ask.

'There's often a coach outside the station, sir.'

'Thank you. Come on, let's go.' We burst out into what should be the car park beyond, but instead I find trees and a small gravel area with two stagecoaches waiting. I lay eyes on the familiar matt black paintwork of the nearest coach and head straight for it.

'Hello, gentlemen,' I say, creeping up on David and James Atkinson as they stand talking by their stagecoach.

'Hello Simon,' James says. He grabs my arm and shakes my hand vigorously, his brother does likewise. I'm surprised they're not wary of me considering what's happened.

'This is my friend, John,' I say.

Both brothers shake hands with him.

'I believe I owe you gentlemen an explanation,' I say.

'Well I know I said you didn't need to explain anything, Si, but the way you left us so suddenly was rather strange,' James says. 'That trick you performed was outstanding.'

'Trick?'

'Yes. Clara told us you and your friends were travelling magicians, and that's how you knew so much about fixing coaches,' David explains.

Clara must have invented a cover story for me. 'Err, yes... That's what we do, isn't it, John?' I stutter.

John nods dumbly.

'She said the night we met, you'd been left behind…' James explains, 'and were simply waiting for the others to return later in the summer.'

'Yes... yes I was. I'm sorry I didn't tell you the truth, I was a bit embarrassed.'

'We didn't even realise he was missing for days,' John adds.

I give him a heavy sideways look.

'You could have told us, Si, we wouldn't have mocked you,' James says. 'I'm sorry that I followed you. I was concerned, that's all.'

'Don't worry, and thank you.'

'Clara said you probably noticed me following you and thought I was the police.' James explains. 'I guess you performed that disappearing trick to throw me off the scent. Very impressive.'

'All part of the show,' I say. I'm glad I don't have to explain anything to the brothers about where I'm from and why I was here, although I'm saddened knowing Clara had to lie for me. Thinking of her I know I must return to my quest. 'Do you have a fare?' I ask.

'No, would you like a ride?' David asks.

'That would be great. We need to get to Conley Hope damn quick.'

Both brothers nod agreeably. 'Then you've come to the right place, my friend,' David says, pulling on a pair of leather gloves.

'I'm sorry to ask more of you gents.'

'No problem,' James says. 'Like I've said before, if you're good enough for Clara then you're good enough for us. We're always at your service.'

'I know,' I say. 'And I really appreciate it.'

'So what brings you back to us then, Simon?' James asks.

'A certain beautiful young lady.'

'We thought that would be the case sooner or later,' he adds, with a grin.

'Would you like to take the rear stand?' David asks.

'Yeah, why not.' I usher John up the ladder to the rear platform and sit him on the toolbox.

David and James both climb up front.

'Hang onto that,' I say to John, pointing to a rail attached to the back of the carriage. I stay standing and lean on the carriage roof. The best view is from here.

'Why are you talking like a ponce?' John asks.

'Shut up and hold on.'

With a flick of David's reins, we lunge forward and set off down the hill. This could be my final breath-taking run to the valley of sunshine and flowers.

**

The journey back to Clara is fast and invigorating. I'm now accustomed to watching the unspoilt scenery flash by as the fastest stagecoach in England hugs the winding lanes so impressively. John's knuckles are white from clinging to the rail. People wave as the famous coach passes.

As we enter the Conley Valley David suddenly slows the horses, we cross the railway line and reach the road junction by the colliery. The way ahead is covered with water. David guides the coach slowly forward and the horses canter deeper.

'What's going on?' I shout.

'Not sure, Si,' David replies. 'I think the lake's burst its banks or something; the mine's underwater.'

I remember the tale old Molly told us about the end of Conley Hope. *Jesus, this is the day she was telling us about.* 'Don't take the main road, Dave,' I shout. 'Take the road to the mine, we need to get there quick.'

'Alright, Si.'

'Stay here,' I say, to John.

'Don't worry, I'm not going anywhere.'

I swiftly shuffle along the side rail and join the brothers up front. 'There are people down there that need our help,' I say.

'How do you know?' James asks.

'Trust me.'

The brothers obviously do as David takes the road to the colliery. We speed up; the horses do well to pull the coach at pace through the deep water creating a bow wave more fitting of a fast moving boat.

I hear shouting from the engine house as we reach the edge of the colliery yard, I realise we're now in the middle of what becomes the modern day lake. I recall Molly's tale once again - she said the schoolhouse was lost. *Where would Clara be right now?* Molly said a woman was killed there on this day. *Is this why Clara has no history?* I panic. 'Get as many people out as you can then get the hell out of here,' I shout, to the brothers.

'Where are you going, Si?' David shouts back.

'The school!' I jump into the water. It's getting deep; it's lapping the bellies of the horses.

David and James jump into the deluge with me. 'Be careful, Si,' James says.

'You too, gents. If I don't get to see you guys again, thanks and good luck.'

'Good luck, Si.' They swim off towards the colliery buildings.

'Come on, John.'

He leaps in with me. 'What's going on?' he asks.

'This is the day Molly told us about, the end of Conley Hope.'

'Shit.'

We battle our way towards the small wood. The water is deep, but we struggle on. I'm completely focussed on getting to the little schoolhouse on the other side of the wood, but the water is frustrating me - I feel like I'm in a nightmare where you're trying to run but you just don't seem to get anywhere. Luckily the water becomes shallower the nearer we get to the woods. Once among the trees we're only paddling in a few inches. I fight my way through the low branches.

John lags behind.

I'm seriously out of breath too but don't dare stop for a second. The thought of Clara coming to harm drives me in a way I would never have thought possible.

'You go-ahead,' John pants. 'I'll catch up.'

As I leave the wood I hear disturbing noises, the kind I'd expect to hear on a construction site as earth movers rip rock and soil from the ground. Branches are crashing from trees. Surging water flows past. It sounds like I'm close to a large waterfall. The field behind the school has become a fierce river. Water is flowing down the valley into a great opening in the ground, dragging trees and shrubs with it.

I vault a fence and run as fast as my burning leg muscles will allow. A cattle shelter disappears before me, swallowed up by the earth. As I pass close to the lane I see people running along it. There's more horrendous cracking noises as the corner of the schoolhouse crumbles to the ground. I hear screaming. Close by, the little church roof falls in. The crashing of slate tiles breaking on mass, adding to the chaos.

I burst through the rear gate into the flooding school playground. I slide to a stop on the wet grass. I freeze. I watch in horror as the entire roof of the schoolhouse collapses in a huge cloud of dust and debris.

I'm knocked to my knees by a ground tremor that shakes what's left of the stone building to pieces before my eyes.

The onslaught of water becomes meaningless as I'm swamped with personal distress. How can the only person on earth, with the ability to control time, be too late?

**

The summer sun is engulfed in cloud and the scene falls darker, along with my thoughts. I don't know where John is – I don't care. I no longer hear shouting. I don't hear the water lapping around me, and I don't feel my wet clothes. I get to my feet and move awkwardly across the playground. I feel drunk. *Maybe Clara isn't here, maybe she's OK.* I find my feet and sense of urgency as I approach what's left of the school. The beautiful structure is now an aberrant sculpture of broken beams and stone.

I clamber over the rugged landscape; it resembles a war time bomb site. There's rubble peaks and deep gullies scattered amongst the mangled roof. Bits of paper, and anything else small enough to fly on the breeze, adds to the dust cloud hovering above me.

People in the lane watch me with vacant faces; others run to escape the deluge of water flowing down the hillside towards us.

I scramble between the timbers and shards of slate searching for any sign of life. I lose my footing and slip between two large pieces of masonry. Waist deep in water and surrounded by broken building fabric, I struggle to pull myself out. I'm stopped by a sound... I hear a whimper amongst the chaos.

'Clara? Is that you?'

There's no reply. The eerie wreck of a building

falls silent again. I manage to wriggle out and kneel upon a beam. Estimating the position of Clara's classroom, I crawl in that direction. Between the noise of falling masonry and lapping of water I hear a faint call.

'Please help me.' It's Clara's voice.

I panic knowing she must be trapped somewhere. 'Clara?' I'm shaking as I scramble towards the cry for help. In the centre of the carnage I find a dry hollow filled with roofing slate and sharp timbers. Between two beams I see what looks like flowery material. I recognise Clara's dress. *Jesus, I was right; Molly was right.* I squeeze myself into the hollow. I take hold of one of the beams and slowly move it a few inches.

Clara cries out with pain.

'I'm sorry, but I need to move this to get to you.' I move the beam further, revealing more dress and pale flesh. It's heart-breaking hearing Clara's cries. I find a little hand and grip it tight. 'I'll have you out in a minute,' I say, trying to hide my panic.

Her hold on me is weak.

I manage to push the beam off her and brush away dust and debris. I find a pretty face – an English rose among the thorns of devastation.

Clara looks at me. Her eyes are pleading with me to free her.

I check I've moved everything I can before sliding my arms under her. I ignore the blood soaked dress as water starts to fill the hollow. 'Right, Clara, I have to move you. This will hurt so I need you to be brave.'

'I don't know if I can, Simon. Just leave me.'

I press my face against hers and whisper in her ear. 'Close your eyes. Imagine you're at the rock pool with me; we're sitting in the sun together. Stay there on that rock and don't go anywhere.'

Clara nods and closes her eyes. I lift her - she screams.

I scramble out of the hollow, holding onto Clara like my own life depends on it. I wade from the rubble and watery onslaught, cradling her limp body.

The lane has now cleared as people escape the water. But one man stands alone at the edge of the school grounds. He wanders, dazed.

'Fetch a doctor,' I shout.

'Yes. Yes, of course,' he says, running off in no particular direction.

I head for higher ground as fast as I dare, I don't want to hurt this precious thing in my arms. I reach a grassy mound and the shade of an oak tree. I gently set Clara down under the protection of its branches. I wrap her in my arms and cradle her head.

She opens her eyes. She looks sleepy – like the night in the barn, after we'd made love.

'You'll be alright,' I say. 'Help is on the way.'

Her tears make tracks on her dusty face. So do mine.

'I love you, darling,' she whispers, between shallow breaths. 'You treat me like a princess without expecting me to be one. You have a lovely soul, Simon.'

'It's you who makes me that way.'

'I'm so sorry.'

'Don't be sorry, Clara.'

'I'm sorry I won't be your wife. I'm sorry I won't be the mother of your children.'

'You will. You'll be fine... I promise.'

Clara tries to move. She struggles. Her breath is strangled.

'Don't move,' I say. 'Just lie still.'

'I'm so afraid.'

'Don't be. You'll be alright. I can fix this, I can fix anything, remember?'

She gifts me a weak smile. 'I'm broken, Simon. You can't fix me.'

I feel her slipping away before me. 'Don't leave me, Clara; just hang on one minute more.'

'I love you, Simon. I always will.'

'I love you too, Clara.'

That green sparkle in her eyes burns out. A stiff wind blows the branches above me. Clara is gone.

TWENTY

I often wondered what makes us uneasy when we're alone sometimes. Without seeing or hearing a thing out of the ordinary, I'd still be spooked. I always presumed it was the sheer silence that did it. We human beings need something going on, someone to talk to, a pet to make a fuss of. Without it we seem unnerved. The thunderous rattle of a train blasting past our house is often more settling than silence, it reminds us things are normal.

I've felt a presence before, never seeing - just feeling, something lingering like a cold patch of air that has no place on a warm street. But I didn't think much of it; after all, I'm only human. People often turn, sensing someone behind them, only to find no one there. We're just wired that way, or so I'm told. Until recently, I never realised that there's more to it than that. Until recently, I never realised that those little chills - the ones that make the hairs on your arms stand on end – can be the signature of something life changing. Looking back, I didn't realise how little I knew about those unnerving moments. I'm still creeped out by them, even though I now spend most of my time chasing them – searching for the next one, then seeing how it unfolds.

The weak January light is fading from my home town of Durham. I'm back in the attic room, in the empty townhouse. I look out of the window at the cold scene, the ice on the inside of the window glass showing it hasn't been a kind winter so far. I've spent so long living in the past, I'm really not sure of the future. I think how at the age of twenty-nine, I have so much time left. Although time doesn't mean that much to me anymore.

I've spent endless hours analysing the last few months. What I've done and where I went wrong – the damage I've caused. My mind is racing and my heart is aching for many reasons. I've seen and done such amazing things lately that having an ordinary life now seems far too simple. I take a final look around the room that gave a beginning to my adventures. I kneel on the dusty floor and roll up my sleeves. I take a pen knife from my pocket. Heart racing, I extend the blade. Using the knife, I carefully prise up a loose floorboard. Underneath is a small brown package; I take it and rip open the old musty paper. Wrapped up inside, I find a beautiful locket.

I smile. It's Clara's.

I fill up as I recall the last time I saw her wearing it, at Conley Hope railway station. I could have given it to her if she were here. Clara's world is now destroyed - mine is too. I'm not sure how long I held her there under that tree, until I gently closed her eyes and kissed her goodbye. It seems so long ago. I put the locket in my pocket.

Everything that's dear to me is trapped in history, but I haven't attempted to go back and retrieve it. John's made a good effort of dissuading me from returning to Conley Hope to change our tragic ending. As far as I know, the rig is still intact, so one phone call to Faza and another three hundred pounds might see me back in Clara's arms. But why put myself through it, knowing I'll only lose her again another day?

I replace the floorboard and leave. I walk the length of a frosty North Bailey. I don't feel like I've had a winter as I've spent so much time in the summer of 1912. And the only person that mattered to me, in all that time, was Elizabeth Clara Pearson - the beautiful woman from the past, who changed me and my life so much in a few short months.

I wonder what my life would be like now if I hadn't helped John and Emily with their university project. What would I have been doing for the last four months if I hadn't seen that photo of Clara and me? Would my actions since then have been significantly different? *I guess I'll never know.* If we all saw our future, would we simply sit back and let it take its course? - Or would our every decision, from that point on, ensure we arrived at what we saw?

Although my travels have been painful at times, I don't regret one second. I've loved spending time with Clara, sharing a few months of my life with her. After all, those moments were far too special to miss out on. I walk briskly down a lane between old houses. There's a small park leading down to the river – I cut through it. Through the evergreen branches I see the bridge over the Wear.

There's a young woman on the bridge; it looks like she's waiting for someone. I've lost track of how many times I've walked this way wishing Clara was there to greet me. The nearer I get to the edge of the park the clearer my line of sight to the bridge, and the clearer the woman becomes. I notice her curly red hair, her pale pretty face. *No, it couldn't be. Could it?*

Suddenly, I'm startled by a figure stepping out of the trees in front of me. It's a man dressed similarly to me, with a scarf covering most of his face. He blocks my path.

I stop, heart pounding.

'Hello, Simon,' he says, lowering the scarf.

For the second time in my life I'm face to face with myself. I look a little older.

'I know, it's all very weird, but you've seen it before,' he says, with a grin.

I didn't have to speak to myself the last time; I was simply standing in the same barn for a few moments. I'm not sure what to say. I eventually calm and find my tongue. 'Hello, erm... me.'

The other me laughs. 'Don't worry, you get used to it eventually.'

I lay eyes on the woman at the bottom of the hill. 'Is that...'

'Yep, that's Clara alright.'

I'm confused. 'So are you the past me, or the future me?' I ask.

'Well, I'm not the past you, am I? Otherwise you'd remember this.'

I have a point. 'Yeah, sorry I'm not thinking straight.' The woman on the bridge is stealing my attention.

'Don't worry, she's fine,' the other me says, catching my gaze riverwards.

'So I get there in the end?' I ask.

'Well the fact she's standing there right as rain and waiting for me, well, *you*, is a pretty good sign, don't you think? It won't happen all by itself though.'

He seems more assertive, confident. I like the future me. 'Why are you here?' I ask.

He glances down the hill towards the woman waiting patiently on the bridge. 'Motivation. I came back to tell you not to give up.'

'Is what I want still possible?'

He points towards the bridge. 'There's the proof, young Simon.' He puts his hands on my shoulders. 'Now, listen. You know how this works now, you're the expert. There are sixty-six days between the day you first kissed Clara, and the day she died. Think of all the energy in all the millions of different places you could find during that time. The way I see it, that gives you *sixty-six chances* to change her fate. You've only used up a few, so what are you waiting for?'

Seeing Clara again is all the motivation I need. 'You're right. I can do this.'

'Yes, you can.' He's shuffling around as I do when I'm restless. 'I have to go. If you'll excuse me, Mr Benson, I'm keeping a lady waiting.'

'You certainly are,' I say, smiling inside and out. 'Oh here, give her this.' I fumble around in my pocket and produce the locket.

He takes it. 'No, Simon. You'll be giving it to her yourself one day.' He slips it back in my pocket. 'Get some rest... You've got a lot to do.' We shake hands firmly.

'Good luck,' he shouts back, as he skips off down the path. I watch from the shadow of the evergreens as he descends the hill and jogs across the road to the bridge. He's met with a warm embrace. He kisses Clara, who smiles and laughs as they turn away from me, her hair catching on the breeze.

My eyes are filling remembering that feeling.

The future me takes her hand and they walk over the bridge, eventually disappearing, lost in the old city's sprawl.

With a deep intake of Durham's crisp winter air, I take out my phone and dial. 'Hi, John, it's Simon. Listen, I need a favour...

OTHER TITLES IN THIS SERIES:

This is the first adventure in the Sixty-Six trilogy.

The second, *Sixty-Six Kilograms*, will be available in early 2018.

www.ingramcontent.com/pod-product-compliance
Lightning Source LLC
Chambersburg PA
CBHW031018120726
47905CB00007B/1958
* 9 7 8 0 9 9 5 6 9 9 2 0 5 *